Praise for the Novels of Stephanie Tyler

"Unforgettable."
—*New York Times* bestselling author Cherry Adair

"Red-hot romance. White-knuckle suspense."
—*New York Times* bestselling author Lara Adrian

"No one writes a bad-boy hero like Tyler."
—*New York Times* bestselling author Larissa Ione

"A story that kept me on the edge of my seat."
—*New York Times* bestselling author Alexandra Ivy

"Stephanie Tyler is a master."   —Romance Junkies

"Sexy and witty."   —Fresh Fiction

"A thrill ride with twists and turns to keep the reader guessing."   —Night Owl Reviews

"Takes murder, suspense, psychic gifts, and passion; twists them all up; and then tosses them out in a way that will keep you wondering what will happen next."
—Joyfully Reviewed

"Heart-stoppingly exciting."   —*Romantic Times*

"A very satisfying romantic thriller."
—*Publishers Weekly*

SURRENDER

A Section 8 Novel

Stephanie Tyler

A SIGNET ECLIPSE BOOK

SIGNET ECLIPSE
Published by the Penguin Group
Penguin Group (USA) Inc., 375 Hudson Street,
New York, New York 10014, USA

USA / Canada / UK / Ireland / Australia / New Zealand / India / South
Africa / China

Penguin Books Ltd., Registered Offices: 80 Strand, London WC2R 0RL,
England
For more information about the Penguin Group visit penguin.com.

First published by Signet Eclipse, an imprint of New American Library,
a division of Penguin Group (USA) Inc.

First Printing, April 2013

SIGNET ECLIPSE and logo are trademarks of Penguin Group (USA) Inc.

ISBN 978-0-451-41349-9

Printed in the United States of America
10 9 8 7 6 5 4 3 2 1

PUBLISHER'S NOTE
This is a work of fiction. Names, characters, places, and incidents either are the
product of the author's imagination or are used fictitiously, and any
resemblance to actual persons, living or dead, business establishments, events,
or locales is entirely coincidental.
   The publisher does not have any control over and does not assume any
responsibility for author or third-party Web sites or their content.

ALWAYS LEARNING   PEARSON

For my awesome readers!

Freedom means choosing your burden.
       —Hephzibah Menuhin

All my dues surely must be paid.
     —"Ready for Love," Bad Company

Prologue

Zaire, twenty years earlier

The explosion threw him forward hard, the heat searing his body, debris cutting into his back as he covered his face and stayed down. Darius didn't need to look back to know what had happened—the bridge had exploded. Simon had purposely cut off their last means of escape. It would force their hands, Darius's especially.

"Darius, you all right?" Simon shook him, yanked him to his feet and held him upright. His ears would continue to ring for months.

"How much ammo do you have?" he called over the din. Couldn't see the rebels yet, but he knew they were coming toward them through the jungle.

"Stop wasting time. You go." Simon jerked his head toward the LZ and the waiting chopper about thirty feet away, crammed full of important rescued American officials and the like. Already precariously over capacity. "Go now and I'll hold them off."

Simon had always had a sense of bravado and a

temper no one wanted to deal with, but one against twenty-plus? Those odds were not in the man's favor. Darius shook his head hard, and it was already spinning from the explosion.

"You are no fucking help to me," Simon told him. "I can't watch your back this time, Darius."

"Fuck you."

"Leave. Me. Here."

"If I do that, I'll come back to just a body."

"You're never coming back here." Simon's teeth were bared, ready for battle—with the rebels, with Darius, if necessary.

"If we both fight, we've got a better shot," Darius told him.

"You would tell me to leave if things were reversed, Master Chief, sir." Simon stood straight and tall, hand to his forehead, and Darius growled, "Don't you dare salute me, son." Their old routine. Simon managed a small smile, one that was as rare as peace in this part of the world.

"Don't take this from me, Darius. Let me save your goddamned life. You have your son to think about—I won't take you away from Dare."

Dare was in middle school—his mother had already left them both, and pain shot through Darius at the thought of leaving his son without a parent.

Simon knew he had him, pressed on. "The team will always need you, and me—well, you can always find someone who can fight."

"Not like you."

"No, not like me," he echoed. "You go and you don't ever return."

Darius didn't say anything, and for a long moment they were silent, listening to the rustling that was still a couple of miles away. The blood was running down his side, and if he stayed in this wet jungle much longer with a wound like that . . .

"There's one spot left for a ride home." Simon told him what he already knew. "That seat is yours."

"I'm half-dead already."

"You think I'm not?" Simon asked, and Darius flashed back to a younger version of the operative in front of him, walking along a dusty road two miles from Leavenworth.

Darius had gone from being a Navy SEAL, fresh from capture in an underground cell where he'd been held for twenty-two days, to a medical discharge, to a phone call inviting him to join a very different kind of team. The CIA was creating a group—Section 8. For operatives like him. They'd have a handler and all the resources they'd need. Their only rule: Complete the mission. The how, when and where were up to them.

He was maybe the sanest of the group, and that was saying something. Simon always had the look of a predator, occasionally replaced by a childlike wonder, usually when Adele was around. If you looked at the team members' old files, you'd see everything from disobeying orders to failing psych exams to setting fires.

But if you knew S8, you'd see the mastermind. The

wetwork expert. The demolitions expert, the one who could handle escape and extractions with ease. They could lie and steal and hack. They could find any kind of transport, anytime, anywhere, anyhow, that could get them the hell out of Dodge.

In the beginning, they'd been nothing more than angry wild animals, circling, furious with one another and their circumstances. But once the trust grew, it was never broken.

Separately, they were good. Together, they were great.

And now, three years later, two S8 operatives stood near the wreckage of a bridge in Zaire and they were both about to die.

"If you could save fifteen people . . . or just one . . . ," Simon prodded.

"Don't you pull that trolley problem shit on me—I've been to more shrinks than you and I'm not leaving you behind like this," Darius said, his voice slightly vicious. But they both knew he'd relent. He'd done everything Simon had asked of him, and this was for the good of the rest of the team.

"They'll never recover without you," Simon told him. "You're the goddamned heart of the team."

"And you're my best goddamned friend," Darius growled. Simon's expression softened, just for a second.

"Just remember the promise," Simon warned.

We don't try to find out who's behind S8. No matter what.

Neither Darius nor Simon believed what happened today was a screwup their handler could've known about. But their promise referenced him specifically. They knew they'd been brought together by the CIA, but their handler picked the jobs, gave them orders and anything else they needed. Once they started distrusting him, it was all over.

"I'll remember," Darius told him now.

"Good. Go." This time, Simon's words were punctuated with a push. Darius barely caught himself, and when he turned, Simon was already running in the direction of the rebels, the crazy fucker confusing them with his contrary tactics. Because who the hell ran toward the bad guys?

Darius made his choice—he was a liability, so he made his way to the helo, pulled himself on board and shoved himself into the pilot's seat. Within minutes, the steel bird was grinding gears, rising above the heavy cover of jungle. As the chopper blades cut the air smoothly with their *whoompa-whoompa-tink*, Darius turned the helo and stared down at the man who'd left himself behind as Darius took the rescued civilians— aid workers, a diplomatic attaché and other Americans who'd been working in the area—away. He'd never take credit for the glory on this one, though. Simon could've sat in this pilot seat as easily as Darius did.

There was a chance Simon could fight them off. There was always a chance. And as he watched for that brief moment, he hoped beyond hope that Simon could win, fight his way out of the mass of humanity that was trying to kill him simply because he was American.

One last glance afforded Darius the view he didn't

want—the mob surrounding Simon. It was like watching his friend—his teammate—sink into a manhole as they swarmed over him.

Section 8 had ended at that moment, at least for him. He'd later learn that their handler had agreed, and the group of seven men and one woman who'd been thrown together to work black ops missions around the globe with no supervision and very few, if any, rules, had been officially disbanded, the surviving members given large sums of money to buy their silence and thank them for their service.

He would have to explain to the team why he'd left Simon behind, although they'd know. They'd get it. They all prepared for that eventuality every single time they went out. It was part of the thrill.

There was no thrill now as he watched his best friend die. And he didn't turn away, stared at the spot until he couldn't see anything anymore, and knew he'd never get that image out of his mind.

Chapter One

Twenty years later

Dare O'Rourke believed in ghosts because they visited him regularly.

He woke, covered in sweat, shaking, and immediately glanced at the clock. He'd slept for fifteen minutes straight before the nightmare. A record.

The screams—both those in the dream and those that tore from his own throat whenever he allowed himself the luxury of sleep—would stay with him as long as he lived, wrapping around his soul and squeezing until he wished he'd died that terrible night.

A part of him had, but what was left wasn't a phoenix rising from the ashes. No, Dare was broken bones and not of sound mind. Might never be again, according to the Navy docs, who said the trauma Dare had faced was too severe, that he wasn't fit for duty. He had no doubt those doctors were right, wasn't sure what kind of man he'd be if he *had* been able to go the business-as-usual route.

He'd never be the same.

The CIA felt differently. *You'll survive. You'll recover. You're needed.*

And even though he knew the world needed rough men like him, no matter how fiercely the government would deny his existence if it came down to brass tacks, he told them all to fuck off and went to live in the woods. He was no longer a SEAL, the thing that had defined him, the job he'd loved for ten years.

Dare had prayed for many things that night in the jungle, including death, but none had been answered. And so he'd stopped praying and holed up alone and just tried to sleep through the night.

Three hundred sixty-three days and counting and not an unbroken sleep among them.

Three hundred sixty-four was a couple of hours away, the day giving way to the dusk, and the car coming up the private road couldn't mean anything but trouble.

Three hundred sixty-three days and no visitors. He saw people only when he went into the small town monthly for supplies. Beyond that, he remained on his property. It was quiet. He could think, whether he wanted to or not.

As for healing . . . that would all be in the eye of the beholder.

He rolled out of bed, flexed the ache from his hands before pulling on jeans and a flannel shirt he left unbuttoned. Barefoot, he went out to greet his guest.

He met the car with his weapon drawn, put it away when the car got close enough for him to see the driver.

Adele. A member of the original Section 8—a black

ops group of seven men and one woman recruited from various military branches and the CIA. All loose cannons, none of them taking command well. All of them the best at what they did. A real life A-Team, except the reality wasn't anything like it was portrayed on television.

Dare's father—Darius—had been a member, was MIA and presumed KIA on a mission last year. At least that's what Adele had told Dare.

All Dare knew was that S8 had officially disbanded when he was thirteen, and for years, its members worked black ops missions on their own steam. Until they'd gotten a call—that call—the remaining six members and one last job. Back into the jungle they'd sworn not to go back into. *A mistake to go,* Darius told him. *We're too old.* But they were still strong, with plenty of experience. And they went anyway.

Four men never returned. Adele and Darius did, but they were never the same. Refused to talk about it and went off on more unreachable missions until they'd both disappeared more than a year ago.

Dare had wanted to assume that the secrets of the group were all dead and buried with them.

Fucking assumptions would get him every time. He knew better. His father and Adele had come back from the dead more than once.

Adele took her time getting out of the car. She was stately looking, at one time considered more handsome than pretty, with short hair and kind blue eyes, a thin frame that belied her strength. It was hard to believe she was as deadly as the men she'd worked with.

"I have a job for you," she said when she reached the porch he refused to leave. No preamble, all business. The only thing contradicting her deadliness was the frail frame she now carried.

She was sick—he could see it in her pale coloring, the darkness shading the skin under her eyes. His heart went out to her; she'd been the closest thing to a mother he'd ever had, even though she'd been far more like a mother wolf than a nurturer.

But it had been enough. "I can't."

"You're not broken, Dare." Adele sounded so damned sure, but why he wanted her reassurance, he had no idea.

He jerked his gaze to her and saw her own quiet pain that she carried, kept so close to the vest all these years. "It was all a setup."

Adele neither confirmed nor denied, but the truth of his own words haunted him.

It was a setup . . . and you were supposed to die.

A Ranger had received a dishonorable discharge for rescuing him against a direct order. Dare would never forget the soldier's face, and he doubted the soldier would ever stop seeing his.

Two men, bound by pain.

He closed his eyes briefly, thought about the way he'd been found, nearly hanging from his arms, up on a platform so he could watch the entire scene being played out in front of him.

The villagers. His guides. American peacekeepers. His team. All slaughtered in front of him.

The fire came closer now . . . and he welcomed it. Had

prayed for it, even as his captors laughed at his predicament, spat in his face. Cut him with knives and ripped his nails off one by one. There was nothing he could offer them, nothing they would take from him.

He'd offered himself multiple times. They refused. He must've passed out—from pain, hunger, it didn't matter. He clawed at the wood, his wrists, forearms, fingers, all broken from trying so hard to escape chains not meant for humans to fight against. It hadn't stopped him—he'd been nearly off the platform, ripping the wood out piece by piece, when the worst of the rape happened in front of him.

It would've been too late.

Could've closed your eyes. Blocked it out. Let yourself pass out.

But if they were going to be tortured, the least he could do was not look away. And he hadn't, not even when they'd nailed his hands to the boards, not for twenty-four hours, until everyone was dead, the village was razed, the acrid smell of smoke burning his nose, his lungs. The sounds of the chopper brought him no relief, because he knew they'd save him before the fire reached him.

The group of Army Rangers had been going to another mission, stumbled on the destruction by way of the fire. They'd come in without permission, the Ranger who'd saved him taking the brunt of the blame, or so Dare had heard later.

Dare hadn't gone to the hearing for that soldier who'd saved him. It wouldn't have helped either of them. In the next months, Dare was sure the soldier would be found dead under mysterious circumstances, another in a long line of men who'd interfered in something S8 related.

He turned his attention back to Adele, who waited with a carefully cultivated pretense of patience. "Why come now?"

She hadn't seen him since right before that last mission. Hadn't come to the hospital. Hadn't called or written. And while he'd told himself it didn't bother him, it had.

"Your sister's in trouble."

Half sister. One he'd never met before out of both necessity and her mother's insistence. He didn't even know if Avery Welsh knew he existed. "I thought she was well hidden."

"We did too."

"Where is she?"

"On her way to the federal penitentiary in New York—or a cemetery—if you don't hurry."

"Are you fucking shitting me?"

She twisted her mouth wryly. "I assure you, I'm not."

"What did she do?"

"She killed two men," Adele said calmly. "The police are coming for her—she's about forty-eight hours away from being sent to jail for life. Of course, there are other men after her too, and they make the police look like the better option."

So the men who were after her had tipped off the police. "She's what—twenty-two?" A goddamned baby.

Adele nodded. "You'll have a small window of opportunity to grab her in the morning at the apartment where she's been hiding."

"You want me to . . ." He stopped, turned, ran his hands through his hair and laughed in disbelief. Spoke to the sky. "She wants me to help a killer."

"Your sister," she corrected. "Is that a problem?"

He laughed again, a sound that was rusty from severe underuse.

Avery had been secreted away with her mother before she'd been born, the relationship between her mother and Darius brief once she found out what Darius's livelihood was. But after that last mission, everything S8 related seemed to die down. Until Darius went missing. Until Dare was almost killed.

Until Adele showed up on his doorstep, dragging the past with her like an anchor.

"She's a known fugitive and I'm supposed to hide her?" he asked now.

"She's family—and she needs your protection."

He turned swiftly, fighting the urge to pin her against a column of the porch with an arm across her neck. The animal inside him was always there, lurking barely below the surface, the wildness never easily contained. "What the hell is that supposed to mean?"

Adele hadn't moved. "Don't make me spell everything out for you, Dare. You know you're still wanted. Why wouldn't she be?"

"I can't do this. Find—"

"Someone else?" she finished, smiled wanly. "There's no one but me and you, and I'm about to buy the farm, as they say. Cancer. The doctors give me a month at best."

"I'm sorry, Adele, but—"

"I know what happened to you. But we protect our own."

"I didn't choose to be a part of your group."

"No, you were lucky enough to be born into it," she said calmly.

"Yeah, that's me. Lucky."

"You're alive, aren't you?"

He wanted to mutter, *Barely*, but didn't. "Where's my father, Adele?"

She simply shrugged. "He's gone."

"Yeah, gone." Darius had been doing that since Dare was six years old.

"They're all gone—the men, *their families*. All *gone* over the course of the last six years. Do you understand?"

He had known. Dare had kept an eye on the families left behind by S8 operatives. Even though Darius had growled at him to stay the hell out of it, he'd found a line of accidents and unexplained deaths. They were all spaced widely enough apart and made enough sense not to look suspicious to the average eye.

But he wasn't the average eye. This was an S8 clean-house order, an expunging, and Dare knew he was still on that list and there was no escaping it.

For Avery, he would have to come out of hiding.

"Hiding won't stop your connection with Section 8," Adele said, as if reading his mind.

"I'm not hiding," he ground out.

"Then go to Avery—show her this from Darius."

She handed him a CD—the cover was a photograph of Avery. He glanced at the picture of the woman, and yeah, she resembled her father—the same arctic frost blue eyes—but her hair was light, not dark. She was really pretty. Too innocent looking to have committed murder, but he'd learned over the years that looks could never be trusted. "And then what? I'm no good for this."

"You're better than you think."

"Bullshit—I'm just the only one you've got."

She smiled, but it didn't reach her eyes.

He looked at the picture stuck into the clear CD case again, and something deep inside him ached for his lost childhood. He hoped Avery had had one. "I'll think about it."

With that, she walked away, turned to him when she was halfway to her car and stood stock-still in the driveway. The back of his neck prickled. "Best think fast, Dare."

It was part instinct, part the way Adele paused as if posing. She gave a small smile, a nod, her shoulders squared.

He sprang into action, yelled, "No!" as he leaped toward her, Sig drawn, but it was too late.

The gunshot rang out and he jumped back to the safety of the house, cutting his losses. Adele collapsed to the ground, motionless. A clean kill. Sniper.

She'd made the ultimate sacrifice—going out like a warrior to force him to get off his ass and into action—ending a life that was almost over anyway. His father would've done the same.

Now there was nothing to be done here but get away and live. A hot extract involving just himself.

He shot off several warning rounds of his own to

buy himself time. He took a quick picture of Adele with his cell phone camera and then went inside, grabbed his go bag and the guitar, then ignited the explosives he'd set up for a just-in-case scenario because, as a kid of a Section 8er, he was always a target.

That entire process took less than a minute, and then he took off in the old truck down the back road, the CD still in his hand.

Adele was too good not to know she'd been followed. She'd trapped him by bringing the trouble literally to his front door.

He cursed her, his father and everyone in that damned group as he motored down the highway, even as another part of his brain, hardwired for danger, made lists of what he'd need.

New wheels.

Guns.

New safe house with a wanted woman.

He threw the CD on the seat next to him and fingered the silver guitar pick he wore on a chain around his neck.

Goddammit, there was no escaping the past.

Chapter Two

Avery Welsh knew the end of the line when she saw it, but it had never been in her nature to surrender.

This time would be no different.

She'd been questioned by the police after the second murder. They hadn't had enough to hold her, so she'd left the small upstate New York town that very afternoon without looking back and headed for someplace in Manhattan where she could disappear.

Having no ties to anyone or anything made that so incredibly easy, it actually made her chest ache to the point where she could've sworn she was having a heart attack.

Now, in this shitty one-room apartment on the third floor in a building in the middle of Hell's Kitchen, the pain started again. Her bags were packed on the floor in front of her, but an unmarked car had staked out the front of her building all night. But maybe she was more suspicious than ever, because they didn't act like feds or cops—either group would've just come in and kicked down the door. She was wanted—there was no reason for such surveillance. She didn't know if that was better or worse and decided that, either way, it was bad news.

The only way out was down the condemned, rickety fire escape, but her fear of heights hadn't let her work up the nerve to head that way. Yet.

Another deep breath. Her hair stuck to the back of her neck despite the freezing-cold apartment. The heat wasn't working, but complaining wasn't an option since she wasn't an official tenant.

When she knew there were most-wanted posters of her in the local post office, discretion and a low profile were warranted.

Mom, I'm sorry, but I had to . . .

She felt a sudden gust of air and whirled around, gun pulled. The man who stood silently in the middle of her living room seemed unconcerned about the weapon.

He must've come up the fire escape, but she'd sworn she'd locked that window.

"You picked the wrong place to rob," she told him as she took in the handsome face and military posture.

"Avery, I'm here to save you."

He knew her name. Undercover? PI? She tried to pretend he hadn't thrown her. "I gave up on the prince-and-white-horse fantasy when I was seven."

His mouth twitched. "Good. But now it's me or the guys coming up the stairs."

Guys, not cops or feds. She hadn't been wrong. *Shit.*

"Who are you?"

"I know your father," he said. "No time to explain further. Come on."

The man was unblinking. The honesty coming from him could be an act, but she prided herself on her bullshit meter. Right now, this guy seemed the safer of the two options.

Another bounty hunter? Repo? He looked capable of anything, but she couldn't afford not to take risks. So when he slung both her bags over his shoulder, she followed her only way out. She'd been looking for information on her father—a man named Darius—for as long as she could remember, but it was like tracking a ghost.

When the past came knocking, she knew she had to answer the door.

"I'm scared of heights," she told him when he'd gotten down to the level of grating below hers.

"You should be more scared of jail. They'll eat you up in there." His comments both scared and infuriated her, so much so that she followed him out onto the rusted stoop and down the stairs and was threading her way down behind him.

She hadn't realized how fast they'd been going until her feet hit the ground with a hard thump on the concrete. She found herself looking down the barrel of a mean old Sig. "I'm already following you."

"Just making sure." He motioned for her and caught her arm, hustled her to a waiting truck. She'd barely scrambled into the seat when the man was in his, cranking the old vehicle out of the alley.

She turned to see the unmarked car starting to make chase but she felt the truck speed up under her, as if there was something extra under the hood. Whatever it was, she was more than grateful. Maybe her mother really was looking out for her. "Who are you?"

He didn't answer as he edged the car through traffic, winding along the side roads, and finally zoomed along the ramp toward the highway.

She turned to check the trailing car's progress.

"Don't bother—I lost them," he told her.

"You're that sure of yourself?"

"I'm that good."

That should've sounded cocky, but instead it came out like a simple truth from a handsome man who was no doubt a warrior.

Like your father . . .

At least that's what her mother had always said about Darius. Avery wanted to believe that, felt like she had some of that warrior inside her.

Now revenge ran too hot in her blood and she was discombobulated. But she was free—for now. "Who are you and how do you know my father?"

"He's my father too." He glanced at her for a second before his eyes were back on the road. "My name's Dare."

She couldn't speak for a long moment, the surprise stealing her breath as she stared at Dare's—her brother's—profile. His hair was dark, strong cheekbones . . . a full mouth. He had blue eyes, nowhere near as light or cold looking as she'd always thought hers were.

Her mom used to tell her with affection, *They're just like your daddy's.* "Are you sure?"

"You knew you had a half brother?" A question for

a question—from that alone, she could see the resemblance between them.

"I knew. Mom always said I'd never meet you."

"You weren't supposed to, but you're in a hell of a lot of trouble."

As she stealthily wiped away a tear, Dare asked, "Why are you wanted?" and handed her the paper with her picture on it.

She studied it as the truck barreled down the road. "It says 'wanted for murder' right here."

"I don't believe everything I read."

"It's true." She wondered if she should just surrender. Explain. But those men she'd searched out were the ones who'd hurt the one person who'd kept her safe all her life, and she'd hurt them.

She'd felt indestructible. Lethal. An angel of death no one saw coming.

Afterward, she'd felt angrier, not better. She had to make things right, had to balance out the bad deeds with some good ones.

"Why'd you do it?"

She glanced at Dare and wondered if he knew what it was like to live with a heavy burden of guilt. "I hunted down and killed the men who tortured, raped and killed my mother. Think a jury of my peers would understand that?"

"I have no goddamned idea what drives most people," he muttered. "You're going to have to fill in the story."

"My mom did bail bonds."

"She was a bounty hunter?"

"Yes—she owned the company and had men working for her. She wouldn't go out alone—but she was the one who usually talked the fugitives into surrendering." Both tough and tender, her mom could bring out the best in anyone. Avery had worked in the office for as long as she could remember, typing up files and helping to keep things running as she got old enough to get her own bounty license. Learning things both legal and illegal from the men and women her mother employed as she helped them try to turn their lives around. "One night, she got a call from a woman she'd helped in the past. It was late and she wanted me to go with her, but I'd been up all night doing paperwork— I'd fallen asleep on the couch and she'd left me a note."

It had been four hours later when she'd woken. Avery had tried to call and got voice mail, so she'd driven to the address her mother had hastily written on a pad of paper by the phone. Luckily, it was on carbon copy paper used for messages.

The fast, smooth motion of this truck was nothing like the way her drive had been that night, her arms jerking the wheel, fear knotting her limbs.

"I found her in the alley. She'd tried to fight—that was obvious. But they just . . ." She put a hand up to her eyes like that could stop the tears. Didn't want to show the kind of emotion she felt to a relative stranger, but revisiting the image was something she did daily. When she got control back, she continued. "They'd cut her. Raped her. Then they stabbed her and let her bleed out. And I had no idea why. Before the police got there, I took fingerprints and samples from under her nails and went to a friend who worked in a lab to run them later that day. I was thinking about meting out my own brand of justice—it was the only thing that got me through."

"You were supposed to be with her," Dare said simply.

Why that was so hard for her to admit to herself, never mind out loud, she didn't know. She nodded, knew now there was no turning back from all this.

"That same woman called again—tried to lure me back to that spot later that night," she said. "I didn't tell the police anything about that. I already knew how to shoot criminals. To track them. To think like them. It took me three weeks to find them—twenty-one days of following that woman around until I got a lead."

"Did they say anything?"

"I didn't give them the chance. I thought they went after her because of a jumped bounty or something. There was paperwork, but I found out later that was all stolen from another bounty hunter. I never suspected..." She brought a hand to her throat, and there was silence in the truck for a long time, even as darkness fell and they put more distance between her and the men who'd come after her. She assumed he was bringing them to a safe place for the night. If there was such a thing. "I think her murder was part of something bigger."

"What makes you think that?"

"Because you and I both know that those men back at the apartment were hired hits, not cops or feds." And now it was her turn for questions. "Where's our father?"

"There's a CD he made for you in the glove compartment."

"I have a laptop in my bag," she said after she pulled the CD out.

"Crank the volume."

She found the CD and then took the small computer from her bag and prepared to watch it.

She drew in a sharp breath when the first image of her father came on the screen, and she paused it for a long moment so she could stare. Traced a light finger around his cheekbone.

There was no denying her parentage.

As Dare turned onto the highway and got lost in the blend of traffic, she hit "play," and the voice—*her father's voice*—filled the truck. Warm, dulcet tones that belied the ice in his eyes—her eyes. She felt at once comforted and sad that this would be their only contact.

But she'd never thought she'd even have this.

"Avery—doll—I'm sorry, but your momma and I decided a long time ago that it was much safer for you if I wasn't involved in your life. But if you're watching this, you're in trouble because of me and things I've been involved in. If you're watching this, you're with Dare, and you're both in trouble—and a man named Richard Powell is the one to blame." A heavy sigh, a shake of the head. Fingers rustled in the short growth of beard on his chin before he continued. "Stay with Dare. Do whatever you have to in order to stay safe. Because the men Powell sent after you will not give up. Ever. Go home—you'll find grace there."

Go home . . .

She'd seen a magic show once, and what interested her the most were the interlocking circles—silver and shiny; they made the coolest noise when the magician separated them and hooked them back together until they made a long, interconnected chain.

Her mother had bought her some and she learned the trick behind them easily. Wished she hadn't ruined the magic for herself, but she'd been too curious not to understand.

She was connected to this man, but not locked to him—not really.

Not yet. "Do you know where home is?"

He nodded. "Buckle up for a long ride."

Avery didn't push him for an explanation, was too busy staring at the computer screen, and Dare took those blessed minutes of silence to decide what the hell to reveal to her.

All or nothing. That had been Darius's motto.

His earliest memory was of his father playing his electric guitar, the music ringing through the house. Darius would turn up the amps and let it blast at top volume until the walls and floors shook.

Dare's mom had given Darius a silver pick on a chain, engraved with the date of their wedding, since he wouldn't wear a ring. Darius gave it to Dare after Mom died, maybe when he was about twelve, and Dare couldn't remember the last time he was without it.

He never liked being a slave to a talisman, but he was. Held the pick between two fingers and rubbed it like a worry stone.

He was never without Darius's guitar either, although he hadn't played it once this year. He could see it in the backseat if he turned his head, but he refused.

Maybe he'd never play again, but he couldn't bring himself to leave it behind.

Avery touched the computer screen one last time and then closed it with a quiet click. "What happened to Darius?"

"I don't know."

"Is he . . . dead?"

Dare shrugged. "He's been MIA for a year, but that doesn't translate to dead."

"Have you looked for him?"

"No." The past had reared its ugly head, and there was no turning away now. At least he wasn't dealing with a shrinking violet here. Helpful . . . and in some ways worse.

"Don't you think you should?" she persisted.

"I've lived with his fallout my entire life," Dare told her. "If you'd like to take up the mantle after we find out who's trying to kill us, be my guest."

The first time he'd been taken from his home was when he was six right after his mom had left them. Dare had lived with Adele and her then husband for eight months before his dad came home. It continued like that until Dare was fourteen or so and would stay at home alone during his father's missions.

"What is he a part of?" Avery asked, and Dare knew she had every right to know.

"They called themselves Section 8 because that's the discharge they'd all been given by the military."

Technically, it was called something else now, but the intent was still the same. Mental defect. Unfit for duty.

"Were they?"

"Crazy? In one way or another, yes." He glanced at her. "You worried you inherited some of it?"

"I know I did," she muttered, and he felt his mouth quirk up a little despite his attempts not to smile.

"Darius was afraid of heights."

"Really?"

"His whole life. He got past it—but he said it was always his nemesis."

"Thanks for telling me that, Dare."

"Welcome. There's a lot more I've got to fill you in on. There were eight of them altogether. Just happened that way, but Adele always though it was poetic."

"Were there other women?"

"Just her. She was killed yesterday after coming to tell me you were in trouble." The thought of her lying on the ground made his throat tighten. She would've told him that this wasn't the time for sentiment, which was reserved for the dead of night when the mission was over, and then you killed it with strong whiskey. Drown the sorrow before it drowned you.

"And this Richard Powell . . . he knows about Section 8?" Avery said, and realization slowly dawned on Dare . . . and on Avery.

"The men you killed—," he started.

"Are the men sent by Powell?" she finished it as a question, and there was surprise in her voice, since she'd obviously just come to that conclusion with

Dare's information. "Do you think they tortured her, trying to get information about my father, to see what he'd told her about Section 8?"

Dare forced his eyes to stay on the road, kept his breathing slow and steady. "Maybe."

"Still think I should be in jail?" she asked quietly, and he shook his head no. "I didn't know I'd be dragging anyone else in. I didn't know anything about the group. I only knew I was trying to avenge my mom's murder."

"I was already dragged into it," he told her. "You heard Darius—I've been marked for death, same as you."

"All because Darius was part of Section 8?" she asked, and he nodded. "Are you part of it too?"

"No. There was only one S8, and they'd disbanded long before I would've been able to work with them." It had been a moment in time. It had been so perfect . . . and it had all gone so horribly wrong. "On what was supposed to be their last mission—twenty years ago— they lost a man. Almost lost Darius. He left Simon behind and then got a call that S8 was officially disbanded."

"But they kept working."

"Yes. Plenty of work for operatives like that," he agreed. And whether he'd wanted to or not, his formative years had been spent learning from each of them. Adele in particular had come in most useful with her love of demolition—she took it to an almost spiritual level with the way she wired the bombs, predicted the blast outcome.

Darius was the mastermind, second only to S8's

handler—he kept the team together, let them work on their individual strengths and made up for their weaknesses. And he'd never replaced Simon—they'd continued to work one man down.

And now they were all gone.

"Did you know their families?"

"No. We were all kept apart, for good reason."

"So you couldn't be used against one another."

"That was the theory."

Darius had been more secretive than ever these last years, like he knew letting Dare in on everything would sign his death warrant. As it was, the burden of the legacy of Section 8 was falling firmly on Dare, even though he knew only the sketchiest of details on the missions, where the bank accounts were, who S8's enemies had been.

But the name Powell . . . that was new.

Avery was telling him, "But we're part of it . . . because we were born to an S8 member."

"Trust me—you don't want to be a part of it. It's not conducive to staying alive. Anyone who had a connection to S8 is being systematically hunted and killed for their knowledge, no matter how much or how little."

"Doesn't the CIA care?"

"S8 fell off their radar a long time ago."

"But not off this Powell guy's," Avery pointed out.

"I'm guessing he was their handler."

"You don't know for sure?"

"They were never supposed to find out. I'm guessing Darius did, and that bought him a world of trouble."

We're running for our lives, he wanted to tell her, but she knew. No reason to say the words out loud.

At some point, they were going to have to turn around and run toward the enemy, just like Simon had done. Sometimes that trick didn't work. But sometimes it did.

"Can we stop Powell?"

"We don't have much choice."

"We could hide."

He'd been doing that, but nothing had changed. The evil was still festering, and if he didn't try to stop it, he couldn't live with himself. "We'll get Powell."

"Don't you think he knows we're coming for him?"

"Sometimes that's the best way."

She nodded and felt her resolve steel like a palpable force. "We're kids of Section 8—we need to live up to the group's rep, right?"

"No, we don't," Dare told her, heard the fierceness in his voice for the first time in more than a year. "We need to exceed it."

Chapter Three

Mental institution or jail—the choice was an easy one for Jem, except for the parts when they tied you down and tried to shock the shit out of your brain.

Not that it ever did anything for him but get him hard, which really freaked the docs out, and that alone made it worth the pain.

This stint had only been three months so far. Before this his crimes had always been wiped from the system, thanks to the CIA.

But this time, the CIA wasn't coming to break him out. His handler had warned him that he'd pushed it too far, and given Jem's history, the only concession made was to put him in the mental ward while he recovered from his GSW.

After that, he was headed to prison, as the government disavowed all knowledge of him.

He'd known they could do so. Hell, it made the risk that much more intriguing. And if he didn't have family troubles, he'd probably serve the few years so he could walk away a free man.

He had six months left, his handler had told him earlier in the week.

"And then what? You gonna put me back in the field?"

"You know that's impossible, Jem. Serve your time in jail, find some peace and then—"

Jem had hung the phone up and walked away. Finding peace was not only impossible; it wasn't on his life list of things to goddamned do.

He was on his own, and anyway, it kept his skills in shape. Amazing what you could learn from crazy people, especially when you had that gene inside you. Letting it run free for a while was as necessary as a wolf running during the full moon. Inevitable and impossible to stop.

"Jeremiah," one of the student nurses called, and he glanced up from the bench he'd been lying on.

"Jem," he corrected, held out his hand for the pills, took them without water and opened his mouth wide to show her that he hadn't hidden them under his tongue.

Damn right he took them—they gave him a mild jolt, but he'd always been able to handle substances like this without many side effects. The crazy outpaced it all.

The student nurses were the best because they believed the patients. He loved to watch them get led through the floors, only to find themselves trapped between a locked door and giggling patients.

Now he watched one of them try to get a woman to calm down and take her meds. But Bettie would go down fighting—slapped the nurse and threw a chair while Jem watched and waited for his out.

When the orderly tried to stop her, she swung another chair, which Jem caught and held.

Bettie turned to him. "I'm the Queen of England!"

"Yes, you are," Jem agreed solemnly. He let the orderly get close to her and then he backed away with the man's keys in his pocket.

Three locks later, he was out the door and in his younger brother's car. Key had been cleaning up after him—and trying to save him—since they were little.

"Never asked you to," Jem would tell him, but Key would keep trying.

One of these days, he might not be there.

But today, he was. "Dude, get the hell out of here."

Key glanced in the rearview at the orderlies and security guard headed toward the car. "I thought you said you were being discharged."

"I said I was ready to be discharged. Are you going to argue semantics, brother, or are you going to drive?"

Key muttered some choice curses under his breath, but he ultimately floored it out of the lot.

"Get the net." Jem laughed, turned the radio all the way up and opened the window. "Fresh fucking air. Got any cigarettes?"

Key just shot him a look and pointed to the glove compartment. "I don't understand why they keep putting you back into these places. Nothing ever changes."

Jem drew a few puffs on the cigarette, silently agreeing with Key. But in reality, he forced the CIA's hand in most of these cases, returned in the hopes that someone could fix him, could explain the burning need to do crazy, dangerous things like they were the air he breathed.

He wanted normal, but as every shrink since the dawn of time had pointed out, normal was relative.

The one thing they did agree on was that he was just enough outside of that box for them to keep agreeing to take him in.

How all this crazy—as his family always called it— skipped Key, he'd never know. But he was grateful for it.

"What did you do this time?"

"Nothing major," Jem assured him, which he knew was no reassurance at all. "Did I screw up your leave?"

"I'm out."

Key had been a great Ranger—and he'd been up for a promotion to the Delta Teams once he passed the necessary tests. Jem didn't know if Key knew that and decided not to even ask. No matter what, he'd done Jem proud.

It had been his brother's life, and now Jem needed to be there to put the pieces back together, before the family curse took out Key at the knees.

If it was a rescue Key needed, that's what he'd get. If he needed to drink and fuck his way through New Orleans before he felt better, they could do that too. But Jem would be damned if he'd watch Key self-destruct and sit by and do nothing about it.

"I don't understand it. You saved a guy's life," he said finally. He hadn't been able to help Key all that much. Jem had tried to pull some strings, but he'd met with a hell of a lot of resistance, enough to make him suspicious that this was far more complicated than Key simply disobeying a direct order.

"The SEAL didn't bother to show up to testify," Key said tightly. "Didn't answer letters. No one could find him to serve the subpoena."

"Sure he's alive?"

"When I find him, he'll wish he wasn't," Key muttered.

Jem didn't bother to try to talk Key out of that—didn't tell him that he was out of a job as well. Until you lost it all, you had no idea how much you were willing to give. Owning next to nothing had always worked for Jem. Having some money in the bank for emergencies was also important. "Where are we headed?"

Key gave a small twist of a grin. "Home."

Most of New Orleans was still shot to shit, which left it a perfect hiding spot for vagrants and lawbreakers.

Luckily, he could be both.

Chapter Four

Two months later
New Orleans

The cabdriver didn't want to drop her there, asked her three times if she was sure she had the right place.

"Really, I'm fine," Avery told him firmly, watched him press his lips together in the rearview mirror as he pulled over in front of the address Dare had given her.

She was fine, because after everything she'd been through, she'd be damned if anyone would stop her now, no matter how hard they were prepared to try.

She knew there were nice parts of New Orleans as well as tougher ones, as was the case in any city. But after Katrina, things were different, her mother had said in that wistful tone she always got when talking about this place.

Avery had wanted to come here for as long as she could remember but had been half-afraid, thanks to Mom's warnings.

New Orleans makes you do crazy things.

"Ma'am, just go directly into the shop—don't stop to talk," the driver said now, as she glanced out the window to get her bearings.

There were two men standing a few doors down from where she needed to go, and a larger group a block down, all of whom stilled when the cab pulled up. She paid the fare and exited the car, kept her head up as she walked toward her destination. But it wasn't going to be that easy.

"I have to be useful. I can't cower and let you protect me forever," she'd argued to Dare earlier.

"It's not forever."

"Give me a job. I don't want to be helpless."

"I get that."

"You said we need to get crazy. Let me get crazy."

Now she was sure she felt Dare's eyes on her as the closest two men moved toward her swiftly. Maybe she screamed *tourist* or maybe it was simply because she was a woman alone.

Crazy indeed.

She flexed her hands by her sides and kept moving forward, as did they.

She took the first man out easily because he wasn't expecting her to kick his ass. One swift chop of her hand across his throat and a second hard kick to the groin and he was on the ground, moaning like a girl. She managed a second kick to his ribs for a finale, to ensure he wouldn't get up when she was dealing with his counterpart.

He took her more seriously. He was big and could easily overpower her if she'd let him. *That's the key,* her mother had always told her. *Never let them have the advantage.*

Her mother had fought to the death. But you couldn't fight with bullets. And the familiar anger welled up inside Avery as she spotted a gun tucked into his jeans, exposed as he raised his hand, readying to punch her in the face.

She put up her own fists, ducked his attempt, because she was smaller and faster. Two quick jabs of her own, one of which clocked him squarely on the jaw, and she was chest to chest with him. Her hand was on the butt of the gun, cocked and ready. One quick wrist move and she said, "Your choice . . . if you want to lose your little friend."

He'd stilled instantly. She stared directly at him. "We're both going to walk away and you're not going to follow me."

He held his hands up. She took his gun with her, turned and walked down the four steps under the awning that said simply, *Tattoos*, and never looked back.

She'd been in New Orleans almost three full days—seventy-two hours—and trouble had already found her. And she was actively seeking out more.

"You find Gunner, take over his top floor," Dare had told her earlier that evening as they'd walked out of the hotel they'd been staying in since their arrival.

"What does Gunner do?" she'd asked.

"Technically, he's running a tattoo shop."

"So what makes you think he'll help us?"

"He saved my life."

"That doesn't make any sense," she'd persisted, and all Dare would say was, "I know."

"Did you call him?"

"No."

"Wouldn't it be easier if you introduced us?"

"Yes," was all he said before he drove away in his old truck, leaving her to grab a cab.

Still, she'd done her research on the way over. What had people done before laptops and WiFi and 4G service?

Maybe walking into Gunner's shop brandishing a gun was a bad idea, but the tattoo artist didn't look up from his work. The woman getting a tattoo seemed almost lulled into a state of relaxation—her chest was bared and Gunner leaned over her intently.

Even seated, Avery could tell Gunner was tall—over six foot five probably—with white-blond hair that was cut short. His features were Nordic but when he glanced up at her his eyes were a warm blue, the color of the summer sky. There were tattoos running up and down his bare arms. She had a feeling they traveled under his wife beater and maybe even down his jean-clad legs.

You can't miss him, Dare had said.

That was a fact.

She figured the guy was armed and that any fight with him might not be a draw. As a show of goodwill, she took the ammo out of the gun and pocketed both. The walls were lined with framed photos of his tattoo artwork—some were almost grotesque, but she couldn't deny they were beautiful.

Gunner had a gift. Why he chose to have his shop here, in a location that no doubt kept away business, kept him from getting famous, she didn't know. But there had to be a reason.

If he knew Darius and Dare, that was definitely the biggest piece to the puzzle.

"Don't have any openings," Gunner called out finally. From what little information she'd managed to find, the shop had a quiet, cultlike following. It served an exclusive clientele and was famous for not accepting appointments.

"I don't want a tattoo."

"You're all done, sweetheart," Gunner drawled to the pretty woman in his chair, and she smiled up at him, a slightly dazed look in her eye. "You got a ride home?"

"My husband's picking me up, yes," she said as he helped her stand and showed her the work.

It was obvious it hadn't all been done today—no, this was a massively beautiful work that encompassed the woman's breasts, or where they'd once been. It was a swirling pattern of color that covered the same amount of skin a sports bra would, making it look like she was wearing some kind of short, floaty camisole. It no doubt hid the scars from a double mastectomy. The woman's hair was short and gray, like it was growing in from a recent round of chemotherapy, but on the whole she looked healthy.

"It's perfect," the woman breathed and turned to give Gunner a gentle hug.

Avery felt like she'd broken in on such an intimate

moment. Until then, she'd never much considered the mysterious privacy of tattoos, never given a thought to what seemed to be a sacredness of process.

The woman was flushed—pride, adrenaline. Gunner seemed to glow as well, like he was some kind of fallen angel.

In reality, he was probably a mercenary. That didn't make him the devil, but he'd no doubt done things he could never talk about, things that would haunt him.

Maybe tattooing was a way of repenting. Or maybe he just liked the stress release.

And even though she knew she should step away, she couldn't tear her eyes away from the work. She supposed that was the point. The woman looked . . . empowered. She might not have her breasts, but the way she looked now, the covering was beautiful enough to draw attention away from that fact. "My husband's going to love it. I love it."

Gunner simply smiled, and when she was ready, he helped her into her shirt and walked her outside. He came back inside a minute later, locked the door behind him. He looked Avery up and down, his blue eyes boring through her. "I don't want women with guns in my shop."

"I have a proposal for you."

"Christ, do you have to make it sound like marriage? I've had enough of them, each one worse than the last."

"Why keep doing it, then?"

"I'm a romantic," he deadpanned. "Are you looking to be my next bride?"

"Not especially."

"Then talk to me. You're what—a bounty hunter who wants to turn merc? Or the more PC private contractor?"

"We need a home base."

"Not another merc group looking to save the world." Gunner paused. "You pay well?"

"Very."

"Bullshit. If you had money you wouldn't be here."

"I've heard you're the best."

"In many, many ways, sweetheart." He paused. "You gonna tell me why you're really here? Because you're obviously new at this shit."

"Will you rent me the top floor?"

He sighed, stared up at the ceiling for a long second before pinning her with his gaze again. "I'll make you a deal. You let me tattoo you, you can have the top floor."

"Who gets to pick the tattoo?"

"Me. And I get to pick where." He smiled wickedly and she nodded and made a deal with the new devil in her life.

She stuck her hand out. After he shook it, she said, "I'm here for Dare."

"Ah, fuck me. And he sent you in here all alone—what the hell is that asshole thinking?" Gunner muttered.

"He said that you owe him because you saved his life."

"Something I never plan on doing again," he assured her.

Chapter Five

Grace Powell was dancing in her garden in the middle of the goddamned New Orleans bayou summer night in the rain.

Dare watched her, alternately fascinated and pissed that he was fascinated at the way her dress clung to her, molding to her breasts in a way that made him want to sink to his knees and howl at the moon.

Or lower her to the wet ground and take the dress off.

He wanted her with a longing so deep and dark he didn't think he'd ever fill it, even if he took her over and over in the hot rain scalding his skin.

So fucking inappropriate. His body was strung too tight for this kind of seductive dance. It took everything he had to stay in place.

Her feet were bare, her long brown hair had coppery highlights and was pulled back in a single braid that shone with water droplets . . . and she was smiling.

Take her now.

After all, why did she deserve to be happy, despite

what Avery had tried to tell him earlier? Avery, whom he'd left behind in town to connect with an old friend, only partially because he didn't want her to take part in this kidnapping.

He'd assumed that when Darius said, *Go home . . . you'll find grace there*, he'd been talking in a more spiritual sense. Instead, he'd found Grace Powell's address in the safe at the house Darius kept on the bayou, written in Darius's handwriting.

Grace Powell.

Dare and Avery had researched Richard Powell, what little there was on him. There was less on his daughter. From what Dare could gather, Grace had been "missing" for the last six years, and somehow, S8 had discovered where she was staying. Might've been dumb luck since she'd ended up living in the same bayou parish, but Dare suspected there was more to the story. Because Powell's daughter was a powerful tool in the S8 arsenal.

Using Powell's daughter was a brilliant plan on paper. In the flesh, harder than Dare had thought. He'd done worse things in his career—many of them—but this felt right and wrong all at once.

Grace Powell could be his salvation or his undoing. Or both.

No matter. Moving forward was the only option. He slopped through the mud and went to her, knowing his father would hate him for doing this. But for the first time in his life, he didn't give a damn about what Darius would think.

And while she struggled, she didn't seem all that surprised.

He grabbed her from behind, pulled her tight against him. A hand over her mouth, another around her waist, and she fought as he carried her to his truck.

She wouldn't stop fighting.

The garden. She smelled like gardenias long after they'd left her garden. He nearly buried his nose in her hair because the smell drove him crazy, over the edge, out of control.

Goddamn, this had been a mistake. He'd let himself go too long without a woman. This was simple lust.

Keep lying to yourself.

She wore a small cross-body bag, as if she'd been expecting to go somewhere. She shifted against the bindings he'd purposely made tight so she'd hate him. So she'd spit on him, stop staring at him like . . .

Like he was more than her captor.

"What's your name?" he asked, even though he knew.

She eyed him coolly, and when she spoke, her voice was laden with both honey and steel. "You should just call me leverage."

The man who'd approached her had fire in his eyes and looked at her like she was prey. Right before he'd put her in the car, Grace had spoken one final time.

"I don't know anything about my father's business," she lied carefully, because he'd know.

"You are your father's business. That's enough for me."

"What did he do to you?"

His eyes had glittered. "He tried to kill me."

She'd wanted to say, *Me too,* but she didn't have the strength. Dare wouldn't believe her anyway.

She'd spent the day helping one woman gather the strength to press charges against her abusive husband. By the time she'd convinced her, helped her get into the car with Marnie to go to the police station, the tension headache had gotten worse. She'd popped several Motrin and kept going, processing another intake on a woman who needed Marnie's help.

By the time she'd gotten home, she hadn't wanted to go into the house, the one she'd built so lovingly—her sanctuary.

It was ultimately what would ruin her, her own fault. And so she'd stayed outside in the garden, until the rain came and the pain in her head receded.

Until Dare came and grabbed her.

White knight or black king . . . it was too early to tell. What wasn't too early to tell was that she wouldn't be able to live in her house again.

She'd miss her garden the most, didn't believe for a second she'd be allowed to go back and tend to it. No, she'd been found and she'd have to let the house, and everything in it, go.

The garden was brimming—August was the time to start picking and freezing the herbs before they withered in the brutal heat and humidity that oppressed everything it touched.

She had been studying this forever, learned a kind of practical magic from her mother. It was a way to keep her close, since she'd left the private island when Grace was twelve. Grace's last memory was of the helicopter rising above the house.

She'd had no idea that the last time she saw her mother would be the last time.

Don't go there, she warned herself harshly. This wasn't a time to show weakness, despite how very weak she felt at the moment. Soaked to the skin, she tried not to shiver, bit down fiercely on the inside of her cheeks to stop her teeth from chattering as Dare led her from the truck into the house she knew as Darius's.

The last time she'd been here, it had been on another hot summer's day and she'd been reluctantly saying good-bye to Darius and Adele. Excited to start her new life, hating the fact that it would include moving around the country every six months for her own safety . . . and yet, two years had passed since that day and she was still here, in the Louisiana bayou, hoping the destruction and natural wildness of the place would shield her from evil.

Had it? Dare didn't look evil—but he also looked nothing like his father, so she was having trouble reading him. It had taken her a year to really believe Darius's intentions—and to someone who had a psychic gift, that it had taken so long had been almost embarrassing. It was a defective, infuriating gift, damaged and in hiding from years of abuse of her pushing it down and away, denying its existence for her own safety.

If she couldn't see the future, she'd be no good for Rip. But that didn't mean he didn't want her back anyway.

Dare O'Rourke had plans for her too, and she could feel those as surely as if he'd already spoken to her out loud.

She should not feel a flutter deep inside her belly while pressed against the man taking her hostage, but it was undeniable. She fought not to lean in and smell his skin. She detected the scent of the jungle on him.

He'd tied her wrists together, tight behind her back, as if deliberately trying to scare her.

She could pretend, but why bother? She'd always known this day would come, was as resigned to it as she was to her gift eventually returning. But there was a part of her that was afraid of her reaction to this man . . . afraid of what he would do to her.

Her arms ached. This man would hurt her if it meant getting a rise out of her stepfather.

She'd always known it was one of the risks. Had lived the past six years as though the enemy was coming for her at any moment. She couldn't remember the last time she'd slept with the lights off. She could fire a gun, knew every self-defense technique and was still on edge. Angry, if she thought about it enough, more than fearful. A good emotion to have behind her, she supposed, but she was tired of being on guard all the time.

If she was lucky, at times she could go a full twenty-four hours without thinking about it. Her house was old, a work in progress, and she'd known from her first moments here that the bayou was a place of magic and a place of lost souls. One could easily get lost.

It was perfect for her. Except she wondered if she'd

ever find something to anchor her. Longed for it, but decided it was too much to ask.

In order to escape her father, she'd had to make certain sacrifices. This was much better than living in a house on one of the small islands off Grand Cayman, where she'd been a prisoner for most of her years growing up.

Still, people were always looking for her—both good and bad. She'd been told as much by Darius and Adele. And Grace felt the relentless press of horseman's hooves at her back now more than ever.

Six years of relative freedom was all that she would be granted, it seemed. It was more than she'd ever thought she'd have.

It wasn't enough.

Chapter Six

Hours earlier, Dare had brought Grace into his house, left her bound but ungagged in a chair in the living room facing the wall. He hadn't said a word to her since they'd driven away from her place, and the tension had built to a nearly unbearable level.

Moving away from her had been a relief, although he could see her through the porch window from the old swing he lowered himself onto.

He'd brought one of Darius's old guitars out with him because it had been sitting by the door as if waiting for someone.

Dare still didn't know if he was that someone, but he set it next to him on the swing and listened to the rain slamming along the old roofing like it was trying its best to break it. His hands ached, as they tended to do in this weather, and no amount of flexing would help that, but he could still shoot and fight, and that was all that mattered.

Pain was always a part of his life—this injury made no difference.

Since he'd left the jungle, he'd exercised his hands

constantly to keep them from seizing up, and they'd slowly begun to heal, one better than the other. He'd had to switch from being right-handed to left because the loss of sensation in his right hand made it difficult to handle a gun. Difficult, not impossible, but he was a better shot with his left than he'd ever been with his right. It was a different perspective. Some people said scars made things stronger because that tissue tended to be tougher. Dare wasn't so sure of that, but he wanted to believe it.

The bayou reminded him of the jungle: hot and noisy and teeming with danger and beauty—just depended on your perspective. Nothing had changed—hurricanes might try to decimate this place, but it always came back.

Bayou living wasn't for everyone. It tended to be rough, sometimes bordering on unpleasant and downright cruel, but some of his best memories were of this house, the surrounding swamps . . . he'd bet he'd find the same pirogues floating around the dock if he took a stroll that way.

So he was back here, but he wasn't *back* yet, not fully. His mind was still in that jungle, his soul locked away and his heart, ice. Adele had chipped at it, Avery had broken through, but that was where it had ended.

"I always wanted a big brother," she'd told him on one of their first of many days spent traveling cross-country in an attempt to throw anyone and everyone off their trail.

"Now you've got one. A little late—"

"Never. Never too late," Avery told him. She'd ordered room service—cookies and hot chocolate for her and coffee for him, *since he wanted to be boring*, she'd said, and they'd sat and talked. Planned. Watched TV. Two months of that and he'd almost felt human again.

Damn, it had been nice. She was smart, like Darius. He trusted her more easily and completely than he'd ever trusted anyone, even his father. Maybe that was the way it was supposed to be when family was involved.

But now the plans were set in motion, and there was no more relaxing. They both had their jobs.

His phone buzzed in his pocket. Avery. Right on time. "You okay?"

"Like you don't know?" she asked with that hint of laughter in her voice that hadn't failed to make him smile yet.

Of course he'd watched her go into Gunner's. He'd never let her take that on alone, no matter her insistence. "I don't know what you're talking about."

"Thanks for trusting me to get to him on my own," she said.

"I needed to see how you handle yourself when I'm not around," he explained. "I didn't mean to throw you to the wolves."

"I took care of the wolves."

"You damned well did. How's Gunner?"

"Not happy."

"He's never happy—get used to it."

"I had to promise him a tattoo."

"That better be all he made you promise," he muttered. But once she stepped inside his shop, Dare knew she was under Gunner's protection, whether Avery knew it or not.

Gunner was so good, she wouldn't.

Avery was safe with Gunner, although Dare had no idea how safe that really was. Gunner was out of the business, but there were a lot of people looking to recruit him against his will and an equal number who wanted him dead.

Gunner was in his early thirties, had come by his rep by the time he'd turned eighteen, solidified it in the Navy and got to legendary status during his first year in black ops.

He worked for no one but himself, which was always a risky proposition, but Gunner would never hook up with a group.

He'd been too much of a loner for the teams—no matter how many times they'd tried to recruit him. He'd known his limits, in love and fighting, but no woman ever believed him, which was why he'd married three times. Four, if Dare believed the rumors.

No matter—Avery wouldn't be his next ex-wife. Dare would kill the guy first.

But that was business of an entirely different order, and Dare had more than his share to handle under this roof tonight.

"Is everything okay on your end?" she asked, changing the subject deftly.

"Darius left nothing on her beyond her address."

"Is she okay?"

"I didn't hurt her."

"I know," she told him. "You're not like that."

He wanted to tell her that she didn't know him well enough if she could make a statement like that, but he didn't want to ruin her perception of him. Not yet. And maybe it was because she was so open with him, because her life depended on him, literally, but being her protector didn't feel like the burden he'd thought it would.

She believed in him in a way that made him want to believe in himself.

"Has she said anything yet?" Avery asked now.

"I haven't started talking to her yet."

"Do you want me there?"

That might be the best thing. Easier for him, for sure. "You're better served where you are. Check in tomorrow."

"It is tomorrow," she chided gently before hanging up.

He put the phone back in his pocket, fingered the silver pick hanging around his neck and looked out at the dark bayou that lay beyond the house.

He remembered green grass, sticky air, the long, lazy summer days that rolled into easy summer nights when breezes were scarce and lightning bugs floated around like flickering magic.

Darius would play the guitar, the notes wafting along the thick air, and Dare would listen and pick up the guitar the next day, trying to play the notes from memory, sometimes succeeding.

But the days for being lazy were few and far between. Darius always had a mission for Dare, wanted his son to be mission ready, and Dare wouldn't not be.

His mother . . . he had vague memories of her, singing in the tiny house in North Carolina that was just off base. She had a small vegetable garden too.

Later, all he remembered was the crying . . . and then she was gone.

Darius went off the rails after that.

Darius left the Army, although he'd never stopped working. It was then that the other six men and Adele began to circle his space. They were at various times friendly and angry and serious and silly. But no one ever took anything out on him.

Not idyllic, but he knew there were much worse ways to grow up.

He stared at the back of Grace's head. She'd turned when he first started tuning the guitar, but she couldn't see him, no matter how hard she tried.

Interrogation had its uses, but he'd have to soften her up first. She was strong and angry, and she would not go down easily. If she was left alone, her mind would take over. He wouldn't have to do much more than that, let her get hungry and tired.

By the time he interrogated her, her own fear would've done more to her than he could've ever brought himself to do. She'd be working over her options in her mind, tiring herself out like a hamster on a wheel.

Will you be doing the same damned thing out here?

He answered himself with a snort and picked up the guitar, balanced it on his thigh.

The choices were pretty simple. If he turned Grace in, he could very well have his life back. More important, so could Avery.

Worst-case scenario: Richard Powell got Grace back and killed all of them. What could Dare do? He couldn't kidnap and hold her as collateral for the rest of her natural-born life.

No, he needed something else on Powell to ensure this trade went smoothly. Grace had to know something he could use against Powell—and in turn, against her.

She'd spill if she thought it would save her from going back to her father, and that was just what he was counting on.

And then he'd have to decide if he could live with himself if he made that trade. A life for a life, Avery's for Grace's.

His palm curled around the smooth wood, his fingers playing along the strings. It would have to be tuned because no one had been here to play it in a long while.

He began to do that, hitting each note, tightening or loosening each string.

He'd never learned to play well with the pick, preferred strumming with his fingers since he could find the rhythm more easily that way. The vibrations under his rough fingertips spread through his hands, causing them to ache a little more. But hell, at least he felt something.

Grace heard the low notes of the guitar float through the screen door.

Dare was on the porch. She hadn't heard him move for hours, but she'd heard him talking. And now this.

She didn't turn around, hadn't the entire time, no matter how difficult it was to stay put. Instead, she concentrated on keeping herself together, because he was counting on her falling apart.

What if she could share everything with him? Was he the one she was supposed to tell her secrets to? Didn't everyone have one person in their lives they could trust, or did that only happen in movies?

The guitar continued now—he'd stopped the practice strumming and was playing a song.

Darius used to play on the old porch, but he wasn't half as good as Dare was. Dare was a natural—he played from the heart. She listened to the chords as they built to a crescendo. She recognized the song— "Plush," by the Stone Temple Pilots—and filled in the hauntingly beautiful lyrics in her head.

It was as if Dare was asking her about tomorrow, where she was going with her mask.

It was as if he knew her.

Set to the music, the question was mournful and hopeful, all at once. Maybe it was time for the mask to drop.

She closed her eyes and prayed he wouldn't come in until the tears had stopped rolling down her cheeks.

Chapter Seven

Gunner decided he was starving and didn't want take-out. They walked to the restaurant, which was just up the block. Avery adjusted the baseball cap she'd grabbed from her bag, noting that no one came near them as they walked together through the darkened streets, which were beginning to show signs of life, as though the music wafted along the sidewalk.

"Don't worry—I'll show you the floor when we get back," he told her. "Wheels in your mind are working overtime. Relax. It's after six. No more work tonight."

As they settled into a table in the loud and crowded casual restaurant, a car backfired outside the open window behind them. She immediately froze, flashed back to killing the first man. She hadn't hesitated to pull the trigger, because he'd killed her mother.

She'd done it face-to-face because she'd wanted him to know who was taking his life, wanted him to see the retribution in her eyes.

"If you're scared of a car backfiring, you'll never survive in this neighborhood," Gunner said, but his tone was gentler than she'd expected.

"I'm still a little jumpy. I was hoping the land of good times would make it better."

"It's not that anymore. Not by a long shot." Gunner's face was grim. "It's a goddamned shame too."

"But you stayed."

"I love her too much to desert her."

"Too bad you can't say the same about your wives," their waitress interjected with a smirk and a snap of her hips.

"Billie Jean, don't go telling all of my secrets." Gunner's drawl was lazy, easy, and if he was pissed about what she'd said, Avery would never know it.

She looked up at Billie Jean and wondered if she really was an ex-wife. She was pretty, with long dark hair and olive skin.

"Who's this—another secret?" Billie Jean asked Gunner with a perfunctory nod in Avery's direction.

"Can we just order please? The usual, times two?" Gunner gave a half grin and Billie Jean relented, wrote something on the small pad and walked away.

She came back less than three minutes later with beers and a plate of small red shellfish-looking things. Avery ignored the food in favor of the beer, since her adrenaline was still racing.

Dare trusted you to do this—don't screw it up, she told herself.

Gunner drew everywhere. She wondered if he even noticed he did it. The black pen made soft scratch marks on the white paper placemats, the napkins. When she looked, she saw a sketch of her: the cap, the big eyes . . . but he ripped it off and stuffed it in his pocket.

"Don't want to take chances with a wanted woman."

"But you taking me here . . ."

"People will know you're with me."

"Like a bodyguard."

"Something like that."

She was too wound up for a place like this, with its cheer and friendliness. She didn't want to celebrate—she wanted revenge on a man who'd ripped her family apart before it even had a chance. She was hot with it, though Dare hadn't wanted it to consume her, was worried that she'd fall over the edge, never to come back.

"You're haunted, *chère*."

"Hunted," she corrected. "There's a difference."

"Not in my book."

She shifted topics. "How long have you known Dare?"

Gunner took a swig of beer from the bottle. "Long enough."

"You tattooed him?"

"I don't break my clients' confidences," he told her. "Have a mudbug."

She wrinkled her nose, even as he showed her how to crack them and suck out the meat. But the taste—she had to admit it was worth it. All the food placed in front of them was amazing, and she ate heartily, forgetting, for that short time at least, why she was really in this city.

She noticed all the women looking at Gunner. Some of them glared at her, like she was stealing their good time away.

"Want to tell me why you're in trouble?" he asked finally, after he'd devoured his own plate and helped her with hers.

"How do you know I'm in trouble?" She licked the salted brine off her pinky and took another long swig of beer. She was feeling more relaxed than she had in months.

"Everyone who comes to me is. And that's a fact. Don't make me pull it out of you. I'm sure your brother told you not to keep secrets from me."

In fact, Dare had. *You can trust him with everything— the more information he has on you, the better. Just don't mention Powell—I'll break that to him.*

She just hadn't been expecting to do it out in public like this, but it wasn't like anyone could hear them over the band. Her confession would blend in. "Someone's trying to kill me. And I'm also wanted for murder."

Gunner cocked his head to stare at her. Did he want her to cry? Break down? She wouldn't, nor would she apologize. She stared back at him, brows raised, daring him to question her further.

Of course he did, but he didn't ask the one she'd expected. "Did anyone follow you—cops or assassins?"

"No. I came here with Dare."

"And they're trying to kill him as well?"

"Yes."

Gunner shook his head. "Got plenty of ammo in the shop."

"Comforting." And it was. He didn't seem to worry

that she was marked. "When did you meet my brother?"

"I worked with his father a long time ago."

"Darius is my father too," she offered. "I didn't know until recently."

Gunner's expression didn't change, but his tone softened. "He was a good guy."

The *was* nearly leveled her, but she decided that the jury was still out on the good-guy part. "I never met him. I don't know anything about him except . . ." *He never claimed me.* "He lived a dangerous life and he got my mom killed."

"Seems to me that women who get involved with dangerous men know what they're getting into. Probably because they've got more than a little bit of hell on wheels in them to start with."

There was no judgment in his tone, but she bristled anyway, probably because he spoke the truth. "I gave my momma hell," she admitted.

"A wild child."

"I guess. I didn't have much to rebel against, but I couldn't sit still. I was always looking around the corner for the next adventure. I grew up in the bounty office she owned. I learned there's a really fine line between upstanding citizen and criminal."

Gunner raised his beer. "Sometimes, there's no line at all."

She clinked her bottle against his. Wondered how much longer she'd keep holding up, holding on. It was expected of her. Necessary. She'd been doing it since she found Momma murdered, and that image was something she could shake from her mind only when she was doing something that required complete concentration.

After she'd killed the men who'd murdered her mother, she'd nearly buckled, forced herself to walk away before the police came.

She still didn't understand how the police could've found her so quickly, but after Dare explained it, it all made sense.

She'd killed Powell's men, and Powell sent more after her. It chilled her to think how close they'd gotten to her, what would've happened if Dare hadn't gotten involved.

"Whoever's after you must be pretty powerful. And pissed," Gunner speculated. "Not every day I meet a female fugitive."

She wanted to ask him how he knew that, but maybe she should be reassured. If he could peg her, he could identify danger.

At least he was on her side. She knew better than to deny what he'd said.

When more plates of food were plunked down, with Billie Jean still smirking, Avery looked up at her. "Look at me like that one more time and you'll have no lips left to make that face."

The words were quiet, the threat coming through loud and clear. Avery's own expression must've told the tale, because Billie Jean backed away fast.

"Scaring away my ex-wife's a good way to stay on

my good side." Gunner grinned as he spoke, then began digging into his gumbo. "Shit is hot—hope you're ready."

"What happens after we eat?"

"We change everything about you."

Chapter Eight

After he finished playing the song, Dare waited another hour, then went into the house with a decisive bang of the door.

She didn't jump, and he damned well knew she wasn't asleep.

He took his time showering and changing and finished a hot cup of coffee in the kitchen, where he could continue to keep an eye on her.

With a dry pair of jeans and no shirt or shoes, he figured it was as good a time as any to get this talk with Grace Powell started.

By doing so, he would officially be reviving Section 8, without the consent of the CIA or any other official party. Actually, by kidnapping Grace, he'd done that. But the thought of bringing more people into it when it was his war to finish—well, that didn't sit well with him.

He moved closer to her, saw her involuntary shivers and called himself a bastard.

"I don't want to do this," he said through clenched teeth to no one in particular but himself, and if Grace heard, she didn't turn her head. He hated being forced to reinvent Section 8 for any reason. A group like that wasn't good for its members—no, it was like signing their death warrants.

The fact that Adele had come to him and forced his hand . . . he wanted to hate her but couldn't.

She'd been born an operative. He hadn't been, but rather had been molded into something resembling hardened steel, which sat over the wildness that always wrestled inside him for dominance and freedom—the wildness that typically won, before all this had started. He covered his insides well, but they would never be able to lock out what he'd been.

He had several people waiting for him to make a move, and this beautiful woman tied up across the room.

"You were avoiding me. Why?" Grace asked him, her voice not exactly defiant but in no way passive.

He fucking burned for her, and she knew it. He could see that in her dark gypsy eyes when he moved to stand in front of her, and he neither confirmed nor denied her suspicion. "Tell me what you know about Powell."

"I told you—nothing of use to you," she said. Her voice held that quality of sex that no woman could fake. She'd been born with it, and it pulled him to her like a siren's song.

"Let me be the judge of that. Start talking."

"Where do I start?"

"From the beginning." He needed to know everything he could about her father, had to live and breathe that enemy. Had to become him in order to decimate him.

After that, a part of that bastard would always linger inside him. There was no way around that.

That's what Grace lived with every day of her life, but he forced that thought away. Sacrifices had to be made for him to keep his promises.

"I don't like remembering," she said.

"I don't give a shit about your likes. Tell me the last time you saw Richard Powell."

"I called him Rip. And it was six years ago."

"How cute—a nickname."

"I called him that because I wanted him dead and buried. The peace part was ironic."

Her gaze leveled him. Everything about her did. Her hair had come loose and tumbled over her shoulders, dried in waves. Her eyes were infused with copper, framed with thick lashes, and her skin was tanned from the summer sun. "Will *Rip* want you back?"

"Yes, for sure."

"And you want nothing to do with him?"

"He's a killer. And for all I know, you're as bad as he is," Grace told him, and Dare glared at her as though she'd just discovered his biggest fear—and his most well-kept secret.

That meant there was hope. She breathed a little easier. She'd been in worse spots—she'd been hurt worse than anyone could hurt her again.

No matter what, she'd survive, whether it be by kicking, crawling or screaming. She wouldn't give this man the satisfaction of breaking down, ever.

If she had to, she'd take him down with her. And he'd never see it coming.

He wasn't about to let up on her soon. Instead, he leaned into her, his hands on either side of her thighs, his face inches from hers. There was menace there, yes, but also a born compassion he'd been unable to drive out of himself, and she knew he must hate it.

"Grace, I might be worse than your father. You don't want to test me, because I will pass with flying colors."

With that, he moved away from her and went into the next room. When he returned, he threw a blanket over her to help with the shivering she was trying to control and refused to look at her again. It was late. She was tired, and sleeping in this upright chair wouldn't be pleasant.

And he had a cell phone in his hand—*her* cell phone. She'd forgotten it was in her pocket and hadn't felt him slip his hand in to grab it.

"What's his number?" he demanded, holding the phone out to her.

"A great merc like you can't get something as easy as a phone number?"

He kicked her chair, and her body lurched as the chair slid back and hit the wall. "Tell me the number—I'll dial and you speak."

"Never." She jerked her body toward him furiously, as far as the ropes would take her. Bared her teeth like an animal, because if that's what he wanted, that's what he'd get.

The ropes were so tight they chafed. She angled for a better position, wondered if she could do any damage to him at all. All Dare did was look at her with a frown.

After a long moment during which she was pretty sure he was about to come over and rebuke her, he came over and instead closed the shades.

"Too dangerous for you to be near an open window."

And then he bent and untied one wrist completely and loosened the other.

It was a dangerous move for him—and from him. The way she was raised to fight, she could do a lot of damage with that one hand.

He must know that.

It was either a test or a dare. She wondered if she should fail miserably or pass with flying colors, then decided she didn't give a damn either way. She still refused to be anyone's puppet.

She'd rather die. And it might come down to that.

After dinner and her check-in call with Dare, Gunner walked Avery back to the tattoo shop, only this time, they entered from three doors down, inside an underground garage. He pointed out his motorcycle and car to her, and Avery took note of them plus the exits and entrances that led to various alleyways.

"I'll get you some keys," he assured her as he let them into the back of the shop and upstairs to the second floor, grabbing the bag she'd come in with along the way.

There were several bedrooms—he picked one for her seemingly at random, but she had a feeling there was no such thing when it came to him.

"Now it's time to fix you up. Bathroom's that way—get changed. I'll get the dye."

"Dye?"

He reached up and touched the brim of her baseball cap. "You're going to get hot and look suspicious as hell if you keep wearing that."

She glanced back in the oval mirror above the dresser and realized that her long blond hair would need to go, and fast. Then she took off the cap and stared at the ponytail that had been there for as long as she could remember.

But now wasn't the time for sentimentality. Instead, she changed quickly and let Gunner help her with the cut and color.

He was surprisingly good at both. With the short, pixie-like cut and warm brown color, her eyes stood out even more.

She didn't look like her old self, and she really didn't feel like it either. Scaling down the side of a building with Dare had changed everything. She'd conquered a lifelong fear in a moment of danger—and could only hope she'd be able to do it again if necessary—escaped jail and met a brother she'd never known she had, literally in the space of minutes.

And now she'd embraced a new lifestyle that promised nothing but trouble.

"Better," Gunner told her. She was barely dressed, with a towel over her shoulders, wearing only a bra and a pair of shorts she'd borrowed from him—and Gunner was looking, but she didn't care; she liked the way he looked at her.

"What about the tattoo?" she asked now.

"I don't tattoo drunk women," he told her, and she wanted to argue that she wasn't drunk, not really—at least not with alcohol. But she was intoxicated for sure.

People do crazy things in New Orleans, her mother had warned her, but there was always a soft light in her eyes when she said it. Because this was where her mother had met Darius. This was where Avery was conceived.

Now Avery was in New Orleans, and her mother had been right. Avery felt crazy, and she liked it. In this town, she could go wild; she could turn into a mercenary like her father had been and still be a woman, a lover.

She could be everything. Live or die, but do either proudly.

"You'd best cover up or you'll end up naked in my tattoo chair," Gunner told her, a lazy smile on his face that told her he was anything but.

"I thought you didn't tattoo intoxicated women."

"For you, I'd make an exception."

Chapter Nine

Dare wanted to see if she could fight. He wanted to see her fight. But instead Grace fisted her hand against her thigh and stared up at him with those dark eyes that saw right through him. His groin stirred. Again.

Her dress had dried, but it still molded to her figure well. He wanted to stare even though he shouldn't, and despite all the rules of civility, he did.

Because he'd never learned to be civilized. Didn't see a reason to start now.

She blinked, and then she proceeded to look him up and down in the same manner he'd done to her.

He didn't know whether to laugh or strip or both. He stuck his hand out and waited. Finally her cool palm slid against his warm one, and the electric jolt seemed to hit both of them at once like a lightning strike—and it threatened to do far more damage than what Mother Nature promised.

At least she felt it too. He wondered if she'd deny it. "I'm Dare."

"Grace," she said, and with a great effort he took his

hand from hers, but not before her fingertips brushed the scars. "But you already knew that."

"Yes." He turned from her to pull himself together, wished Adele hadn't visited him, wished he was still alone in the woods.

You and your nightmares. You and your ghosts.

Hell, they were loyal. They'd follow him anywhere.

She was willing to die before she'd go back. He'd known that from the second he took her, but he had to push her to confirm it.

He had to prove it to himself to decide how far he would go. That was one reason he didn't want Avery close by. She didn't deserve to see this shit. But she also didn't need to be kept in the dark. Couldn't be.

He handed Grace a bottle of water from the nearby counter, pressed it into her hand after he'd taken the top off. She moved her arms gingerly—he knew they'd ache.

Dare had been trained to notice even the smallest details, nuances. It made him a good lover and a better SEAL. It would serve him well as a merc.

He hadn't thought of himself as a merc until Grace had called him one, but he couldn't deny it. Instead, he catalogued what he saw.

She had a small, crescent-shaped scar on her inner wrist, as if she'd been cut. Glass or metal, and he'd bet it wasn't self-inflicted.

Her fingernails weren't long, but they were rounded at the tips, obviously well tended and strong. Her hands looked like an artist's hands—capable, used to work.

The garden at her house would've taken quite a lot of upkeep, and it was obviously well loved.

What would it be like to love something so much, to put that much work into it daily, only to know it would die slowly, to watch it wither, all the while understanding it might not come back. And even if it did, it might never be the same—strong, healthy, vibrant—instead, a shadow of its former self.

But there was always the promise that it would.

She was as lush as the garden. She radiated light and hope. She was the total opposite of him, and she'd never forgive him for what he was about to do to her.

Or maybe she would and he shouldn't care either way, but damn it all to hell, he did.

She watched him the entire time she drank, even as he avoided her gaze, hating the way her wrists showed the marks of his bindings.

He was tired of the guilt. One job, one final job, and then he was really and truly burying Section 8 forever. "Do you know names of people Powell killed?"

She blinked, played with the half-empty bottle for a moment before telling him, "My mother, for one. And you've already told me he killed your father."

"Do you know who my father was?"

"Darius."

He took a step back like she'd physically pushed him. "You knew him?"

"Yes—I knew him and Adele. I knew you were coming for me—I just didn't know exactly when."

"If you knew I was coming, why didn't you run?"

"Where would I go? I'm tired of running. I was finally happy here."

"You have no survival instinct," he told her, and no, he wouldn't feel guilty about this. He was so tired of that, and it was heavy and he'd burdened himself with it for so long, he was pretty sure he'd never see himself clear of it.

"What if you're my survival instinct?" she asked.

"Don't you do that—don't you make me that."

She smiled a little, as if she knew that thought was more frightening for him than facing down the barrel of a Sig. "Your father used to fish down by the docks."

"Don't," he warned through clenched teeth.

"He's a good cook too. Adele couldn't cook at all. She always joked that she could burn—"

"Water," he finished. Pictured Adele laughing as she said it. "She always said her talents lay in other areas."

"She was so lethal," Grace whispered now. "Lethal, and still so good. I wasn't sure that combination was possible."

She trailed off and Dare was done asking questions for the moment. Questions were never the right way to do something. There were too many variables in the answers.

But she wasn't done sharing.

"If you look in the closet in the last bedroom, you'll find some record books with my handwriting," she told him. "I know there are four bedrooms here. A basement with enough food to last for several months—and the bathrooms are down the hall—third door on the right and forth on the left, respectively. The room Darius stayed in had a picture of a guitar over the bed and a red quilt."

There was no way she could know that. "You really lived here?"

"For a while, yes."

"As a hostage?"

"At first, Darius and Adele treated me like one," she agreed. "And then things changed."

Why wouldn't his father have told him about this, about whether or not he could trust her? Darius had to have known this would come into play at some point. Had to have known how precarious his son's future was.

Darius had always been a selfish bastard, but nothing proved it more than this. Dare went to the closet and pulled out a few books, brought them to the kitchen table and found she'd written some key terms on a piece of paper.

He was no expert, but this wasn't a hoax—the writing matched. "You worked S8's books."

She nodded. "I traveled with them. They passed intel through me."

"You knew what they did?"

"I knew they weren't bankers." A wry smile twisted her lips. "They got me away from Rip in the first place. I left when I was eighteen and I've never looked back."

"Had you tried to escape before that?"

She shrugged. Looked away. Didn't want to go there, and yeah, he got that.

When she spoke, it wasn't a direct answer to his question. "I couldn't pass up the opportunity when your father came along."

"How did you pull it off?"

She gave him a sideways glance. "Got into a caterer's trunk before they boarded the helicopter. Rip keeps the island on lockdown—very few people are permitted to stay longer than a night. For his parties, guests were flown in."

"No private chefs?"

"One. He's always on premises. If he needs help, he calls the same catering company that's been vetted by security."

"And they had no idea you were on board?"

Grace bit out the next words before she could stop herself. "Of course they knew. Darius sent them. It was all part of their plan. They wanted to use me at first, the way you want to."

Recalling those early days, when she'd been nothing but a Section 8 pawn, the same way she'd been Rip's pawn all those years, made Grace tense up. But it hadn't taken Darius and Adele long before they'd stopped speaking to her like she was a prisoner.

She'd assumed what went a long way toward softening them was seeing the unhealed stripes from the whip on her back and arms. Adele had to help her medicate the newest ones after they'd gotten infected during her first weeks at the house.

Even after she trusted them and they trusted her— and she had no doubt they truly did—she never admitted to them that she had a gift of precognition. Broken or not, that might make anyone rethink their decision not to use her.

The psychic skills that lay dormant for years had never blossomed here, as she'd feared they might. She was more than grateful they remained silent, because that gift reminded her of her past, her mother . . . she refused to be a shell of her former self, another one of Rip's victims.

So why had she let Dare take her so easily? She'd recognized him, yes, but his intent hadn't been pure, like his father's had. She'd felt his arms around her like strong bonds of protection. He was conflicted . . . but he was the better choice for what was coming.

"Are you sure . . . about Darius?"

"Are you?" he asked, his voice a fierce rasp. "Did you have something to do with his death?"

"No." Darius had seemed indestructible. She couldn't believe he was gone. And if he was, by Rip's hand, that was her fault, another person to add to the list that made her cringe with guilt.

"So S8 rescues you and then you just happen to stay with them . . . and then Rip just happens to pick them off, one by one."

"You can't think I had anything to do with it."

"I don't know what to think!" he roared. "You're his daughter. You could be working for him—now and then. It's the perfect plan. Especially because Darius is the one who pointed me in your direction."

"Maybe to save me, not use me. Maybe I'm in as much damned danger as you are, if not more."

"Haven't seen Rip try to kill you recently," Dare told her. He spread his hands, palms up, and showed her the scars on both of them. They'd driven spikes through his hands. There were exit wounds on the backs of his hands when he turned them over. "It was just for show. Never would've hung—my skin and muscle would've ripped like paper trying to hold my weight."

"He's not me," she whispered. "I'm not responsible for what he's done. I can't be."

But in her heart, she knew she always would be, no matter how vigorous her protest, no matter how clear her conscience should be. Because it wasn't, no matter how much she'd tried to repent for crimes she'd never committed, even though the only thing she was truly guilty of was not killing Rip when she'd had the chance.

"I'm sorry," she said now. "I can't say anything else."

"You can. You will. I've got nothing but time."

This time, there might really be no way out.

They both heard the noise at the same time—a truck, coming through the bayou at top speed, despite the rain. It was someone who knew the area well.

Dare took her by the biceps and brought her over to a heavy pipe that ran from floor to ceiling in the corner. He handcuffed her wrists around the pipe and then pushed a chair under her so she could sit.

Grace's phone didn't have GPS—he'd checked that already. "Who else knows about this place?" he demanded.

She didn't answer, pressed her lips together until he said, "If you don't tell me, I'll kill them on sight."

"No, please . . . it's just my friend Marnie. She knows if she can't find me at home that sometimes I come here and sit on the porch."

He was out the door in seconds, flicking the lights off as he went, just in time for the truck to come barreling around the corner. He ducked along the side of the porch and crouched, weapon drawn.

The truck slowed, the passenger's side window came down and he saw a woman with long hair peering out into the porch.

"Grace, are you there?" she called, and he held his damned breath, hoping Grace wouldn't be stupid enough to answer. The last thing he needed was two female hostages; he wasn't very effective at keeping even one controlled.

Granted, he'd gotten more out of her when he didn't have her tied like a wild hog, but still . . .

"Grace!" the woman called loudly. Beeped a few times and was met with silence beyond the pattering rain. She shut the window and drove away slowly. He had no idea if she'd be back. No idea if he could trust Grace to lie to her on the phone so she wouldn't return.

He'd have to convince Grace it would be in her friend's best interest for her to lie.

Chapter Ten

Earlier that evening, Grace had been fighting for a woman's life. Now she was supposed to be fighting for her own, and she realized she'd gotten the familiar feelings of warning all mixed up.

This was what was coming down the pike for her. She'd become so focused on another woman's safety that she'd compromised her own.

Marnie. Her friend. Her safety net. Marnie, who understood when Grace took foolish risks, because she did the same thing. They were women who'd danced around violence their entire lives. They knew no other way, and they probably never would.

She and Marnie always expected the harshness of the violence because of their backgrounds and this job they did, but they were still somehow always surprised by it.

No matter how prepared they were, it was never enough.

Carmen waited for them in the small courtyard as they'd asked—staying inside her apartment wouldn't allow her to run or scream if Marcus arrived. And she'd been spotted by him by the time Marnie and Grace arrived. Marcus was a repeat offender—a violent rapist and abuser—and he had Carmen pinned under him, a hand across her throat, the other between her legs.

He had nothing to lose. Carmen—and Grace and Marnie—had everything to.

Beside her, Marnie retched and Grace fought back a scream. Instead, she steadily aimed the gun at the side of Marcus's head, where it wouldn't affect Carmen at all.

"You get off her," she told him, "or I'll kill you."

Maybe she should kill him anyway, do a little vigilante justice, because this man would keep finding Carmen until he killed her. He'd never be put away long enough for her to ever get safe, let alone feel that way.

Grace knew all too well how that felt. The need for vengeance ran deep and hot in her blood, a need retriggered when she went on these calls or met with a victim or woke from one of her nightmares.

She was as screwed up as these women, which was why they trusted her so much.

Marcus wasn't moving. Instead, he shifted, which caused her to lose her position with the gun as he goddamned spat at her. She aimed quickly at his leg and let off a shot. The night was heavy, thick with violence, and the force of her shot barely shattered it, swam through the heavy murk of darkness and despair and hit where she'd aimed. When he stared between her and the tree next to him, he appeared stunned, and it gave Carmen time enough to bring her palm up into his nose and slam him backwards. His bone crunched, blood spattered and Carmen was free and running, Marnie going after her.

Which left Grace alone with Marcus, and he was up and coming for her fast. Didn't seem to care that the gun was between them. And she would not die tonight.

"I'll take care of you once and for all, bitch!" he yelled and continued onward like a freight train. She braced herself to shoot and then realized that Marnie had done it for her, taking Marcus down with a shot to his calf.

"Get to the van!" Marnie called, and Grace ran, Carmen now behind her. At some point, Carmen must've run back to the apartment to grab her daughter and a bag she'd packed.

Marnie got behind the wheel, and in seconds, they were flying down the road.

Grace hadn't heard any sirens, which wasn't unusual for this area. None of the neighbors liked or trusted the police enough to call them, even when they were in serious danger.

Grace had escaped from hell, and now she consistently put herself in the line of fire of her own free will in order to make sure no woman or child suffered for longer than they had to. Tonight, Carmen had gotten out of her apartment with her most precious possession, her five-year-old daughter, a small tote and a little money and into a van with a woman she'd never met who would drive her to salvation.

Carmen would eventually settle somewhere. Grace would never know where, because it was safer for all of them that way, but she liked to imagine that all those women and children had a great life, that the women remarried and the kids grew up happy and healthy and unaffected by anything they'd seen in their early years.

She knew, according to the statistics Marnie told her,

that many of the women ended up with another abusive partner, because that was all they knew.

Now Grace held her breath as she heard Marnie calling to her, waited through the deafening silence until the old truck drove away and exhaled when no shots followed. Marnie was safe and Grace would do anything to keep her that way.

And then Dare was slamming back in the house, using a candle low on the table so the light wouldn't be seen from the street, especially when he pulled down the blackout shade.

He obviously knew this place as well as she did.

"Where were you tonight?" he demanded now.

"Right where you found me." She paused. "Thank you for not shooting my friend."

With that, he unlocked the cuffs and held her phone out to her. "Marnie keeps calling and texting. She wants to know if you're okay—if you're safe. Who's after you?"

"No one you'd know."

"You'd be surprised who I know," he told her, his voice edging toward dangerously low. It sent a wave of pure panic through her nervous system. She'd been through too much tonight all ready. Her body hadn't come down from the earlier scuffle with a madman, and now she was confronted by her past, ready to rise up and drag her all the way back in with sharp claws and a biting sting that she'd never get used to.

"I used to do dangerous things. Take bad risks after Darius and Adele rescued me, because I could. They didn't try to stop me, like they knew it had to work itself out of me, like a fever." The weight of the admission still hung on her, though Dare didn't seem to be judging her. But he'd been trained well—who knew what lay behind his poker face?

"I still do them," he muttered. His hair dropped over his bare shoulders, chest glistened, jeans stuck to his hard lower body, molded there. He'd been barefoot when he'd run out with the gun.

"Me too," she whispered, talking back the recent lie. He seemed to approve, clicked the safety, but he held on to the gun. He still had that predatory look in his eyes. He was Darius's son, but he looked nothing like him.

She stared around the old cabin where she'd once been permitted to roam freely. Her wrists ached, but she ignored the pain in favor of continuing to study the man who could hold her fate in his hands. Wondered how much to reveal.

She and Darius had talked about Dare a bit, but Darius had always said he'd never told his son what he had to do, that the boy had to follow his own conscience in order to be any kind of good man.

She believed Dare was a good man . . . or else there was some kind of hoodoo magic he was dabbling in, because her body wanted to surrender to him, not fight him.

The jolt of pleasure at that thought threw her off more than any pain she'd ever had. It was an odd sensation of low-level electricity rumbling through her, making it hard to concentrate.

The only benefit was that Dare seemed to be having

the same trouble. As he moved closer, she knew she should move away, but his gaze was intense, even under the soft light.

She'd been living hard, playing harder, skirting a dangerous line between brave and simply stupid; she'd done all of it because S8 gave her the opportunity to do so.

She'd never seen any other kind of life for herself. She lived from day to day; it had been the only way she'd survived for a long time. She hadn't come across a reason to change any of it in all these years.

Except now she had the reason, the sign, in the form of a ruggedly handsome man who towered over her. She knew that he'd demand more from her—how she would handle the request was up to her.

Or was it? Dare's gaze was too sharp, his thoughts too focused. She wouldn't be surprised if he was able to read minds as well. He appeared that capable.

His fingers traced the bruises on her forearm, which were well above the marks left where he'd bound her earlier. There was no mistaking that someone had grabbed her hard—and he'd know it wasn't him.

"Is someone abusing you? A boyfriend?" he asked, and she nearly laughed at the idea of her being attached to any one man long enough to call him boyfriend.

"No, not me." Not ever.

"You need to start explaining the bruises and Marnie."

"That isn't why you brought me here," she said. He acknowledged that with a nod. "Then let's move past it."

"I can't stomach someone hurting a woman."

"I deserved it," she told him. "He was pissed that I took away his punching bag. I told him I hoped he'd rot in hell and then I kicked him in the balls. He grabbed me and I broke his nose."

The corner of Dare's mouth quirked up a little as if he approved, but his voice was dead serious when he said, "No woman ever deserves to be hit."

"Obviously not everyone feels the same way."

He stared at her for a long moment, and she neutralized her expression and stared back at him.

He was such a beautifully handsome man. Dark, mysterious. Haunted. A tug in her womb made her want to edge toward him.

He would kiss her if she got closer—she was sure of it. What would it solve? Nothing. But maybe kisses weren't supposed to solve anything—maybe they were supposed to simply be.

"You're beautiful," he told her roughly, like it hurt him to say so.

"But you're not letting me go."

"I can't, Grace. Not yet. I have a lot more things to figure out. For now, let's just stick with Marnie—who is she, exactly?"

"My employer," she admitted.

"Is she the last person you were in contact with?"

"We spoke this afternoon."

"Where do you work?"

"Out of my house. Sometimes out of hers if necessary. Most of it's done by phone, with a few face-to-face meetings."

"What kind of work is it?"

She hesitated because she'd gotten in too deep. With him, with Marnie, with all of it. She'd been trying to dig herself out since she was eighteen.

"What kind of work?" he repeated, but he wasn't angry.

"I help Marnie—and she helps women who've been abused."

He nodded, like that confirmed what he'd thought, even as he swore under his breath. "So you're in contact with a lot of anonymous people."

"Marnie's very careful about that where I'm concerned."

"Because she knows who you are?"

"I never told her anything about that, but I've been working with her since Adele recommended me for the job," Grace said coolly; she knew that would shut him up.

And it did, for a minute, until he said, "Call Marnie and tell her you're okay. Not to worry."

"Will I be?" she asked, but he didn't answer. She called anyway, and he leaned over and put the phone on speaker so he could hear both ends of the conversation. "Marnie, it's me."

Marnie's voice rang through the phone, the concern and relief evident in her tone. "Grace, where are you? I've been calling—stopped by the old place and yours. You can't do that to me."

"I'm sorry—I'm okay. I went for a walk behind the house and waited the rain out. I didn't mean to worry you." She could be a good liar when she needed to be, and she was letting Dare see that. Putting out a trust that maybe she shouldn't. "Look, I'll call you later and check in."

"Okay—just wanted to let you know that Carmen's safe and sound."

"Great." She hung up and handed Dare back the phone. He put it in his pocket and watched her again. "Carmen's the woman I helped tonight. Her boyfriend's the one who tried to stop me. Marnie and I work to get these women out of their situations and into safe houses, usually out of state. The police can issue restraining orders, but no one follows them. There's no deterrent." She'd become a warrior for her cause, fierce and determined—invincible where other women were concerned.

As Dare ran a hand through his hair, she went to grab the blanket that had fallen to the ground earlier and wrapped it around herself.

"The man who gave you those bruises—he won't go down easily," he said finally.

"Probably not," she agreed.

"I'm sure Adele didn't want you working this end of Marnie's business."

She closed her eyes briefly and thought about the first time she'd left the house to search for one of Marnie's women.

She'd been alone in this house when she'd gotten the call.

"Kim, what's wrong?"

"Please, you have to come help me," Kim whispered, the frantic note in her voice impossible to ignore. *"He's here."*

Grace went cold. "Have you called Marnie?"

"She's not answering. This is the emergency number she gave me."

Marnie always answered—the woman was a goddess when it came to what she referred to as her calling. Saving women who'd been abused, raped or otherwise harmed was the only thing that had gotten her past the point of feeling like a victim. She'd helped Grace so much when Grace first arrived in New Orleans.

Adele had been the one who'd put the two of them in touch. She'd known, somehow, what Grace had gone through, although Grace had never told anyone about it. Because if she told, it meant it had really happened and she'd have to deal with it.

Adele left Marnie's name and number for Grace one morning.

"What's this for?" Grace asked.

"She runs a hotline out of her house—she needs some help. I think it'll be good for you." Adele sipped her coffee and turned away after saying it; it hadn't been simply a suggestion.

"But I'm already helping you and Darius."

"You still will. But you need to be busier. Good for the soul," Adele said.

Marnie ran far more than a hotline from her bayou house, hidden away from the road and most civilization with thick brush and a clever drive that seemed to point away from it. It was the perfect hideaway for Marnie herself—and once Grace realized the only way to truly make things better for herself was to help others, she did more than simply devote her life to it. She threw herself headfirst into it, ate and slept the women and children she helped.

Sometimes, it was simply a matter of a phone call and a referral to a rape crisis counselor or a police officer or two she trusted. Other times, it was far more complicated and skirted the law.

Grace gave herself more freedom with each passing week. Found herself risking herself when she shouldn't have—picking up strange men in bars—and soon that became like a drug. Adele knew, of course, didn't disapprove of Grace's promiscuity, as long as she didn't leave herself vulnerable to being found out by Powell.

"At first, I was only supposed to work the phones while Marnie was out on calls. It was the perfect job— and I felt like I was helping. And then I got restless, especially once Darius and Adele left. I'd expected to hear from them, at least once in a while. When I didn't . . . I thought maybe it was for my own safety. Maybe it was for the best . . ." She stopped because she heard the catch in her own voice, turned away from Dare because he would see too much.

He already has.

Chapter Eleven

Gunner had more private tattoo appointments coming in, and so he left Avery upstairs, alone and restless. She nursed the beer he'd left for her as she stared out across the small balcony. She'd opened the French doors enough to hear the music floating in, noted the bar across the alleyway and decided that she'd be safe enough there.

It was time to try out her new look anyway. Cops didn't lay in wait in college bars looking for America's most wanted, and the assassins themselves wouldn't make a move in the crowd. *If* there were more, and if they'd followed her.

She couldn't handle being a prisoner any longer.

There was the small matter of the alleyway itself, but it appeared to be a nicely crowded pathway to the bar. She climbed down the fire escape easily after pulling on a tank top and sandals and followed the groups of laughing people.

The heat, the bodies, the music—all of it came together in one giant cacophonous swell that carried her into the bar with the rest of the revelers.

She wondered if it was always like this on weekends or if she'd just gotten lucky. Ordered a drink and swayed a little bit to the music. Turning down an offer to dance was easy enough the first time, but gradually the men began to get more persistent.

"Look, I just want to hang out here," she told the guy who wouldn't let go of her wrist. She finally pushed at his shoulder hard enough that he was momentarily stunned.

Defending herself was going to get old. She couldn't draw so much attention to herself, and she would if she continued to kick this guy's ass.

As she began to back away again, he lunged. And then he disappeared, replaced by a man who had a golden smile and an easy air, although she suspected there wasn't anything truly easy about him.

He'd taken the man out without breaking stride. Eventually, the bouncers would pour the pest out onto the sidewalk, but for now, he weaved into the crowd.

"Thanks."

"You were doing all right."

"Then why'd you step in?" she called above the din.

"If you were gonna wrestle, I wanted it to be with me." His grin disarmed her. The thought of being caught in his stronghold made her blood run warm. Two days in New Orleans and two men had given her this reaction; no one should come to this city without some kind of chaperone or chastity belt.

"You okay, *chère*?"

The man's dialogue was authentic, came from deep inside, although there was no innocent southern farm-boy thing going on here by any stretch of the imagination.

He was blond, his hair longer than Gunner's. His face held the scruff of several days' worth of not shaving, and she rubbed her cheek against it lightly. He laughed, put an easy arm around her waist and bought her another shot. She accepted, told herself firmly that it was the last one. Of course, that didn't count the famous hurricanes that were designed by their very nature to knock her flat on her ass.

"What's your name?" she asked him finally.

"Does it really matter?" he murmured. She wanted to think it didn't, but it did. It always would. She was a damned romantic, like her mom, no matter how she fought it, which was why she didn't get involved. A few one-night stands were all she'd had over the past two years.

"If I said it did?" she asked, heard the husky want in her own voice.

"It's Key." He looked at her. "And you?"

"Avery."

"Glad we got that out of the way." His mouth came down on hers, and she melted into him. She'd had the perfect amount of alcohol, and the crowd seemed to swell around her like a protective hug. She was anonymous, and for the first time in months, she felt safe.

It felt good.

Key's tongue teased her, and she wished she could go with him somewhere . . . anywhere, but that would be stupid and she'd already taken a chance tonight.

Key pulled her into a corner, away from the masses,

where she could actually hear herself think, and then she looked into his face and realized that thinking was the last think she wanted to do.

Thinking was overrated. Highly so.

As if agreeing, he gave her another slow, sure kiss that tasted like the best of everything rolled into one. His hands held her waist, his stance still somehow protective, even as his body melded to hers in a slow dance of tumbling, riotous passion, as if the two of them were completely alone rather than in this crazy bar.

But that was the beauty of this place—for all intents and purposes, they *were* alone. And she stopped any last semblance of reason and let insanity win out for the time being.

Of course, it wasn't long before she realized that Key had a gun and a knife. He could be military or a merc or a bounty hunter. Or a criminal.

None of the options were good. Did he recognize her? Was this all a setup?

She didn't think he would need to do this much work to get her in hand. The fact that she'd literally been in his arms and technically still remained a free woman was comforting . . . and still she had to extricate—and fast.

But his touch—he held on to her like a parched man in the desert who'd found the fountain of life and wasn't prepared to let go. In the private corner that had become theirs, she was trapped between his body and the wall in the most delicious way possible. And so she let herself go, wondering if she could orgasm from the kissing and light fondling alone.

She'd been trying for her entire life to figure out Darius's hold on her mother—why she'd hated and loved this city and that man.

New Orleans and her surroundings were the keys to everything. Avery needed to figure out how to unlock the puzzle, to make sure she never made the same mistakes her mother had made.

New Orleans could be the death of her—its rhythms seemed to be in time with her heartbeat, her soul, and that was seductive and wrong. Wrong, according to her mother, who'd thrown all caution to the wind here.

Avery could love it here, and somehow that was so very wrong. So was flirting, drinking and dancing, but she didn't care. For the moment, she was normal.

"You're adorable."

"You're seeing two of me, aren't you?" she asked.

He waggled a finger at her and murmured something in what she assumed to be Cajun French.

"See, I don't know what you're saying. You might be telling me I'm the ugliest thing you've ever seen."

"Yeah, that's it, sugar."

"So . . . what do you do?" she asked, and he held up his bottle of beer and pointed to it, asking her, "What do you do?"

"For tonight, the same thing."

"And kissing me," he said seriously.

"Do you live here?"

"In this bar?"

"In New Orleans."

"Nah. Just passin' through. On a road trip with my brother."

"What's that consist of?"

"Mainly looking for trouble. Tonight, I found her."
He pulled her close, and she looked into those hazel
eyes and something tugged at her. He was happy
tonight—that wasn't a lie—but there was a sadness un-
derlying his expression she couldn't deny.

She guessed everyone had secrets. Sometimes, that
was reassuring to know; other times, terrifying.

"What are you thinking about, *chère*?" The more he
drank, the thicker his accent got, but he actually
seemed to gain more control with each beer, each shot.
In fact, he'd probably pass as sober even if given more
than a passing glance, while she felt like she might tip
sideways at the slightest push.

"You."

He laughed. "Want to know all my secrets?"

"Something like that."

"I'm an open book. So live a little—come home
with me."

"I can't," she told Key.

"Not gonna show me your tits?"

"You don't have any beads."

"I have something better than beads," Key promised, and dammit, she believed him.

She wouldn't bring him back to Gunner's and she
wasn't going home with him, no matter how badly her
body begged her to. And so after kissing him until she
couldn't breathe, she stroked his cheek and walked away.

"You're really leaving me like this?" he called.

"Gives you something to look forward to," she told
him over her shoulder as she kept walking.

But Key wasn't letting that happen. In seconds, he was on her again, kissing the back of her neck, luring her back in, and she knew she couldn't—didn't want to—resist. But right now that was all the same thing. "I'm not letting you run," he told her.

"Where are you staying?"

"Just around the corner. You're safe with me."

"You were in the military, weren't you?"

Key gave her a small, slightly drunken smile and then placed a renewed interest in making sure she couldn't resist him. And it took everything she had to do so. Granted, it took quite a while, until she was sure someone was going to tell them to get a room. They did little more than kiss, but every nerve in her body was on fire, the slow burn more arousing than fast sex could ever be.

"Gotta go, Key," she told him. She was unsteady as she pushed away from him and walked away, out of the bar and his life, no doubt saving her from undeserved heartache.

And he let her.

Twenty minutes later, back at Gunner's, she'd already showered to get Key's scent off her. Her now short hair dried fast, and she lay there in the unfamiliar bed, the fan blowing on her, realizing she was still the same exact person after all.

What had she expected to change?

Chapter Twelve

M aybe it was for the best . . .
    Maybe Darius and Adele had thought not contacting Grace again was for the best, but it had still hurt her. Dare read her unspoken thoughts before she turned away, and he cursed his father and S8 again for ruining yet another life in the course of saving it.

But Grace . . . she was her own worst enemy, and she had to know that. "You knew better but you put yourself in danger anyway."

That made her turn back around. "I couldn't sit back and do nothing. That first time, the girl—she was so young and scared, and I couldn't reach Marnie. And I couldn't just hang up the phone and leave someone in trouble like that. So I didn't." She paused, as if reliving it, and then she told him, "Once I started, I couldn't stop. The rush of getting the job done—being able to finally do something instead of just sitting in a house doing paperwork or sneaking out to bars . . . I was finally able to live again."

"That's not living, Grace. You were trying to hurt yourself—like committing a slow form of suicide."

She looked shaken. "That's not true."

"You broke all the rules. Darius and Adele told you to not leave the house—in exchange for working with Marnie, I'm betting she'd bring you groceries and anything else necessary, right?"

She nodded reluctantly. He knew how things worked, why Adele would set up this barter for Grace. Marnie would suspect that Grace was a battered woman in hiding. In actuality, it was the perfect plan, until Grace went rogue.

"You don't understand."

"Why the hell would you do that? Not listen? Put yourself in danger?"

"What do you care? If I followed directions, you might not have been able to find me."

"No more contact with Marnie—you just had your last phone call."

She blinked slowly, as if remembering she was still his kidnapping victim. Her eyes blazed, and if he'd realized anything in the short time they'd spent together, it was that an angry Grace gave all her cards away, and then some.

She tried hard to be icy, but her warmth broke through every time.

The problem was, either way he wanted her just as damned much.

"You don't get to tell me what I can and can't do," Grace told Dare now, because even though he did indeed fill that role now, the fact that she actively resisted it was just as important.

Caged again. Was freedom even possible? Would it ever be?

She knew how to deal with being trapped only one way—and that was to fight by any means necessary. She'd done it before and she'd do it again.

Success or not, she'd have tried something.

"I think I do get to. Remember?" He held up the handcuffs, and she glared at him.

"What do you want from me?" she demanded. "I have no information to give you—I haven't seen Rip in six years. So if you're going to give me to him, do it. Do it now."

"I will, as soon as you call him," he said, calling her bluff.

"I don't know how to get in touch with him."

"But you're going to play this out—and try to play me too? Like Esme would?"

"Don't you talk about my mother," she warned.

"Touchy subject? I'm betting you learned a hell of a lot from her."

He knew. She forced herself to breathe, to tell herself that he didn't know the whole truth. "I did."

"Esme was able to con Powell—she must've been good."

She had been—a grifter who'd perfected her fake psychic routine. She'd just happened to have a daughter whose gift was all too real. But Grace refused to do anything but nod.

Dare continued. "If all you're looking for is danger and excitement, I can give that to you."

"And I can give it right back to you," she murmured as he moved toward her. This was what she was used to. This was how she'd kept herself alive without losing her mind. Giving up her body was easy—she'd learned that lesson the hard way.

"So what—you're a poor little lost girl—mean no harm? Need to be rescued?" he asked.

She hated characterizing herself that way. "I haven't needed rescuing in a long time. Haven't asked for it."

"Right. Because you can take care of yourself. Run with the big boys. Take down men with your fists just like Esme used her body."

She hated that he was right.

"Poor little rich girl, looking for some action," he continued. "Is that what this is all about? You left the Powell estate and you got bored, and so you decided to play the great avenger."

"That's not the way it happened."

"You had my father and Adele fooled, right? Had them take you away, pretended you'd play their game, but you couldn't resist the danger. I get it—some people are born drawn to it, like a moth to a flame, getting just close enough to feel the burn."

She wondered if he was talking about himself now. He moved closer, and she stood quickly, the chair creaking backward.

"Now you're scared? I would think this is exactly what you want." His voice teased, and she hated that he was right. The flare of fear was exactly what she needed. What she craved.

He smiled, backed away a little, leaning against the

counter. But his eyes still traveled her body again, and she took advantage of that. She shoved him against the counter, tugged at his belt purposely. He took her wrists, pulled them to her sides as she struggled.

The sex would be angry . . . maybe even a little vicious. It would be exactly the way she wanted it to be. She felt that thrill when he forced a rough hand in her hair and took her mouth with his. She wanted it that way because it would mean another victory. She would make him hers, take this over. Then it wouldn't matter that he'd kidnapped her.

When he finally fucked her, she would win and nothing else would matter. The familiar pattern would hold, and that would mean she was all right, that nothing could touch her or hurt her.

She would remain unbreakable, although she was secretly broken inside, all taped together so the pieces wouldn't rattle and give her away.

"Kiss me," he demanded.

"I don't follow your orders."

"You'll love it if you do—I can promise you that."

Would she? Probably. And that bothered her more than anything else. She wanted the control—needed it.

But making Dare think he had it? That would put her head back in the game. "Fine."

She went up on her tiptoes; he bent his head to meet her halfway. The kiss was the start of the battleground for both of them. It was beyond good. She knew it would be.

As he kissed her literally stupid, at some point he surrendered her wrists. She wound her hands into his hair to keep him close. In return, he pressed against her so she could feel the hard swell of his arousal.

The game wasn't working. Or maybe it was—on her. Pleasure flowed like white-hot sunshine through her body. She'd be on fire soon if she didn't douse her desires. Had to bring this to a manageable level for herself and didn't see a way clear to doing so if she remained in Dare's embrace.

But his hands, oh, his hands roamed her body like he was following a map—or creating one. He noticed every nuance, every small jolt of pleasure she allowed to break through her expression.

If she could stay stoic, unmoving, cause him to lose his mind with her touches, that would be perfect.

There was lust on his face—his eyes were heavy lidded. But he had all the damned control, and he knew, goddamn him, he knew. He knew because he softened his kisses, his hold on her hair, her waist.

Would she be powerless against him? She'd wanted to think she'd learned her lessons so well that she could never repeat her mother's patterns and fall for a man who wanted nothing more than to use her for his personal gain and leave her a dried-out husk.

You are your mother's daughter.

But she'd absorbed enough of Rip's ruthlessness to even that score, to balance her enough so that she felt she could be practical in all matters pertaining to love.

All that resolve fell away when Dare touched her for the first time. Now she had to make sure he didn't know that.

If she had her way, he never would.

She pulled him tighter, wanted that dizzy, falling feeling to fade. But it wouldn't. Instead it persisted until she was holding on to him to keep upright.

"You're not like Esme, are you?" he murmured. "I can see it in your eyes when I mention her."

"Now you're psychic?" she asked without irony.

"Not even close. You are hiding something . . . or at least you think you are . . . but Esme would never put herself in the kind of danger you do—not without a payout."

The payout for her wasn't monetary, but it was there. She stared at him, uncertain what to do next, when the flash hit her like lightning. She half collapsed in Dare's arms. Vaguely heard him urgently repeating her name.

Something was terribly wrong.

The feeling of dread continued to course through Grace's entire body—took her over completely, making her pulse race. She started to sweat and shake.

It was returning—a gift she didn't want—and there was no denying it. It was so unwelcome. She had pushed it down for years. The last time she'd had a feeling like this, Rip had locked her in a room and she hadn't seen daylight for a year.

To pass the time, she'd recited lyrics to some of her favorite songs over and over until they became a mantra. She'd forced herself not to feel.

Even when she'd had that slight tingling of her senses before Dare kidnapped her, she'd been able to convince herself that it was nothing but the intuition she'd developed over the years, a sixth sense S8 had helped her hone.

But she'd been wrong. She was starting to feel again. Just when she'd had the coldness, the hardening of her heart, down to a science, Dare and her gift forced her to feel.

She would resist both as long as it was humanly possible.

But this feeling—it wasn't leaving—was enough to make her drop to her knees. Her skull seemed to be squeezed by a tightening band that threatened her sight and her sanity.

No pictures or flashes—nothing. But something was very, very wrong, and it was happening to someone she was close to.

There weren't many she could think of.

"Dare," she managed to croak.

"I'm here—I've got you," he said. "What's wrong?"

"A headache," she lied.

"Come on, you need to sit down." He half carried her to the chair, would've done so completely if not for her stupidly stubborn resistance.

"I'm fine. It must be the stress."

"Looks like more than stress," he said.

Telling him the truth now would make her far too vulnerable to Dare—and although Dare told her he planned on turning her over, she'd gotten the sense she could change his mind.

She closed her eyes, massaged her temples and tried

to divine the feeling, tried to get it back, but everything had faded, leaving her exhausted and tense.

Outside, thunder rumbled and the rain came down harder than before. A phone began to ring—and immediately she knew what was happening. "There's another phone in my bag—front pocket. It's the phone I use for my job—a throwaway—and the only one who has the number is Marnie." She heard herself babbling even as Dare grabbed the phone and handed it to her.

She put it on speaker when she picked up. The female voice on the other end didn't wait for her to get out "hello" before she started screaming.

Marnie.

There was a scuffle and another scream, and then the phone went dead. Grace jumped up. "We have to go to her. Dare, you have to take me to Marnie's house."

She met his eyes and saw he believed her. *Thank God.* He went outside first, checked the area before coming back to usher her into the car.

She followed him out into the rain and into his truck. He threw her a blanket, which she pulled over herself. She was soaked again from that short walk, but she didn't care. The most important thing was that they were headed to Marnie's. She clutched the cell phone, continued attempting to call and getting only a busy signal in return.

That wasn't a good sign. She stared at Dare's profile in the darkness—his jaw was tight. "Breathe, Grace— we'll get to her."

"She's already dead."

He didn't argue with that, didn't try to give her false hope or ply her with platitudes. Was it Marcus who'd come back for Marnie, or someone else?

It was much different riding with him when she wasn't bound, but she was even more frightened this time around.

"You're on the right track," she told him now. "It's behind the old Barlow place."

"I know where that is. Hang on," he told her as they rounded the most dangerous bend in this part of the parish. The bridge would be partially covered with rising water. It never got bad enough that cars couldn't pass over it, but you had to be careful or you'd lose your brakes and go careening off the side.

Dare drove like an old pro, like he knew this place intimately. Darius had mentioned that Dare had lived here from the age of twelve, and she could picture him as a young boy, heading out in the truck by himself, determined to find his way around.

She'd bet anything he hated being lost as much as she did.

Chapter Thirteen

You could live in these bayous for years and still not know there were houses hidden in secret pockets. Darius's was one such place; the small bridge that connected it to the road could easily be missed or hidden. Darius had made sure of it every time he barricaded himself in.

Dare had done the same after he'd driven across the bridge tonight.

By boat, the house was impossible to find unless you had exact coordinates. If Powell ever found the place, it would be because Darius had given him the coordinates. Dare could never see that happening.

Now, as he headed to Marnie's house, he made a mental note to find out more about Grace Powell. That was no headache she'd had. Her eyes were open, so she hadn't fainted, and she seemed like she was in pain. He dismissed seizure—he'd seen enough of them in the field to know—and wondered if it was a panic attack.

He needed to get to the bottom of all of this, but somehow this kidnapping had turned into a protective detail. He supposed he was closer to S8's mission statement than he'd originally thought.

Beside him, Grace was clutching the dashboard, willing him to go faster despite what she'd said earlier about Marnie already being dead, and he was already pushing it along these slick and narrow back roads. He was chilled to think of the risks she'd take if she was driving herself.

On a calm night, Marnie's place was fifteen minutes away. With the storms continuing to blow through the area, which still sustained a lot of hurricane damage, it would take double that, if not longer. He had to bypass a lot of side roads, and many they did drive through were partially underwater.

"Sit back, Grace. Put the seatbelt on," he told her. She glanced at him, and when he returned the look, he noted the surprise on her face. She did as he asked.

Her reaction when he'd mentioned her mother had been interesting. Sadness coupled with anger, which made sense when you considered Esme's rap sheet. It had been easy enough to find—public record—and from there he'd found a lot of her aliases and other information. And then nothing—from the time she'd married Powell until her death when Grace was twelve.

Raised by a grifter and a psychopath. Saved by assassins and now working to help battered women. What the hell was he doing with her?

Steel yourself up, Dare—got to prove you've got the balls for the job, Darius always said. *Gotta be a cold motherfucker.*

Was Darius? Dare supposed so—or else he was a hell of a good actor.

"Your father used to play the guitar all the time," she said suddenly.

He realized he'd been playing with the pick around his neck as they waited for another truck to cross the road in front of them. "Yeah. Said he wanted to be a country music star but settled for the Army instead."

"He was good. You're better."

At those words, he swallowed hard. Tucked the necklace into his shirt and continued driving. "It might not be too late, Grace."

"For Marnie?"

"For you."

He felt her stare at him for a long moment, and then the radio clicked on. Low, but the sound was enough to overshadow the blustering winds.

He could still taste her. Feel her body against his. If she hadn't stopped, he wasn't sure he would've been able to. Maybe he'd just gone too long without. Or maybe Grace was purposely pushing his buttons.

He was so damned angry—at S8, at his father, at Powell and, by extension, at Grace, because he couldn't tell whose side she was on. Because he couldn't blame her for being on her own side.

Because she was trying to seduce him and she was winning.

"Pull over here," she instructed. "Marnie doesn't want anyone closer than this by car."

He did as she asked, but not for the reason she'd stated. His biggest concern was that whoever had come after Marnie was still around, and he wanted the element of surprise. Of course, he'd rather do it without Grace, but she'd never stay put.

He cut the engine—had already cut the lights a while back, using night vision he'd practiced and instincts he'd never had to in order to guide him toward the house. Now he waited, a hand on her shoulder to keep her still while he stared out into the darkness, watching, waiting for any movement.

He had the firepower and he would keep Grace close to him, in case this was a trap. But judging by the screams they'd heard over the phone, Marnie wasn't acting. There had been real fear—real pain—and he had a feeling they were about to intrude on a crime scene of some sort.

Grace seemed to know it too, almost seemed to steel herself.

He saw nothing. "Let's go. Stay close and behind me. If I tell you to get down, get down."

"I will."

She waited in her seat until he came to get her. He shut the doors quietly, clicking them closed but not all the way shut. The rain came down harder as they slogged through the mud. He'd put her in a pair of wellies before they'd left so she'd be protected against snakes—they'd be numerous in this weather, washing up from the bayou and swimming wherever they could.

Darius had made him learn about all the snakes out here, poisonous and non. How to handle snakebites. How to kill the snakes before they killed you.

It was a lesson he'd learned all too well.

*   *   *

Dare held his gun in one hand and her with the other. Grace slipped several times as they threaded through the long grasses that lined the area around Marnie's. She wasn't worrying about snakes or anything else, but thankfully, Dare was. The boots he'd made her put on were an old pair of Adele's, and they were slightly big but kept her feet dry and safe.

Her heart thudded in her chest as she sidled up to the porch, the grasses rustling against her jean-clad legs. Her throat was nearly closed with terror.

Something was very wrong. Marnie should've known she was here. By the time anyone got this close to the house, Marnie would be standing in the front yard with either a shotgun or a glass of lemonade, depending on the visitor.

Sometimes she had both, just in case.

The porch light was on, which meant nothing since Grace knew it was on a timer. There was another auto-timed lamp in the front room and one in the back, so no matter which way a woman looking for help approached the house, she'd get the comfort of light.

It wasn't surprising that many of the survivors they'd met were scared of the dark. Grace willed herself not to be, but she knew Marnie rarely, if ever, turned off lights. Marnie also never slept more than an hour at any given time, and Grace always suspected it was more because of what had happened to Marnie than the job.

She wanted to explain all this to Dare, to tell him this was very bad, but nothing would come out even if she tried. Instead, she knocked on the door, a loud rap . . . and the door swung wide open.

"No." That single word leaked out, and Dare was in front of her, headed inside first even as she clung to his back.

Lights blazed inside, and there was no sound or movement. She heard Dare bite back a curse, and then he said, "Don't look, Grace. Let me get you back to the truck."

"I can't. I have to see." She let go of him and moved to stand next to him.

Her throat went dry and she mouthed the word *no* a few times, her tongue hitting the roof of her mouth by rote.

There was so much blood, all of it pooled around Marnie's head. Marnie, lying on her back in the middle of the living room, the pale yellow rug surrounding her. There was evidence of a fight, but Marnie had been expecting someone. There were no signs of a break-in.

Marnie had let her guard down and the attacker in. How could that have happened?

Grace wanted to sink to the ground, to hold Marnie's face between her palms, to pick her up and bring her away from this violence, but she knew not to touch anything or to leave footprints.

If she hadn't known, Dare would be there, as he was, holding her shoulders. "Turn away."

"She suffered."

He didn't try to lie. "But she's at peace now."

"She didn't deserve this. She was so good, and I can't help but think it's my fault. Anyone who gets close to me dies."

He had no answer for that beyond, "It's not you—it's your circumstances."

"That doesn't make it any easier."

"No, it doesn't," he agreed before he physically turned her around toward him and away from Marnie's body.

It had been forever since she'd hugged anyone. Neither she nor Marnie had been particularly affectionate, thanks to their backgrounds. And hugging a man for pure comfort? Never.

But instincts—needs—were strong things; they refused to be denied. Her cheek found his chest and her arms went tentatively around his waist. His body was as tight as a strung bow at first, but he put his arms around her, one on the small of her back, the other resting gently on the back of her head, each one caressing just a touch.

She didn't think they should stay there long, but he didn't rush her or pull away. She mumbled, "We should go, but I can't leave her like this," with her face still against his shirt, eyes closed as if that would somehow make the entire scene behind her disappear.

She felt bruised, like she'd taken an internal beating that would never heal.

Marnie. She'd been Grace's second chance, her phase two, and now she was gone. The guilt that she hadn't gotten here in time was ever present, holding her like a weighted chain wrapped around her ankles. "I can't leave her like this."

"We'll call the police," he promised. "Does she have any family?"

In a small voice, she said, "No. She's alone, like me."

There was a long pause, and then, "I'll send some-one to claim the body and give her a burial."

She wanted to ask him why he was doing all this for her and decided that sometimes it was better not to question, but rather just to accept.

Marnie's death didn't look like it had been done by a pro, but that was what nagged him. It was almost too staged, too imperfect. If Marcus or someone like him had gotten to Marnie, it would've been messier.

And if Marnie had been killed by a pro, Dare would have to think it might be connected to Grace. Because even if she was telling the truth about having no con-tact with him, there was no telling if Powell knew where she was.

Which meant Dare might very well be a moving tar-get in a place where he'd thought he was well hidden.

"Were you supposed to be at Marnie's tonight? Working?" he asked. Grace looked up at him as though she was seeing him for the first time. Which meant she was in shock.

But she managed to answer. "No. We never planned things like that."

He thought about Marnie's call—had she been forced to make it?

Someone had to have been lying in wait for her. Maybe they hadn't made their move because he'd come here with her, given away his hand. And that had al-ready been reported back to Powell. He was sure of it.

That didn't mean everything else had to go accord-ing to plan.

Grace was kneeling near the body now, although she didn't seem to be looking at Marnie, but rather at some point across the room. He'd take advantage of her grief-driven shock to investigate a little now, because he didn't want to scare her even more.

"I'm going to make a call," he said, and Grace nodded although he doubted she actually heard anything he'd said.

He checked the rest of the small house and found nothing out of place. He'd noted the set of boot prints leading up to and around the house as he and Grace had approached—but he hadn't seen them leading away from the porch. Which meant Marnie's killer had gone out the back.

Which meant he was still here.

This was definitely a one-person job—killing Marnie, taking Grace—a well-trained operative could do that in his sleep.

"Wait here," he murmured, but she wasn't even listening, was now staring at Marnie's body, and he figured that was the lesser of two evils.

She'd have nightmares either way.

He kept talking to her, his voice low, as he moved along the edges of the room. They'd been spotted for sure. He needed to ensure that whoever had spotted them didn't live to talk about it.

He slid out the front door soundlessly, edged around to the back porch and saw a man in all black looking through the window at Grace. Dare caught the glint of a knife, and then the guy looked up, realizing that Dare was no longer in the room.

He seemed to hedge between running and fighting, but Dare didn't, lunged for him. They slammed off the porch into the tall grass nearly silently. The guy got him with the knife, but it was a nick along his biceps. Dare pressed against the man's throat with his arm; he had both the bulk and the anger on his side.

"Who sent you?" he hissed.

"Fuck you," the man told him. It didn't matter. Dare knew this had nothing to do with Marnie's work. It had all been a setup, and there wasn't time to waste before getting Grace back to the safety of the house.

He knocked the man out using the pressure point in his neck, carried him down to the bayou and used the man's knife against him over the water, pushing it cleanly through the carotid. He slid the dead man into the bayou, where the gators and the bayou itself would take care of everything, including the bones. He climbed into the small motorboat, let the engine drop off into the water as well, got out and pushed the boat out to float into the bayou, where someone would find it and claim it as theirs.

And then he double-timed it back to Grace. He grabbed a towel from the kitchen, shoved it between his arm and the jacket to stop the bleeding and found her in the same position.

"Grace, come on. Time to go." He didn't wait for her answer. She was beyond comforting. Instead, he picked her up and carried her out to the truck.

Chapter Fourteen

Avery couldn't sleep, had wandered out to the balcony to stare at the bar when a knock on the door made her start. Gunner called through, then came in before Avery gave the okay.

She came off the balcony to meet him, but he was on her in seconds, pinning her outside with his body.

"Do you think I didn't know you'd left?" he asked gruffly.

"I didn't know I needed a bodyguard."

"You do, sweetheart. You really damned do." His words were clipped and even. "And you still owe me a sit-down in my chair."

"I don't welch on my promises."

"Good to know." He was almost out the door before she asked, "How did you know I'd left?"

He crooked a finger at her, and she followed him down the hall to a room that housed a wallful of monitors for security cams. She glanced over several of them—the downstairs, the outside steps, none of her room, thankfully.

And several in the bar she'd been in. "You spied on me."

"You stole a wallet."

"Does the bar know you do this?"

"Since I pay the mortgage, I'm allowed to," he informed her.

"Anything else I should know about you?"

"How much time you got, *chère*?" he drawled. "Although I think you prefer the pretty boys."

"I'd count you among those."

He gave a short laugh. "Oh, I haven't been one of those in a long time. If that's what you're looking for—"

"I was looking to blow off some steam. I should've told you. But I need to be able to take care of myself."

"Most people who are able to take care of themselves do so with help—that's the paradox of helping yourself. It can't be done—not for long, anyway." Gunner frowned and ran a hand through his hair. "Look, I'll help you, the way I'm sure Dare did—or would—but you've gotta stay close. Especially with these two around."

"What two?" she asked.

He rewound the recording from the bar and showed her Key . . . and then a dark-haired guy snapping a cell phone picture of her as she left.

"Friends of yours?" she asked.

"I don't have friends."

Had he seen the kiss? If he'd been watching her the whole time, he'd seen everything. She dug into the pocket of the jeans she'd worn earlier and pulled out the wallet and went through it.

His name was Key Brossard. His driver's license

gave his residence as North Carolina, his address near the Army base. She found an old military ID tucked into a side pocket. Army. Motor pool.

But the card was expired. No recent one. Some cash, one credit card, no pictures or condoms.

She wasn't even sure why she'd taken it, but she no longer ignored any instinct. It might prove too costly.

"Don't worry about getting that back to him—they'll come to you," Gunner said.

She frowned and closed the wallet. "As long as they don't bring the police."

"They won't." Gunner checked over the other security monitors, and she looked over his shoulder to see the restaurant several doors down, past the end of the parking garage.

"You own that too?"

"Yes."

It appeared he owned basically the whole block, which included the parking garage. "I guess tattooing pays well."

He snorted and looked over his shoulder at her. "You're cute. Glad I decided to let you stay."

"Sarcasm?"

"The truth." He spun in the chair and pointed to a matching one. She sat in it cross-legged as a burst of cheers from the bar floated up through the window. "Nice to hear this town in the partying spirit again."

"What makes this place so magical?"

"Ah, the age-old question. You know what I say? Don't question it. It doesn't make sense and it never will—and that's the beauty of it."

"When did you start tattooing?"

"I gave myself my first one when I was sixteen." He lifted his jeans and pointed to a skull and crossbones on his calf. It was faded, definitely not as professional as the others, but that was its charm. "Tattoos are like a road map of where you've been, where you're going. I like to think of them as a résumé. You know, in certain countries, you can tell a man's entire past just by reading his tattoos."

"That would come in handy if everyone followed that rule," she commented.

"Or it would get you in a hell of a lot of trouble."

"Right." She wrapped her arms around her bare legs and rested her chin on her knees. "Speaking of troubles . . . any way to get rid of my charges?"

"I'm no magician, but I can put your name toward the bottom of the pile, so to speak. Or I would've, if there was any trace of the men you killed or you as a suspect."

"What do you mean? Last time Dare checked—"

"This time I checked. You're officially a free woman."

"That's why it was okay for me to go to the restaurant. That's why you didn't stop me from going to the bar."

"Partially," he agreed.

"What does that mean?"

"The cops aren't the ones you need to worry about. Someone was interested in having you erased, so they could take care of erasing you the way they wanted to."

She went cold again, and her thoughts went to Richard Powell. Dare had told her not to bring his name up to Gunner, but he did have enough power to keep her crimes hidden so he could mete out his own form of punishment. She wondered if she should bother Dare with this and decided against it. He had too much on his mind already, and most of it centered around her safety.

The picture was clear enough, taken from the back room of the bar, where Jem had left the poker game for a moment to check on his little brother.

Key was having no trouble getting his game on with her, until she pulled away and left.

Jem's picture caught the reluctant look on her face. She looked completely different from when she'd entered Gunner's earlier that evening—and that was definitely a purposeful move. No one stayed with Gunner for fun. There was always danger or money involved. But the fact that she was here with Key was just dumb luck. Key hadn't seen any of his surveillance from earlier, would have no idea who she was.

"Little girl lost, what's your deal?" he asked softly.

He ran it through the facial recognition software on his phone until it pulled up an online picture . . . for a wanted poster. A single one—the rest of her was all too conveniently erased. But the problem with the goddamned Internet meant you couldn't erase every last trail . . . and sometimes, that was a lucky break for him. "Ah, Key, come on—when you step in it, you really goddamn step in it."

Granted, Jem was one to talk since he was a hunted, wanted man himself, but he knew how to hide. He also

knew that the CIA and his various other acquired enemies would never take him down without losing many
of their men—and eventually, they'd give up.

Keeping Key safe might prove more difficult. He
was more of the smash-and-grab type—the Rangers
utilized some secrecy but preferred big guns.

They'd arrived hours earlier, after Jem finally got
some intel on Dare linking him to the New Orleans
area. Dare had lived near them growing up, which ate
at Key more than he'd admit. Jem always said there
were no coincidences, that they were moved around
the chessboard for reasons unknown. But fuck it all, he
never said he liked it.

The woman named Avery had undone his brother
with a kiss. A couple of touches. Jem wondered if it
was the first time since Key's whole ordeal that his
brother had tried to lose himself like that.

That would've been the first thing Jem would've
sought comfort in, but Key had always had better
control, never allowed himself to live in fairy-tale
land the way Jem did. Key had fought that crazy gene
with everything he had, and Jem sometimes wondered why. Maybe Key should've just let it out, given
it free reign.

How much had it hurt Jem, really? It seemed like
their careers were neck and neck for shit at the moment, and Jem seemed to be having a lot more fun.

"I've taken way too much of your money," he told
the men now, checked out of the game before they'd
never let him play again. There was a delicate balance
to these things, and he never overstayed his welcome.

He went back out to the bar, where Key was ignoring girls trying desperately to get his attention.

"The dark-haired one—she was cute."

He accepted the beer Jem handed him, gulped it as though it might help. "She was all right."

"You run her off?"

"Yeah, that's what happened." Key's drawl got deeper when he drank, or maybe it was just the proximity to their childhood. Jem knew it was throwing him, although it was hard to tell when he was off balance.

"She's a murderer," he told his brother casually.

"You're back here a couple of days and you're a tarot card reader?"

Jem held up his cell. "Better. Facial recognition software."

"Ah, fuck."

"Hey, you dodged a bullet. Finally. Maybe your luck's turning around."

"Which would make that the strongest occurrence to happen to me in this state forever." Key held up his beer bottle for an invisible toast and then felt his jeans' pocket. "My wallet's gone."

"The murderer's also a damned good thief," Jem commented. "And nothing good happens when you drink, Key."

"That's never stopped you."

"I said nothing good happens when *you* drink. When I drink, it's all good." He paused. "We can get it back—she's staying at Gunner's."

"The tat place?"

Jem cut his eyes to him. "That tat place . . . yeah."

"Can we forget the girl?"

"No, we can't. Because the girl shows up out of no-where and stays with Gunner."

"So?"

"Gunner and I go back a long way. I'll check it out."

"I don't want to know any goddamn more," Key told him, but Jem was now like a dog with a bone. He had no CIA job and he had to stay busy or go even crazier. "Maybe I shouldn't have broken you out of that place."

"Ah, Key, I would've done it anyway. Just wanted to give you something to do."

"Gee, thanks." Key shoved him, and Jem, in turn, decided to leave him there to drink his troubles away.

"Headed home—take a cab."

"Thanks for watching out for me," Key called, the sarcasm evident even through his slurred words.

Jem walked the five blocks in the heat back to the apartment they'd rented a week ago. The air-condi-tioning was blasting, and Jem stripped down and showered the smoke and bar smell off him before set-tling at the computer with a glass of sweet tea.

Key rarely drank—Jem knew this was a temporary situation so he didn't have to relive the trial or the rea-son for it. But lately, if Key hadn't had enough bour-bon, he'd brood about it, turning events over and over in his mind until he finally fell asleep.

"Disobeying a direct order," Jem muttered as he looked through Key's classified file for the millionth time, the way he'd done from the time the incident first occurred. Key hadn't called him, but Jem had contacts who'd immediately let him know what had happened.

Hadn't mattered that the reason for disobeying a direct order had been saving one of the military's own. The jury's mind had been made up, despite the impressive array of men who took the stand in Key's defense. The array of medals, awards and exemplary service records were all shot to shit because Dare O'Rourke refused to come forward and say that he'd needed to be saved.

The bastard had been hanging, for Christ sakes, according to Key. Unable to move. Exhausted. And there had been maybe three feet between him and certain death by burning alive.

Jem paged through the transcripts.

JAG prosecutor: "Did he struggle?"

Key: "He was unconscious."

JAG prosecutor: "Not according to mission records. Not according to the man himself."

Dare's statement, put into evidence by his lawyers, simply said that he hadn't needed help and that he'd told Key to stand down.

Key had been found guilty on all charges. Barely escaped the brig, and that was because Jem pulled every goddamn string he knew of and a few more he didn't.

He'd never tell Key that—it didn't matter. He owed his baby brother for the rest of the boy's life, and he'd pay until the bank was empty.

Chapter Fifteen

After getting Grace safely into the truck, Dare grabbed the flashlight and checked under the chassis and the hood and anywhere else a tracker could've been planted. Then he drove faster on the way home, but also circled into the surrounding bayou first before taking a slightly different route in case someone was staking out the house.

No one followed, but that didn't mean there weren't more of Powell's men out here, hoping to get lucky. He covered the bridge up behind them and planned on using only the water routes from now on. He drove with the lights off as he headed toward the house.

He'd spent a lifetime learning to read people, a skill born from necessity to be able to keep up with Darius's many moods, plus Adele's and other S8 men he spent time with. There were also numerous authority figures he'd needed to lie to in order to keep up appearances, especially when he was older and Darius would disappear. Dare got tired of staying with Adele or random neighbors when she was on a mission with Darius, and so he'd learned to avoid child protective services or overly interested teachers.

Grace was a slightly more difficult read because of whom she'd grown up with. She'd built a nice wall around herself, but being near the place she felt bound to—Darius's house—was helping to break her down.

He tried to tell himself he was doing her a favor, that carrying all that damned baggage around forever wasn't good for anyone.

There was no way he could turn her back over to Rip and live with himself, but he wouldn't tell her that and give up his bargaining power.

And she was hiding something from him. Maybe it was for self-protection; maybe it was to screw him over. But sooner or later, she'd spill. He knew it because he always got people to spill. He was the best interrogator the SEALs had—his gift, they'd called it.

It was what he *did*, but it was a gift he kept well hidden because it kept him in good stead with everyone . . . until the damned jungle.

Next to him, Grace remained still and silent, her arms wrapped around herself. She was partially in shock, her breathing fast and jerky.

She was also close to panicking, and panicked people made bad decisions. Grace would be no different. And he hadn't bothered to try to calm her down.

When he stopped the truck outside the house, Grace bolted. He didn't think she'd planned on doing so, figured it was more instinct mixed with grief, but it didn't matter.

She was running. Predictably. He'd given her other chances, backed her against the wall to see what she was made of. Sometimes forcing someone's hand made them reveal their entire battle plan, ensuring he could take the element of surprise away from their future interactions.

He gave her enough rope to hang herself. With any luck, she'd get lost and scared shitless enough to rethink running again, and then he'd go track her, prey to predator, stalking the dark bayou the way he had as a teen, ensuring his inner compass was as finely tuned as it could be.

Even now, years later, he knew it like the back of his hand. Spotted her by the harsh breaths and rush of skin against clothes, against brush, signs and sounds that could be honed in on only after years of fine-tuning himself to be the perfect machine for stealth and secrecy.

The job. He'd started to lose track of the fact that this was still exactly that—nothing more, nothing less—no matter how pretty or tortured his self-proclaimed leverage was.

He moved silently behind her, threaded through the brush and brambles in the soaking rain alongside her for a while without her noticing.

She was crying, although he had a feeling she'd never admit it.

Grace barely knew she was running. She was overwhelmed and couldn't see beyond the tears blurring her eyes.

All she knew was that she needed to escape—didn't matter whom or what she was running from—because really, she knew deep down in her heart that it wasn't only Dare.

She took off through the small backyard that was once a garden and straight into the depths of the bayou grand that lined the back of the house beyond. There were maybe twenty feet of high grass before she'd hit the water. At one time, she could always find a pirogue or two floating next to the small dock, as though drawn to it.

As though they knew whoever stayed here was always looking for an escape route.

All the while she ran, she couldn't shake the feeling that he'd let her run, that this was all part of his damned plan. But Dare needed to know that she'd never gone down without a fight before and she wasn't about to start now.

She couldn't escape him, but if she didn't try, she'd never forgive herself. When faced with the opening, she'd taken it, though she was moving through the darkness that couched the bayou more slowly than she would've liked.

In the daylight, she knew every square inch of the place. At night, she'd refused to step outside, remained huddled under the covers, terrified first that Rip would find her and then, later, terrified that she'd be alone like that forever.

She'd never told Marnie anything about her past, or asked her for help, even though Marnie's self-styled underground railroad could easily have helped Grace get lost forever.

But she was already so lost—she couldn't bear to have it be for forever.

Finally she got her bearings, her breaths coming so hard she felt as though her lungs were ripping out of her chest. She slipped and slid in the tall grass and then caught the path down to the water and her energy revived.

Dare was waiting for her on the dock, facing her, arms crossed. She barely saw his outline, his arms crossed loosely over his chest.

This time, there was no pirogue in the water.

She held her hands up, the international *I surrender* sign, wondered if that would be enough.

He walked toward her, brushed past her and said, "Follow me and don't pull this shit again."

She struggled with everything she had so she could keep up with him and walked by his side as much as possible all the way back to the house.

True to his word, he called the police as soon as he'd locked and alarmed them back inside the house. Then, while she continued to listen, he made another call with instructions for Marnie's burial.

Grace busied herself making strong coffee. He supplied the bottle of whiskey and they sat in their wet clothes and drank the mix and she tried to blur the edges of the night's memory, if only for a brief moment.

"I'm sorry you had to see that," he told her, his voice sounding slightly hollow. In his line of work, she knew he saw dead bodies all the time. But this seemed to affect him more than it should have.

"If I hadn't been with you . . ." She trailed off and he laughed a little.

"My kidnapping saved your life, yes."

But he didn't say that she was no longer kidnapped. Nothing had really changed . . . nothing and everything.

She fished in her pocket and held out Marnie's phone to him. "I took it off the table by the door."

"It's best that you have no contact with any of these women—for your safety."

"Isn't there a way you can secure the phone line or forward the calls? Please, Dare, this is important."

"What's more important than your life?"

"The lives of the women who are saved by what Marnie does," she told him. "She might not have been able to put me together, but she damn well tried. And she did more for me on that front than I'd ever expected anyone to."

"Forget it. We've done what we could. I have other things to worry about." He took out the battery, broke the SIM card and broke the phone in half before chucking it into the garbage.

She was out of her chair trying to stop him, but he was too quick.

"If you'd let her come in earlier, this wouldn't have happened," she told him, gave him a hard slap across the face. He didn't flinch, merely grabbed her wrist to stop her from doing it again.

"You know that's not true. They were lying in wait for her."

"We don't know who killed her—maybe it's someone working with you."

"Maybe it's someone working for you. Maybe you're in contact with Powell and you're not telling me," he said.

"I would never— I told you I'd rather die than go back with him, and I meant it."

"Why should I believe you?" he demanded.

"Why shouldn't you?"

He didn't answer that, told her instead, "You need protection."

She hadn't realized S8 had been unable to provide that any longer. Adele had been her last hope, and whatever she'd put in place to keep Grace off the grid was wearing thin. Something dangerous was bound to happen.

"I was supposed to move a few months ago," she admitted.

"Why didn't you?"

"I'm supposed to build something and then leave it every six months for the rest of my life." She stared at him. "That's as bad as being imprisoned by my father."

"You'd be alive."

"You know that's not living."

"Some people would take it any way they could. Some people would fight for survival," Dare said fiercely.

"Some people . . . or you?" she asked, and he pulled back with a muttered curse. Instead of answering her further, he told her to go goddamned shower and get out of the wet clothes. She knew she needed to get warm and dry, did as he said, all the while knowing he was right on the other side of the partially open door.

The steam escaped the bathroom door, swirled around Dare like a goddamned tease. When he walked by, he could barely see the outline of Grace's naked body through the frosted shower door, but he'd seen enough to feel like a dirty old man.

"What the hell am I doing?" he asked himself out loud.

Saving your sister. Avenging your father. Saving himself too, but that mattered to him a hell of a lot less than the first two.

Avery didn't deserve any of this. Maybe Grace didn't either, but sometimes sacrifices had to be made, and there was always collateral damage involved. He'd learned that from a very early age.

And while he had made a call about Marnie, it wasn't to the police. He wasn't alerting anyone about anything. Instead, he'd asked his own voice mail to make arrangements for Marnie's body and clean up. Later he'd ask Gunner to help him out.

He stitched his arm up quickly, put on a T-shirt to cover the gauze so Grace wouldn't see. Thought about telling her what he'd found at Marnie's but decided against it for now.

The water shut off and he heard the shower door open and Grace moving around. Then she came toward the open door, saying, "Dare?"

She peeked out. She wore a heavy towel wrapped around her, her bare shoulders dotted with water droplets. She smelled like lavender and hibiscus and sunshine, her hair wet and tumbling over her shoulders.

He handed her some of his clothes to borrow—a T-shirt and some shorts that would be huge on her—plus a pair of socks.

He glanced down at her toes and saw that her nails were painted a deep plum color that suited her. She had sexy toes. And they weren't retreating.

"I won't try to escape again. There's nowhere for me to go—you know that already."

He met her gaze. Her eyes held an honesty that nearly broke him. "Then why run?"

"To know I can."

He couldn't argue. "Get dressed and come into the kitchen."

She blinked at his trust, smiled and then went back into the bathroom and shut the door. He changed out of his wet clothes and showered in the other bathroom. Found her sitting at the table waiting for him.

She'd made more coffee. Handed him a cup, which he accepted.

After a long beat, she told him, "Your father and Adele trusted me."

"They knew I wouldn't take their word for it."

"You don't trust your father?"

"Do you trust yours?" he asked, and she sat back and wrapped her arms around herself.

"Okay, yes, I get it. This world—it's different. It's not about trust. It's about what you can do for someone."

He went to the stove, turned the flame on under a pan and went to the fridge. Butter, bread and cheese and a few minutes later, he put a grilled cheese sandwich in front of her. Followed by a small glass of whiskey.

"You're still shaking," he informed her.

She nodded as she bit into the sandwich, closed her eyes and gave a soft moan of appreciation, like it was the best thing ever. He remained standing, eating the gooey, warm sandwich barefoot while leaning against the counter. He caught the sounds of tornado sirens in the distance.

She heard them too.

"Storm's going to get worse before it gets better," he observed.

"Well, if that's not a metaphor," she murmured, and he shook his head.

"We've got a hell of a lot to get straight here."

"Yes. But I think we're off to a better start this time."

"We'll see about that," he muttered. "Why don't you tell me more about your time with Darius and Adele? I know you weren't here for six years straight."

"No, at first for about six months. And then I lived in Alabama for a year," she admitted. "And then Houston, Tampa. London for several months."

"And you came back here two years ago?"

"Yes. And I haven't seen either of them for a year."

"Why back here?"

She glanced up at him with those big dark eyes. "Because I asked them to. I missed it."

She'd wanted stability. He couldn't blame her, and

obviously Darius and Adele didn't want to let her down.

Was Grace using them, or had it been the other way around?

"Did they know something about you, Grace? Some reason you'd be valuable to Rip?"

"Beyond being his daughter?"

There was something else going on. Dare was going to get to the bottom of it, for all their sakes.

Chapter Sixteen

Grace stood, brought her plate to the sink so she didn't have to face Dare. She'd been wondering if she should simply tell him about what happened earlier, about her gift sputtering on and off like a faulty light-bulb.

But what if . . .

That *what if* was why she kept her mouth shut. She was valuable to Rip, with or without her gift. At least she had been at one point. She'd spent so much time with his precious group, he might think differently now. But Dare . . . who was she to say that, even if he didn't leverage her to Rip, he wouldn't try to use her gift the way Rip had, defective or not?

For now, she'd keep that secret to herself. Maybe forever.

She ran the water and Dare came up behind her.

"I'll take care of it," he told her.

"Least I can do."

"You can't pretend Marnie's death didn't happen," he said.

"I can—for as long as I want. Sometimes, it's the

only way to get through things." She glanced over her shoulder, looked into his eyes and then down at his hands. "I have a feeling you know exactly what I'm talking about."

She wondered if he'd yell at her again or simply walk away. That last one would be the worst. She wanted him to understand.

She turned around and found herself so close to him. Maybe he'd planned it this way or maybe it was happenstance. It didn't matter. The wildness in her was so raw—she wanted to break through to this man. Had to, the way he'd already broken through to her.

She didn't know how to deal with a man like this. Darius had been powerful, yes, but he'd kept his distance, let Adele deal with her most of the time.

She'd still been so broken, a surly teenager prone to sneaking out of the house and drinking with men who were bad for her to prove she could never be hurt again.

She'd been so goddamned wrong; she knew that now. But Adele never scolded. For four years, Grace traveled with Adele, but Grace always thought of this as her home base. This was where she'd first begun to heal.

His hand came up to her cheek. "You're flushed."

She felt hot all over. A little dizzy, but a different dizzy than she'd felt earlier, when the vision broke through. She swallowed the tightness in her throat away, wanted to tell him the flush was because of him.

"I've been thinking about you for years," she confessed finally.

"Why's that?"

"Your picture . . . the way Darius and Adele talked about you. You're a good man, Dare O'Rourke."

"A good man who kidnapped you."

"For your father . . . he told you to."

Dare reached a hand up and brushed her hair back over her shoulders. Tucked it behind an ear, stroked her earlobe, and she shivered. "You knew he would."

"He told me he might have to one day. He said . . . 'Dare will do the right thing, but I've never been the type to tell him what he has to do.'"

"True. No one tells me what to do."

"No one?"

"No one." He leaned in and kissed her, and she soared, as she had earlier. The threat of danger had dissipated. So had the anger. It was replaced with heat, and she gripped his shoulders to try to gain some quarter.

But there was none in this situation. Her head began to spin, her nipples tightened and she was done fighting him. And that hadn't ever happened to her.

She wasn't sure how long they kissed for, lost track of time because he just continued kissing her like that was the most important thing in the world. He'd picked her up at one point so she was sitting on the counter and he was standing between her legs.

He pulled back, murmured, "Something's wrong."

"Tell me something I don't know."

His hand was on her forehead, his eyes full of concern she wished would disappear. "I think you have a fever. You're burning up—I'll get a thermometer."

"Don't bother—it's well over 101," she told him. She

got these fevers less regularly than she had when she was young, but they tended to come on fast and raise the mercury high. She was growing woozy, and then Dare was carrying her, putting her into the big bed she remembered so well. Darius would send her to bed with tea when they first got here, and it was like having a guardian angel. She'd never had anyone like that before, although she'd longed for it.

But Dare—he would be either her savior or her destroyer. It was yet to be determined.

If she was in her house—she'd been careful never to think of it as home—she could prepare something for the fever. But there was no garden here, no supply of herbs that were as interchangeable as medicines to her and people like her.

She and Momma had grown up in Mississippi, which was why she hadn't returned there. The community had run them out of town after discovering some of Esme's scams, and Grace cursed the fact that Momma had run right into Rip instead of continuing on to New Orleans, like she'd originally planned.

Grace's life would've been so different.

But her mother had always believed in what was meant to be. That there was no escaping her destiny, her fate.

Grace longed to escape, and she had, if only for years rather than a lifetime. She was not opposed to fighting for her freedom—she valued freedom over peace; she'd never been convinced it was possible to have both concurrently.

*   *   *

Grace was mumbling something about peace and freedom, and Dare had no idea how this fever had come
out of nowhere and spiked so goddamned high.

He found a thermometer; her temperature was close
to 103 now. He grabbed Tylenol and brought it to her,
would find something stronger as soon as he got her
more comfortable.

She shivered under the heavy quilts, despite the
lack of AC. The fans were only pushing humid air lan-
guidly. She looked like she couldn't get warm enough,
and he was tempted to take her to a hospital.

But he couldn't shake that what had happened to
Marnie wasn't over, that the same people who'd hurt
Marnie were now after Grace. With that in mind, he
knew what he was going to do.

"I'm going to get you help," he told her.

"No—no hospital."

"I'm calling someone to come here," he told her. She
nodded; there was nothing else she could do.

The sun was just about to rise—and Dare didn't like
anyone coming here during daylight hours. Especially
not now. And Gunner would be the only one he'd call.
Gunner had been a medic, and he was better than a
doctor any day and a hundred times more discreet.

He made a quick call to Avery and spoke with Gunner. Avery sounded so damned worried—probably because he sounded worried himself—and he made a
mental note to apologize to her when she got here.

He wasn't used to dealing with the kind of family
who worried about him. Hell, he wasn't used to dealing with anyone like that.

"Get that fever down, Dare," Gunner told him.

"I don't have much here."

"Read me the labels," Gunner instructed, and Dare went through the medicine chest, which Darius had always left well stocked. "Okay, give her two of that antibiotic—separate them by four hours. I'll continue with an IV antibiotic that's stronger when I get there tonight, even though I'm betting it won't do shit. And get her into a cool bath or shower, or at the very least, wipe her down. And give her the narcotic to knock her out only as a last resort if she fights the bath or if she's in pain."

"I'll do it," he told Gunner, then shoved the phone into his pocket and followed Gunner's instructions.

He filled the old claw-footed tub with cool water and went back into the bedroom.

Grace was so hot, her skin was burning. He attempted to cool her down with a cool washcloth along her face and neck after forcing several Tylenol down her throat. She'd tried to push him away but calmed once he showed her the bottle.

But she was still so restless. Moaning a little in her sleep—and if she dreamed, they weren't pleasant. Because of that, he'd do anything he could to make it better until Gunner and Avery got here. And then she began to curl into a ball and cry out as if she was in real pain.

He had to get her out of her clothes. She might hate him for it, but it was the best plan for now.

As if she knew what he planned, she turned away from him onto her stomach, buried her face in the pillow, and the T-shirt she'd put on after they'd come in from the rain rose up to reveal bare skin. Bare skin that was abraded with scars.

They were made purposely—someone had beaten Grace—a whip, belt, it didn't matter. The marks had never healed, and he hissed in a breath when he first saw them. And then, as he ran a finger along them, he realized he was clenching his jaw so hard his head ached. He lifted the shirt higher so he could see how far up they went. And then he noted that the scars went down past the waistband of the sweats.

His throat dried. Carefully, he pushed the T-shirt up over her head and off her body. She'd stopped protesting—too weak maybe, or embarrassed, but he wasn't about to stop his exploration.

Her back was like a road map of pure pain, made with some kind of leather switch. One of the straps had caught on the tender flesh of the back of her upper arm. When he pulled off the sweatpants, he noted that the scars ran down past her buttocks. This was torture. Nothing less than—meant to be a lesson.

He wondered if she'd learned it—told himself this kind of woman was too strong to bow down to anything.

He wouldn't use her. He'd have to find another way.

"Did he do this to you? Powell?" he asked quietly, not expecting her to answer.

"Rip," she reminded him softly. "He had one of his men do it."

"Why?"

"I wouldn't cooperate."

"When you're better, I'll take you back to your house—your garden."

She turned to him, her eyes hazy with fever, her cheeks flushed hot. "I can't go back there. You're not the only person coming for me."

"I'll keep you with me until I figure something out."

"You won't get an argument from me. But why am I naked?"

"Have to break this fever," he murmured, and whether she heard him or not, he didn't know, but she stopped fighting for the moment. He took that opportunity to pick her up and bring her into the bathroom. He lowered her into the tub, and she clung to him; the water must've felt like ice on her blazing skin. But gradually, she let go of him, more from exhaustion than anything, and he used a cloth to cover her forehead, gave her small sips of water to keep her hydrated.

He couldn't help but glance down at her body, lush and perfect. Her nipples were the color of a blush, breasts round and high. The dark curls between her thighs made his cock harden.

He could still taste their kisses and wondered if he'd pushed her too far, taken advantage of her without realizing it. "Grace, about the kiss—"

"Wonderful," she murmured. "If I wasn't sick . . ."

"Yeah."

She reached up out of the water to hold his hand. She seemed comfortable being naked in front of him, but maybe she was half-delirious. "This is better. Don't feel as cold."

She was actually starting to sweat a little, which was

great. He took her temperature again. It had gone down significantly.

"I get fevers like this," she told him. "Spike really high. Happened when I was a kid but I never outgrew it."

"Will it come back again?"

She nodded. He gave her the water bottle and she took a big sip.

"Why don't we get you back into bed? You can sleep, and by the time your fever spikes, my friend will be here with the good stuff to help you."

She agreed. He helped her out of the tub and wrapped a towel around her. Held her steady while she dried off and got her into one of his T-shirts, which went down to midthigh. He lowered her into the bed, covered her with a sheet and watched her drift off to sleep.

He'd been up for nearly forty-eight hours straight. Good way to keep the ghosts at bay, but this was the best opportunity to rest he was going to get. He set the alarms and prepared to wait the day out.

He lay on the bed next to her, careful not to wake or crowd her. His Sig was on the table next to him, and he flicked through the channels on the TV restlessly.

The last time he was here, he'd been twenty-eight and on R&R from the SEALs for a month. He'd been wounded, and his shoulder still ached when he thought about it. Now the pain in his hands overrode pretty much any other pain he had. He flexed them as he watched the old black-and-white western and thought about how much his life had changed in the space of two months.

At some point, he slept—too soundly, because when he woke, Grace was tossing and turning next to him. Shivering again. Mumbling too.

"Hang on, baby, help is coming," he told her.

The fever was spiking higher than before. She was resisting everything. He hated having to drug her but didn't really see a choice. He injected her with the dosage of morphine that Gunnar told him to give, then put her back into the bath, despite the fact that she was shivering uncontrollably.

Shivering while simultaneously mumbling that she was fine. Jesus Christ, she could've gone through Hell Week in BUD/S with no problems.

Beyond her fever, she was grieving underneath it all, for her life here, for Marnie.

He was more tied to S8 than ever, through Avery and through Grace. There was no getting around it.

Chapter Seventeen

Jem got a half hour of sleep at most, worked long after Key stumbled in and began his snoring on the couch.

He woke his brother sometime after noon.

"Get showered and dressed and meet me at the tat shop in twenty," he told Key, who grunted. "Coffee and breakfast is on the stove. And I'm not your mama."

"Thank fucking God for that," Key muttered, and then continued to mutter, saying something along the lines of never drinking again as long as he fucking lived.

If Avery was staying with Gunner, it was for protection. Why Gunner had let her out on her own was a mystery. Unless Gunner was losing his touch.

Doubtful.

The door was locked but the alarm system was off. There was a big bodyguard who'd go down like a rock and some celebrity tween of the week lying on Gunner's table.

Gunner's back was to him, but he'd know Jem was in the shop in three, two, one . . .

Without turning around or stopping his work, he said, "I'm closed."

"You need better locks."

As many times as the men had met over the years, they never talked about the past. It was an unspoken agreement that had kept the men alive in each other's presence for the past fifteen years.

The bodyguard was up in a second, and Gunner sighed and shut down the tat gun. "Dude, he's cool. He's just going to grab some coffee and wait for me. Quietly."

Jem smiled his best crazy-assed smile at the bodyguard and hoped the guy was smart enough to stand down, because Jem could easily kill him without breaking a sweat.

Granted, so could Gunner.

It took another half an hour for Gunner to finish up with the tat on the young celebrity, then pose for the obligatory picture that would end up on Twitter and bring Gunner more business than he'd ever imagined or wanted.

For Gunner, tattooing was as sacred as anything. As sacred as that fucked-up reverse-karma thing he had going. Because if Gunner saved your life, he owed you a favor, not the other way around. Jem knew that growing up here was enough to give anyone more superstitions than they could count.

Finally, Gunner let the bodyguard with the stupid hidden gun, too many muscles and not enough range to be good for anything take the tween away. Punk. But the girl was cute and didn't need much more than the scary-looking man to frighten people into giving her a clear path, and hell, Jem was long out of the hero business.

"Want that coffee Irish?" Gunner asked Jem without turning back around.

"Hair of the dog," Jem agreed, and Gunner gave him a shot in the steaming mug and served himself the same. After a long moment of silence as Jem let the liquid burn his gullet, he said, "You know you're housing a multiple murderer?"

"Her money's good."

"So's her ass."

"Wouldn't know."

"Losing your touch?"

"Ah, Jeremiah, you wish." Gunner slugged down half the coffee. "I don't need this shit today—what do you want, really?"

Brass tacks, that was what it always came down to between them. "Looking for someone. Dare O'Rourke."

Avery tossed and turned for most of the night, finally fell into a deeper sleep as morning came. When she woke, she heard voices downstairs. Gunner had obviously opened her door at some point in order to keep track of her.

She guessed she needed to be grateful that someone else was watching her back.

She moved toward the stairs to hear the voices—Gunner and another guy whose voice she didn't recognize. Then she heard the door open, and Gunner said, "Key, long time no see. How long you been back?"

Key. Here, in Gunner's shop. She went down the stairs and waited behind the curtain that separated the kitchenette area of the shop from the main room. Watched as Key shook Gunner's hand.

"Been years," Gunner was saying. "You two finally coming home?"

"For now," Key said. "Jem and I came here looking for someone."

"Yeah, Jem mentioned Dare," Gunner said, and Avery's stomach tightened.

There is no such thing as coincidences.

But Gunner was a pro. "I knew Darius. Haven't seen his son."

And God bless him, that was the truth. Now she wondered if Dare had avoided seeing Gunner purposely, and it was looking like the answer to that would be yes.

"I need to see him," Key said.

"Why?" she demanded, pushing through the curtain. Key's eyebrows rose, and he looked between her and Gunner. She wondered if his irritation was a mask for jealousy.

"Your new wife?" Key asked Gunner.

"A friend," Gunner said. "She's renting upstairs."

"A friend who knows Dare?" Key asked, directing his question to Gunner but staring at her.

"I never said that," she answered sweetly.

Key laughed, but it wasn't free and easy the way it had been the night before. "Sometimes it's what you don't say. Got anything you want to tell me?"

"I'm hungover," she said.

He simply looked away, and she swore she saw a

look of disappointment on his face. What did he expect? All she'd done was kiss him.

For hours.

Kissing the same person for that long did something to her brain. Rewired it. She could still taste him, feel the weight of his body on hers.

There was something innately romantic about kissing and only kissing.

Nothing chaste about it. Such a seemingly innocent thing, but far more intimate than it seemed on the surface.

Part of her wanted to take it all back. "How do you know them?" she asked Gunner.

"Gunner and I moved in the same circles for years," Jem answered instead.

"Jem is twenty pounds of crazy stuffed in a five-pound bag," Gunner told her.

"And that's different from you how?" she asked innocently.

"Wiseass," he muttered, and Jem hooted, said, "I like her, Gunner."

She noted that Key didn't echo the sentiment, and that bothered her.

"Trust me—Jem's in a whole different league," Gunner said. "Want me to tell her about that time in Prague—"

"Just tell Dare we need to talk to him," Jem interjected, putting a hand on Key's shoulder, because Key was suddenly frozen, staring at her oddly. She took a step back, and Gunner pulled her behind him.

The look on Key's face told her she was about to be

used in the same way she and Dare had been told to use Grace.

"Hey, Key, I think it's time to go—Gunner will call us with any updates on Dare," Jem said, never taking his eyes off Avery.

"Come on, Avery—we'll get some breakfast," Gunner told her, and she finally tore her eyes from Key long enough for him and Jem to leave. "You should've stayed out of it. You managed to piss Key off."

"He's just upset I walked away from him last night."

"Why did you?"

"Because I couldn't exactly bring him back here, could I?"

Wrong answer, if Gunner's murderous expression was any indication, but it quickly fell away, replaced by his imperturbable mask. "No, *chère*, that wouldn't've been smart. Next time, fuck him in the bar's bathroom and don't get caught or let anyone take your picture. He ran it and found one instance still hanging around online about your recent infractions of the law."

So that's why Key had asked her if she had anything to say to him.

"Avery, you've got to stay out of shit like this," Gunner continued.

"Why are they after my brother?" she demanded.

"I have no goddamned idea, but I don't like any of this. I'm beginning to feel like we're all being herded together."

"By Powell?" The name slipped out, and she cursed herself, especially when Gunner's glare was secondary to his hand grabbing her. He held her arm, pushed her against the wall much more gently than she'd thought he'd be capable of and still left her feeling threatened.

"You're gonna tell me everything you know about Richard Powell—and if he's why you're here, God help us all."

Key made it into the alleyway before retching last night's liquor and this morning's breakfast. Jem yanked him up and moved him along, back into their car, and drove them toward the apartment they'd rented in the French Quarter. Didn't say anything to him until they'd gotten up the stairs and he'd shoved Key into a cold shower.

Jem waited for him in the living room, pacing the small area like a goddamned caged lion and then decided to make his brother some toast to settle his stomach. He knew what Key had thought about in that room with Avery, and the worst part was, she knew it.

Taking her would make Dare pay for everything. And Key had begun to think of himself as a mean old bastard, moving along on the heels of vengeance, capable of anything.

He'd been wrong. He wasn't Jem—not by a long shot. And thank fucking God for that.

When Key came out, he looked slightly green but calmer. Jem handed him a Coke and some toast, and Key sat at the table wearing a pair of shorts, trying to work the bread down. The sugar would help. So would turning on the AC full blast, which Jem did to keep Key from falling back to sleep.

The apartment was a nice two-bedroom that he'd

paid for—and Key didn't ask how. Key's own savings was nil, since he'd paid for an outside lawyer to attempt to help with his defense.

He shouldn't have bothered.

"You really think Avery's related to Dare?" Jem asked Key.

"She had that same look . . . the one Dare had when I tried to rescue him. I can't explain it, but it was like seeing a ghost. I'd bet my life that she knows him. She's staying with Gunner just when he shows up in town? What are the chances? He's got no siblings listed, but that doesn't mean anything. And if she hired Gunner, he's not saying shit."

Jem ran a hand through his hair "Don't think about it."

"I'm thinking."

"Then let me do it."

"You think I've gone soft."

"I think you kissed her. You don't have it in you to be cruel to a woman you've kissed, and there's no shame in that."

Jem didn't know that Key felt shame all the damned time now—or maybe he did. "Can you?"

"Can I what?"

"Kiss and be cruel."

"All the damned time," Jem said without hesitation. "All the damned time."

Chapter Eighteen

Drugs. Grace struggled against the feeling, tried to put her fingers down her throat to get the pills up, and then she recalled the tiny pinprick feeling on her upper arm.

An injection. There was no getting rid of the medicine until it wore off. She was helpless, a feeling she remembered all too well. A feeling she hated.

Was she tied? It didn't appear so. She tried to call out to Dare before she was lost in the haze, but through her fever-addled brain she could feel the narcotics holding her down as effectively as bindings. And still she struggled because that's what she'd vowed always to do. She was pretty sure she was still in Darius's house with Dare, but her brain was misfiring, taking her to a time and place in the not-so-distant past when she'd been forced to lie still, and she had, because it made things less than enjoyable for the men who'd tortured her.

They liked it when she fought. As soon as she'd discovered that, she'd lain as still as the dead.

She screamed until she realized that excited them to the

point of frenzy. They were sharks for her blood, her pain, her fears.

When she looked into their eyes, she saw darkness—no shine at all.

Would her eyes look as dead as theirs when this was all over? Would it be better that way?

"Cooperation is the name of the game, pretty girl," the man taunted her, his hands tightening painfully around her wrists. The pain of him driving himself inside her should've felt far worse, but she'd stopped feeling it. Stopped feeling anything.

And that was survival at its finest.

"Then why don't you give it to me harder?" she asked the man above her again, and for a second, it made him halt with uncertainty and stare down at her. She ground her pelvis up against his. "Go ahead—make me want it."

She didn't know if she'd begun to live or die that night, but she eventually made it out alive, scars and all.

Would she ever find a man she wouldn't damage? One who wouldn't damage her? She didn't have the instincts to know anymore. She'd stopped trusting herself years ago.

When the man rolled off her, the familiar feeling of power shot through her, stronger than any orgasm. She wasn't in that helpless place she'd flashed back to. She was in control. Older, but she didn't think she was any wiser. She was simply alive.

For now, that had to be enough.

"Grace, it's okay—you're safe." Dare's voice. How many hours had passed? How many times had she cried out in her sleep?

What had she given away?

She opened her eyes to stare at him, and he repeated, "Grace, it's me—you're okay—you're safe."

"I'm never safe," she managed, her fist slamming into his face with all the strength she had. It didn't seem to faze him—he grabbed her wrist, not tightly, and stopped her from continuing her assault. "Who gave you permission to drug me?"

"It was an antibiotic—"

"And a painkiller."

"Your temperature was close to 103. You were in screaming pain—literally. I couldn't get you to stop thrashing around enough to get you into the bath. I figured you'd sleep through the worst of it."

He bore scratches on his face, neck and arms to prove his story, she noted. She'd fought him. And it was a reasonable explanation, but she was long past being reasonable. Reasonable got you hurt. "You had no right to make decisions for me—any decisions."

She pushed against him when he released her, and he relented. She didn't know if it was guilt or something else, but she took advantage, fought like a banshee until she had nothing left.

"Better?" he asked, without a hint of irony.

She said, "Much," between harsh breaths.

His lip was bleeding, his cheek bruised. Minimal damage on both counts, but she still took satisfaction in it.

"Never. Again. Do you understand me . . . ? I don't care about the pain. I need . . . to feel it." Her voice rose with a desperate quality that she hated, but the only thing that mattered was that he not drug her.

"I'm sorry."

"You took my dignity."

"That wasn't my intention. I know what that's like," he said, his drawl soft, seductive, even though she should feel nothing of the sort at the moment.

"I want to hate you." It was the drugs talking, taking her over. "I want to, but I can't."

"Good. Feeling's mutual." He wiped the blood from his lip with the back of his hand. "Get back to bed."

"No."

"Do it or I'll put you there."

"Try it."

He did more than try—he hauled her over his shoulder and walked her, kicking and fighting but ultimately too worn-out to be effective. He dropped her on the bed, told her, "I won't lock you in here unless you give me reason to."

She charged him and he put her back on the bed. She pulled and they tumbled together.

She shouldn't have wanted this. It must be the drugs making her hot, bothered. Clouding her judgment.

She'd never know which one of them made the first move, but they were kissing, even as their bodies fought against each other. She waited to feel the familiar surge of power at not feeling anything. Instead, the burst of heat nearly seared her.

It didn't go away. She knew she'd surrender to it if things went further, and she couldn't let that happen.

As if he knew, he pulled back and rolled off her, but,

as she soon realized, only to grab handcuffs. He snapped one on her wrist, the other on his.

"Go to sleep," he told her gruffly. She saw how aroused he was, and that at least pleased her, since she was equally so.

"No more drugs."

"Just Tylenol and an antibiotic—take it."

She inspected the pills and the bottles they came from and reluctantly took them. She needed to keep getting better. Stronger. This fight—all her battles—was far from over.

She did sleep, wasn't sure for how long, but when she woke she noticed that he'd taken the cuffs off and he'd deserted the bed.

His scent was still everywhere, like he'd marked her in some way.

She was desperate for him, out of control, and the only consolation was that he seemed to feel the exact same way.

Dare heard Grace stirring, brought her some water to drink but waited at the door of the room until she acknowledged him.

"Hey. Look, about before—"

"I'll take the water," was all she said. She took a long drink. "My fever's coming back."

"More antibiotics are on the way."

"What's going on, Dare?"

"I don't know," he said honestly. "I fucking have no idea. I've lost control of this. Of you."

"You never had control of me. I don't give that up," she told him. "But with you . . . I want to."

He sat on the bed next to her. "We'll figure this out, okay? We'll figure out a way to deal with Powell."

"I'll help you."

"Grace—"

"I don't know any other way but violence," she told him. "At least I thought I didn't. But when you kiss me, that all goes away. I'm trying to fight it, but I don't want to anymore."

He didn't know if it was the painkillers helping her confession along or not, but he was grateful just the same.

"Just promise me that when I'm better, you'll kiss me again," she told him.

"That's a promise I can damn well keep." He paused. "Sometimes I feel like violence is all I know too."

She turned his hand over and looked at the scar in his palm. Touched it gingerly. "I guess the bastard nearly killed both of us."

"But we're both still here."

She stared up at him, her eyes still clouded with fever. "You can use me to draw Rip out."

"That fever's worse than I thought."

"You've got to stop him, no matter what," she murmured.

"I will. Don't you worry about that, Grace. But it will be with you by my side, not by his. Are we clear on that? Because every damned thing has changed now."

"Clear," she told him. She put her head on her pillow and he tucked a towel under her and then wiped her forehead and shoulders and back and thighs with cool water. He did that until he heard the nearly non-existent hum of the small Kodiak.

Gunner. Finally.

"Baby, it's okay—you're safe with me. You always were." He patted her dry before she started shivering, knew the fever wouldn't stay down for very long without stronger meds.

He covered her with a light sheet and waited, not wanting to leave her, knowing that Gunner could find his way to the house easily and disable the alarm.

About five minutes passed before he heard the light knock and the door opening.

"Dare, it's us," Gunner called.

"Back bedroom," Dare called back, and then he heard the footsteps. Gunner came in first, followed by Avery, and while Gunner went right to Grace, Dare stood to see Avery.

"You okay?" he asked, and she nodded, looked around him to see Grace. "It's a fever—nothing more."

"I didn't think you'd hurt her," she said.

"I didn't. I won't."

"Then what do we do?" she asked. He hadn't figured that out yet, but he would.

Chapter Nineteen

Gunner stayed with Grace for the better part of an hour. When he came back out, Dare noted that she was sleeping comfortably.

"No narcotics, right?" he asked.

Gunner nodded with a small frown. "She told me the same thing. Bad reaction?"

"Something like that."

"How long have you had her here?"

"Less than forty-eight hours."

"And you almost killed her," Gunner said furiously.

"I didn't cause her fever."

"Might as well have. She's dehydrated too. What the hell?"

Ah, fuck. Dare ran a hand through his hair. "I think she might've had a panic attack."

"Did she black out?"

"No."

"Sometimes high fevers can cause seizures."

"She saw a friend get killed. Not by me."

"You might possibly be the worst kidnapper ever," Gunner told him. "And that's not a compliment."

"Get off my back, Gunner."

"You were the one who called me in to babysit your sister."

"Babysit me?" Avery interjected from behind them. Shit, Dare hadn't even heard her coming. "Is that what you've been doing?"

"Not very well," Dare muttered, but Gunner wasn't having that. Because he knew about Powell—Avery had slipped and told him. Even though Avery hadn't mentioned the mistake to Dare, he could see the look of pure ice in Gunner's eyes when he'd come into the house.

"What the fuck were you thinking?" Gunner asked quietly now, his voice a razor in the dusk. "You're calling me to help you. You care about Grace."

"So?"

"You now care about the only thing standing between you and certain death. Do I really need to explain that?" Gunner asked Dare. "Fuck you for dragging me into this."

"You've been in worse," Dare informed him, and Gunner's fists clenched.

"Richard Powell's kid? Really? You thought you could take Powell's kid and walk away unscathed? You're in some serious shit with this, and you sent your sister to fool me." Gunner turned to Avery. "You realize how much trouble you're in? Quadruple it from what I told you last night."

"Back out now if you want," Dare told him.

Gunner threw his bag across the room. "I'd rather beat the shit out of you."

"Go ahead—but get Grace better first."

"I already gave her prescription ibuprofen for the pain and fever; that will make her sleep it off. Antibiotics won't do shit. As for the rest of it, fuck. Just fuck." Gunner ran both hands through his hair, and Avery felt a thin trickle of sweat bead up between her breasts.

She told him, "Dare said you were like family. I need family."

"Ah, come on, Avery, don't pull that guilt shit with me." Gunner sounded so frustrated that she wondered why he was in the business he was in if he didn't deal well with danger. Somehow this was different, and she needed to figure out why. There was apparently a huge learning curve that went along with being Darius's kid. She needed to shorten her educational time.

Gunner stormed out onto the porch, and both she and Dare followed him.

"Powell's not invincible," Dare pointed out. "Obviously, he's got a weakness, and she's inside that room."

"We're all fucked. Everything Powell comes in contact with, he destroys. That's why I never took any jobs that concerned him. And now I'm involved up to my goddamned neck." Gunner sat down heavily, let his legs dangle off the porch. Even though there was only a brackish trickle of water, and tall grasses and twenty feet between the porch and the water, Avery wondered if there were any gators that wandered up here. She'd seen them, their sleek heads sliding through the dark waters as Gunner's Kodiak cut through the brackish murk easily, and she didn't want to get any closer.

"If we're all fucked, then maybe sticking together's the best thing to do," she said.

Gunner looked up at the sky and laughed quietly, resigned. "Key's involved in this somehow," he told her. "So whatever's going on between you two—"

"Key?" Dare said slowly.

"You know Key too?" she asked. "He and Jem were asking about you."

"Jem's his brother—former CIA," Gunner clarified for Dare, and then it was Dare's turn to curse.

"What the hell's going on between you and Key?" Dare demanded angrily.

"Nothing. Will the two of you concentrate on the business at hand and not my love life?"

"Love life?" Dare asked, and she sighed.

"Forget it. That's not what I meant. Can we focus on what's going on here, please?" Avery asked.

Dare nodded. "You guys will stay here tonight," he said. "Avery, in the morning, I need you to go to Grace's house. Use her key—say you're her cousin if anyone asks. She went out of town unexpectedly and she asked you to grab a few things of hers."

"What do you really want me to do?"

"Find anything that proves to me she's on the up-and-up," Dare said.

"And if she's not?"

"I'll deal with her."

She wanted to tell him that he was so far beyond dealing with her that it wasn't funny, but she didn't. Not now, anyway.

"I think Powell's guys are around the bayou," Dare told Gunner.

"That dead friend of Grace's you mentioned earlier?" Gunner asked, then continued without waiting for an answer. "What about Key and Jem? They're not going to stop poking around for you. Want to share what that's all about?"

"Not especially." Dare stared up at the porch's old ceiling beams before looking back at Avery and Gunner. "After you check Grace's house for me, you two go back to the shop, find Key and Jem and bring them here."

"We are being herded together—I just can't tell if it's you or Rip who's doing it," Gunner told him angrily.

"Neither can I," Dare said. "Neither can I."

Chapter Twenty

Avery slept restlessly that night, keeping an ear out for Dare and Gunner. Grace appeared to be having a rough night. She'd peeked in and seen Grace lying in bed, flushed and crying.

She didn't think Dare was going to be able to use Grace in the way he'd originally intended—and Avery was glad. She didn't want him to have what appeared now to be innocent blood on his hands. They'd find another way to fix things.

Now she made another pot of coffee for all of them and drank hers on the screened-in back porch. The security lights were on around the property, the rain had finally stopped and she could hear the bayou teeming with life.

She curled up on one of the chairs for a while, her hands wrapped around the mug, until Dare came and sat next to her.

"Grace is holding something back," Dare said.

"Maybe it's not what you think—maybe it's something personal," Avery pointed out.

"I need to know everything in order to make a decision about what I'm doing with her. She needs to be doing everything she can to stay out of Powell's grasp. Instead, she's . . . Fuck, I can't decide what the hell her game is."

"Maybe because there's no game."

"Powell's daughter has a game. You live with a guy like that long enough, it bleeds into you." He paused. "Heard you're stealing wallets now."

"It's an old hobby. How's Grace feeling?"

"Fever's breaking again. I think she'll be better by tonight. Gunner's with her."

"You're not going to tell me about Key, are you?"

"You'll know more soon enough. But he's in the same kind of trouble we are."

"Because of Darius?"

"All roads do lead back to him," Dare affirmed, then drank the rest of his coffee in two gulps. "Gunner will take you to Grace's."

"He should stay with Grace."

"You're not going alone."

"Isn't it more suspicious with the two of us breaking in, though?"

"Fine—he'll wait in the car along the back path. You go in by yourself. Fast, though."

"What exactly am I looking for again?"

"Anything to help us."

"Suppose it ends up hurting Grace?"

"I'm beginning to think that's the only way any of this is going to work," he said. He wasn't happy about it, though, or else he wouldn't have the dark circles under his eyes or the worry in his face.

She'd never kidnapped anyone, but she knew that you weren't supposed to care about your kidnap victim's well-being. Not to the extent he seemed to.

"She's been through hell," he told her gruffly before he got up to leave. "She's been through goddamned hell, Avery."

When he went back inside, she followed him. She showered and dressed—she'd slept in one of Dare's shirts, but he'd washed her clothes overnight—and got into the old truck with Gunner.

"You'd get lost out here," he told her.

"I do have a sucky sense of direction," she agreed, and they drove the rest of the way in silence, about a thirty-minute drive, since Grace's house was on the other side of the bayou. She was pretty sure Gunner doubled back a few times to make sure they weren't followed.

She concentrated on the job ahead of her. She had Dare's gun, a knife and her cell phone in her pockets, along with Grace's keys.

"You remember your cover story?"

"Yes—I'm Grace's cousin, going to grab her mail and a few other things."

Gunner nodded, pulled off the road and pointed. "It's that one. Go in the back."

She looked through the keys and found the one marked for the back door. She threaded through the path so as not to step on what were beautifully planted greens and flowers leading up to a small back porch. There were two white chairs and a small table there, with hanging baskets of flowers, all of which were shining, thanks to the rain.

No neighbors were close enough to see her now, but people around here looked out for one another, and she had no doubt a suspicious neighbor might stop by before she was through searching.

She used the key and closed the door behind her. Gun drawn, she went through every room quickly and then gave Gunner the *everything's okay* wave out one of the back windows.

Then she went on to searching more carefully.

It wasn't large—a bedroom, bathroom, kitchen and living room—but it was fastidiously maintained.

By the bed, there were two large suitcases that were open—and full. There was a small bag on the bed that was also packed, with toiletries and airline tickets under the name Adele Manners.

But the odd thing was, the tickets were for three weeks earlier. Avery put the tickets in her pocket and wondered why Grace had missed her trip. Three weeks ago didn't correspond to anything for Avery or Dare, but she'd bring them to him anyway.

Beyond that, there was nothing—no photo albums or journals—but the house still felt like a home, thanks to the glassware and plants and quilts. There was a small TV in the living room—lots of books, a mix of classics and popular fiction.

This was a woman who still lived like she'd have to pick up and leave at any time. There was not even a scrap of paper, beyond the tickets, that could incriminate her. Not even a shopping list.

She heard a car pull up out front and glanced through the window while ducking. The man who got out didn't look like a neighbor. He was dressed down, in jeans and a T-shirt, and carried a piece of pipe along his thigh that would've blended in if Avery hadn't been looking for weapons.

The car was an old one that looked like it belonged in the bayou.

She backed away carefully, got herself out the back door and hid in the mass of trees to the right of the house. Gunner must've heard the guy too, because he'd rolled the truck out of sight. She saw him standing in the trees, camouflaged until he gave her a short wave.

She remained as still as possible and realized she still had a good view into the house through a back window.

The man either picked the lock or used a skeleton key, because the door wasn't kicked in. He closed it behind him and walked around. When he didn't find anyone, he made a phone call, and then he began to smash everything he could.

She stopped watching, put her forehead against the cypress bark and tried not to wince as the woman's only possessions were ransacked and her house destroyed.

Grace had put a lot of care into that house.

The destruction seemed to last forever. Real time, maybe five minutes. When she heard the slam of the front door, she moved carefully and watched the man get back into his car and leave. She committed the plate to memory—it wasn't a rental—and then she turned to check on Gunner.

But he was no longer there. She shifted to look toward the house and saw him coming around the side from the front. She hadn't seen him move from the trees and made a mental note to ask him to teach her that trick. If she was going to be skulking in the bushes, she might as well make it fun.

"Were you trying to catch him?" she asked.

"I would've caught him if I'd been trying," he said, and she rolled her eyes.

"Okay, Cajun Superman, so what did you do?"

"I'm not Cajun, and I put a tracker on the car," he explained patiently, holding up his cell phone to show her the moving dot. "If he doesn't find it, we can see where he's staying."

She noted that he didn't say anything about the Superman part. "Think it's around here?"

"Pretty impossible. It's a tight-knit community, even after Katrina. If someone like him set up shop in an abandoned house, we'd hear about it. I'm going to grab some security buttons from the truck. I'll plant them in the house and then dust for prints—keep an eye out for me. And text Dare—tell him to be on the lookout in case that guy has his address."

She did both, half melting from the sun and the stress, but her adrenaline surge more than made up for it. Nothing came or went, including a breeze, as Gunner did his work inside Grace's ruined house, and when he came out they moved quietly into the truck.

When they got back to the house, Dare was waiting on the porch, shotgun by his side. "No one's driven by."

"No other tracks but ours," Gunner agreed, and told Dare about the break-in.

"You're all right?" Dare asked her.

"I'm fine—he didn't spot me. But he was definitely a pro and looking for Grace."

"He sure sent the message," Dare muttered.

She handed him the tickets. "Are you going to tell her about her house?"

Gunner brushed past her and said, "I'll do it," and when Dare didn't stop him he went inside.

Grace had dreamed, but it wasn't the drugged kind of dreaming from earlier. She fought the fever and the bad dreams and instead focused on Dare. It helped that he barely left her side all night.

At times, she heard him talking to another man. She knew the blond man had come to help.

Now, when she woke, she was alone, and the blond man with the tattoos was sitting next to the bed, checking her vitals.

"Didn't mean to wake you," he told her. "But you're doing better. I'm Gunner—you were pretty out of it when we met."

"I'm much better," she said, and he nodded and took her temperature before agreeing, "I think we finally broke the fever. But you've still got to rest and drink lots of fluids."

"Are you some sort of traveling bayou doctor?"

"Medic in the Navy for a while," he told her. "A pretty good crash course."

"And you're friends with Dare?"

"Depends on the day."

She laughed, but he remained serious. "You have something to tell me," she said.

"Something to ask you," he corrected as he pulled his cell phone from his pocket and showed her a picture. "Do you recognize him?"

She glanced at the picture, then took Gunner's wrist to move the phone closer. Then she pushed his arm away just as fast. Her throat tightened, breath left her body, even as her adrenaline raced. She heard Gunner mutter, "Shit," as she tried to leave the room, tugging on the doorknob.

She couldn't get far enough away from that picture.

"Grace, come on, honey . . . please—he's not anywhere close to here," Gunner told her, over and over in a soothing voice, until finally she was able to meet his eyes. "You are safe."

"For now," she told him. "Where was he?"

He hesitated for a long moment before telling her. "At your house."

"Why?"

"Avery and I went there to check on things. While we were there, he broke in. Smashed it up when he couldn't find you. We assumed he was a pro."

"Yes, he is. I know him." In her worst nightmares, she could still see his face hovering over her. His wasn't the only face she saw, but it was by far the most sadistic of the bunch. "He works for . . ."

"Your father," he finished. "Dare told me. I'm here to help."

"And here I thought you were just a doctor."

"I'm not just anything, *chère*." His half grin pulled her back from the lingering shock at seeing Rip's body- guard. She nodded, hugged her arms around herself as he continued. "We weren't followed here, so you're still safe. No matter how this started . . . look, it'll end differently if you stay with Dare."

"I think we need each other," she said, and he glanced up at her, his brow furrowed. "Did you know Rip too? Did he hurt you?"

"You can't let yourself be hurt without your con- sent. Take back your life, Grace—and don't ever let him close to you again."

When he left, she realized he'd never answered her question about whether he knew her father.

Chapter Twenty-one

Gunner and Avery left sometime after nine p.m. Dare walked them to the dock and watched them move away nearly silently before heading back to the house. He checked the perimeter first. None of the alarms had been triggered, save the silent ones he himself tripped walking them down to the water.

He reset them, checked for tire marks beyond those of his own truck's and, satisfied, went back inside.

Grace had showered and was sitting in the kitchen wearing his shirt and a pair of his jeans, rolled up a million times and belted. Her feet were bare, and he grabbed her socks and bent down to put them on her even while she protested.

"You're supposed to rest and stay warm."

"It's like a thousand degrees out."

"You're arguing, so I know you're better," he told her. "Are you hungry?"

"Not yet. First I want to go see my house."

"It's not safe."

"Nothing in my life is, Dare." She stared at him. "The man who killed Marnie . . ."

"I took care of him."

She nodded, like a part of her knew that already. "It had to be Rip. It's always him."

Unfortunately, he couldn't disagree. "Gunner said you knew the man who broke in."

"He's one of Rip's associates. Head of security. He's a nasty man and he's good at what he does." Her tone was bitter but firm. "Please . . . I need to go back there one last time."

He knew he should say no, but the guy was long gone. Gunner had set up surveillance cameras at Grace's and they'd seen no one come back and no signs of anyone else's surveillance.

Trashing her house had been a message. She'd received it, loud and clear. And by the look in her eyes, she was ready to send one of her own. The least he could do was help her.

Grace's house wasn't close enough to the water to risk taking the boat and walking through the dark bayou. Instead, Dare drove in a seemingly aimless pattern for a while, took the back route and parked far enough away so they could see if anyone was near the house when they got close. According to the security button cam Gunner had installed, no one had gone inside since the initial break-in.

Grace couldn't go inside at first. Instead, she circled around to the front, since the back still looked pristine, the greenery she'd used to pretty up the wild tangle still intact.

She knew it would be the only thing that was.

When she got to the front yard, it nearly broke her, that something as simple as a destroyed garden could make her feel that way after everything she'd been through. But to see the grasses, the herbs and the flowers trampled and slashed and pulled purposefully out of the ground . . . she was sick with grief and hate.

"We don't have to go in," Dare told her.

"I do." She pushed past him through the already open front door, and without stepping inside, she saw the wide swath of damage.

Everything she'd cultivated, cared for, tended to, inside and out, was destroyed. It wasn't the first time that Rip had done something like this to her.

"I should've known better. He taught me better than this."

You don't get attached to people or things. If you don't, you'll never be hurt. No one, nothing can touch you if you follow those rules.

He hadn't realized then that he'd given her a battle plan for survival.

He must've realized he was teaching her to be exactly like him. That was the worst possible outcome; that could hurt her far more than a decimated living space.

She could still smell Hal in here, the same heavy aftershave—an expensive brand—he'd always worn. She'd hated smelling like him after he'd touched her—and he did so purposely, like the scent would brand her.

She pulled Dare's shirt over the lower half of her face so she could smell only him instead.

She forced herself to walk through the rooms, her borrowed sneakers crunching on broken glass and ceramic, strewn clothing ruined with bleach. She memorized every inch of broken space and tucked it away into that place where vengeance brewed, hot and harsh, waiting until the time was right to seek retribution.

When she turned back toward the door, Dare was waiting there, watching the perimeter and her at the same time. His face wore a haunted look, but his stance was all warrior, ready to strike if necessary.

For you.

He was on her side, their connection a far cry from everything that had happened between them the night he'd dragged her away from here and her then blossoming, beautiful garden. Deep down, she'd known it was the last time she'd see it as it was, which was why she'd danced in it at midnight. She didn't know if that was her gift at work or pure intuition, but either way, she'd been right.

She walked through the garden, bent down and ran her hands over the earth. She grabbed some dirt in her fist and squeezed, as if making it a part of her.

"I'll plant you a new one," he told her, his voice rough. She looked up at him and then down at the ground again, until she found a stone to her liking, small, polished white with age. She opened her palm and brushed the dirt off, took the stone with her instead.

"Burn it all to the ground," she told him.

"Grace—"

"I want the last word."

He didn't argue further. And as she watched from the safety of the truck, at his insistence, she saw the flames purify the area, burning away Rip's touch and his hold on her forever.

"I'm sorry," she whispered, but she knew the earth would recover and flourish. Someone else would live there, maybe even happily ever after. But it wouldn't be her.

Dare had grabbed the matches from his car and siphoned some gasoline from the tank. Then he'd walked up to the house and he'd goddamned tried to breathe.

Every fire he'd had to start since that night in the jungle made him flash back badly, sometimes when he was awake. He couldn't afford to let that happen here—not when he had to stay on guard for Grace.

Now, as he stood apart from the flames, he closed his eyes and felt the heat, knew this burning was symbolic for both of them. Strangely enough, this time, it was easy for him to stay in control, the same kind Grace insisted on. He controlled this fire, and when he thought of it like that, he was able to open his eyes and not see the scene from the jungle in front of him.

Fire purifies and fire destroys. Grace had taken control of the situation, and maybe he should follow her lead, burn the past. Except the man he was fighting was both past and present. Dare just had to make sure Powell wasn't the future.

He watched as Grace's house and garden burned.

All that beauty, destroyed. But it was transient. The most important part was in the car, safe and sound.

He knew the police might come out eventually, but this area of the bayou was already so deserted, half-destroyed by Katrina's fury, that he wasn't worried about an immediate law enforcement presence.

He had the hose, wet down the perimeter to deter that fire from spreading and watched to make sure the fire didn't spread any farther than it needed to. He waited until the house was down to the studs, Grace's belongings unrecognizable ash, before he began to douse the flames.

She wanted the last word because she knew Powell's men would come back to check at some point. He didn't doubt it. If Powell knew where she'd been living, it was time to get the hell out of the bayou and Louisiana—and soon. Powell's men might never find Darius's house, but the wolves were circling—and he needed a plan for fighting back.

He had a feeling that the answer lay in brute force.

When the last of the embers were wet and cold, he dropped the hose, shut off the water and walked away.

When he got into the truck, Grace kept her face turned toward the side window even after they'd driven away.

Grace squeezed her hands together tightly and tried to tell herself that none of this hurt, that if she pretended hard enough and long enough, it wouldn't matter that everything she tried to build was consistently destroyed by a man claiming to be her family.

As she'd done in the past, she had the final say—destroyed before they could destroy her further. She'd long ago realized that nothing was as important as taking control and never letting it go.

But she'd handed some of it—a lot of it—over to Dare. And he hadn't disappointed her. He'd taken care of Marnie, of the house . . . of her.

And she didn't know what to do now.

She'd developed survival instincts that had worked well for her up until she'd met Dare. Now all the rules had changed completely, and she felt the need to hang on to the closest immovable object with both hands.

And the closest immovable object was Dare.

"You saved me," she told him finally, when Dare pulled the truck up alongside his house. She turned and faced him. "I would've been there and they would've taken me . . . or worse."

"Yeah, I should get a goddamned medal." He got out of the truck, but he didn't slam the door, and then he opened her door, got them back into the house and locked inside.

She sat at the table with a pad of paper and a pen and wrote quietly for the next hour. When he finally sat across from her with a cup of coffee for each of them, she pushed the paper his way.

"It's everything I remember from Rip's. Layouts. Codes. Names. Numbers. I'm sure things have changed, but Darius said you were good with patterns."

"I am." He fingered the pages. "I'll have to ask questions."

"I know."

"But not tonight."

She looked at him, surprised, but when she looked into his eyes, she knew his intentions.

"Is something wrong?"

"Not wrong, no," he murmured. "But we don't have a lot of time before Avery and the others come back here. And we've had too many stops and starts between us already. Tonight, I'm not stopping what's been happening between us, unless you say your piece first."

She watched him rise from the chair and walk the short distance to her. Instead of answering him with words, she stood to meet him.

He gathered her even as she stood and wrapped her arms around him. She pressed her lips to his, and then he walked them both into the shower, fully clothed. She appreciated the sentiment—a fresh start, stripping away the past—and as everything dropped to the floor under the spray, Dare buried his head against her neck and just held her tightly for a long moment, even as his erection pressed into her belly.

He moved the wet clothes away as she began to soap him up, shushing him when he insisted he wanted to do this for her.

She soaped his hair with shampoo, rinsed it until it shone nearly blue-black, washed the smoky residue and smell from him, and then he did the same for her.

The bond that had already grown between them cemented at that moment. Dare would never hurt her, but she would need to convince him to use her the way he'd planned to before they'd met.

The way she'd always known it would have to be.

She let her fingers thread through his hair. She'd wanted to touch it like this since he'd grabbed her, and she moaned her approval against his mouth.

There had never been anyone for her like this—not even close—and for someone as open about her sexuality as she was . . . it was the first time she'd *felt*. Before this, she'd forced herself to be numb during sex. Frozen her heart, refused herself pleasure other than from the power she gained from each encounter.

That had all changed.

"What do you want from me, Dare?" she murmured, fear spiking her heart because she knew the answer. Didn't know if she could actually handle this, but she'd come this far.

Pushing forward was the only thing to do.

"This is what I want, and it has nothing to do with pity, or simple need. It has to do with you, Grace. Because I've wanted to be inside of you, making you cry out my name, since I first laid eyes on you in the garden, dancing in your bare feet under the moon."

His honesty took her breath away. She was mesmerized by his skin—it was tawny, with both white and reddish pink scars on his chest and arms. Scars from battles new and old.

She wanted to scar him with her fingernails still, rake them down his back, make him hers. But the desire to control him wasn't as strong as it had been earlier.

She wondered if she could truly let him in and decided she couldn't. But he wouldn't know that.

As if rising to her challenge, he lifted her, pressing her sex to his arousal. She responded by wrapping her legs around his waist, arms around his broad shoulders as he carried them, both still dripping, to his bedroom.

The quilt was already off, as if the bed had been prepared for them. The cool air combined with the water on her skin felt heavenly.

When he pressed her into the sheets, his hand found her folds while he suckled her nipple. She jolted at the burst of arousal that speared through her like a fast-blossoming flower in springtime. She was clutching his shoulders, knew she was babbling—a cross between begging and moaning. When he began to kiss his way down her stomach, she began to panic.

It had never been like this—never been all about her. She'd never let it be. Men had always made it about their pleasure.

Dare was making it all about hers.

He won't hurt you.

The only person she could hurt now was herself, by stopping this. She screwed her eyes shut as he parted her legs.

"Grace—look at me," he told her. He ran a finger along her wet sex, and she shuddered down her entire body. "Look at me."

She did, watched as he knelt between her legs, then bent forward, lifted her hips a little and kissed her in the most intimate way possible. His eyes didn't break from hers. She felt herself flush with embarrassment, and then the sensations of complete and utter pleasure made her not care. His tongue stroked her, probed, and she was helpless to do anything but enjoy it.

And she did.

His tongue was wicked, her nerve endings snapping with white-hot flashes as he refused to stop. She threaded a hand in his hair as if to keep his head there, although part of her wanted to pull him away, to stop the runaway train so she could step off and flee.

She'd never felt like this. She was giving up so much, giving up everything.

She wanted to come—needed to—but letting herself would be admitting she was ready to give up control. So she fought it with everything she had, but it was going to happen. She would come for him, his name on her lips, just as he'd said she would. And it wasn't because he was rough or controlling. In fact, it was somehow the opposite, even though she was the one who lay beneath him. He'd given her the control, and she'd taken it, found her comfort . . . and she climaxed with the blaze of a thousand suns behind her eyes.

When he kissed his way back up her body, she tugged at him. "More," she murmured.

"Plenty more," he agreed. She watched him roll on a condom, could barely wait for him to enter her.

"Please," she begged as he attempted to go slowly. She pushed against him instead, taking in his hard length so it filled her. "Yes, that's it."

"Jesus, Grace," he muttered, and she smiled, laughed. She was going to take him over the edge—but she was going to go with him. It was so right, and she'd waited so long for this.

She'd never thought she'd find it. Now she wrapped her legs around him, hooking her feet on his back as he sank against her.

Grace was stretched tight around him, wet and hot, and her moans, Christ, her moans were going to undo him completely. He was trying to go slow, but she didn't want that. And still, it wasn't like before—wasn't rough like she'd tried to make it the first night they'd met. This time, she wasn't putting on a front. She was enjoying this.

And he was damned well going to make sure she continued to. He thrust against her as she clung to him. She nipped his shoulders with her teeth, dug her nails into his back, and he kissed her then, like he was a dying man and she was the only one who could give him what he needed.

She kissed him back, unabashedly. Her walls down, the fight over. She groaned into his mouth, and then he pulled away and took her fast, until she contracted around him, crying out with her climax.

He came with her; she felt his cock throb inside her, heard his mutterings, the low, growling groan of a man possessed with desire who'd finally succumbed.

Two peas in a pod, they were.

"Are you okay?" he asked.

"I want to do that again. And again."

He laughed, a real and true belly laugh that got her going as well. And when she joined him, she realized that he was still hard inside of her and that he wanted the same thing.

A couple of hours later, they lay together, legs entwined, Dare tracing lazy circles on her skin as the breeze fluttered over them. There was the heavy feeling of rain in the air as they remained unhurried.

"You all right?" he asked.

"Very." She turned her gaze to him. "You don't know . . . I didn't want to. You made me feel. Normally, I can turn it off. I just wanted to turn you on. Make you lose control," she admitted.

"Sweetheart, you got your wish. How's it make you feel?"

"Like hell," she said with a smile.

"Makes two of us."

Still, she moved to smooth away the hair from his face, and he let her.

"I'm supposed to be taking care of you."

"Technically, it's a kidnapping."

"I think we're beyond that, no?" He was staring at his hands. She took them into her smooth, cool palms and rubbed the ache away until he nearly groaned. "Thanks. That's nice."

His hands were big. Big hands, big feet . . . no disappointment. And she'd lied about him being rough, at least not in the sense she was used to.

Dare was anything but detached from his emotions. He wasn't only into the physical act. No, there was so much more to it than that. She'd wanted him to be an animal, nothing but primal male urges, because that's what she knew how to deal with. It was what she'd been able to conquer. But emotion, that was an entirely different mountain, and she appeared to be afraid of its height.

"Are we . . . beyond the kidnapping? Because I thought maybe you only said it to appease me when I was sick."

"I never say things just to appease people. More often than not, I say things to piss them off. I don't want to use you, Grace."

"Not anymore."

"Right, not anymore," he said. "I don't know how else to make you believe me."

She stared at him. Touched his cheek with her palm. "I don't want to believe you. Goddammit, Dare, I don't want to, but I do. I always have."

Chapter Twenty-two

Gunner took her back in the Kodiak and then on his Harley, which he'd locked in a shed onshore. Avery guessed he owned it; it all looked steel reinforced.

He hadn't said much of anything, to her or to Dare, since they'd come back from Grace's house. Had checked on Grace, then spent time out on the front porch by himself.

She tried again now, before they got on the bike. "I really can take care of myself, you know."

"You shouldn't have to," was all he told her before handing her the helmet. Of course, he didn't bother with one, but arguing would be futile. She put it on, hopped on behind him and enjoyed the cool bayou night as the bike raced along the back paths until they hit the city.

Different worlds. She wasn't sure which one she liked better, but to her, they were both still pretty magical.

Now, back in the shop, he locked the doors behind them.

"Time for your tattoo," he said.

"Right now?"

"Right now."

She couldn't argue. Instead, as he began to draw up a design, she sat on his chair and watched. He drew in quick bursts with a black pencil—then he threaded the sketch through a copy machine and onto thin paper that would transfer the projected design to her body.

"Shirt off," he told her without looking at her. But she was pretty sure he glanced her way as she stripped and held the shirt up to cover her breasts. "Lie down on your side, arm over your head."

He helped her move the T-shirt so she remained covered as he transferred the design onto her. Then he held the mirror up so she could see what he planned. Helped her up so she could see it in the big mirror.

"They'll be pink and white with some black and gray shading," was all he said as she fingered the design, a string of flowers that would look as if they floated down her side.

It would look beautiful. Perfect. How had he known?

She didn't bother asking, merely nodded her assent, and Gunner patted the table again.

She wondered why he hadn't simply asked to sleep with her instead and realized that what they were about to do might be considered far more intimate.

"When you're done, we have to get in touch with Jem and Key," she said before he started.

"I don't think we're going to have a problem with that," Gunner said over the buzz of the needle. Without turning her head, she felt the blast of hot air above her, heard the jingle of the bells as the door opened.

"Nice vacation?" Jem asked.

"Was going to call you," Gunner said.

Avery remained in position as Key stared between her and Gunner. "I'm getting a tattoo," she said, in case it wasn't obvious.

"You gonna let him mark you like that?" Key asked.

"It's not like I'm grass in a dog park. Besides, it was our agreement. I don't go back when I give my word."

"Good to know. I guess you're sleeping with him?" His words were dangerously quiet.

She wondered why—if—he cared. "Not that it's any of your business, but no."

He snorted. "I don't like stepping in the middle of love triangles."

She wanted to say that it wasn't love, but it was some kind of crazy triangle. You'd have to be blind not to see it, and even then, the energy was palpable.

Gunner was somewhere around six foot five. Key was taller, Jem slightly shorter, but all three together were especially impressive. Imposing. Dangerously sexy.

But she wasn't in the market for relationships.

"Do you have any information?" Jem was asking.

"As soon as I'm done with Avery's tattoo, we're supposed to take you to see Dare," Gunner said.

Key's face hardened at the mention of her brother's name, and she couldn't wait to get to the bottom of what had happened between them. The fact that Key had been preparing to use her against Dare was proof enough that it was something very bad.

"I'm starting now, which means no more talking," Gunner said.

"Let's go get a drink, Key," Jem said.

"I'm not leaving them alone—they could take off again," Key said. At least he'd stopped looking at her as though she were the money in a bank robbery.

Jem muttered something about drinking Gunner's whiskey as Key moved closer to the table and Gunner turned on the tattoo gun.

The buzz of the needle, the humid air on her skin . . . and she'd never had anything like the attraction she had for both men.

Key and Gunner were having a pissing contest, and she honestly didn't think it had much to do with her. But maybe it did.

She felt languid. Light-headed. It had nothing to do with the tattoo process.

Half-naked, the needle buzzing and every sense heightened. An intimate act shared with the two men surrounding her, Key stubbornly refusing to leave and Gunner not stopping his process.

It was heady, she had to admit. Power over men wasn't something she was into, but this came naturally, seemed as old as time itself, as intricate, and yet, so simple.

She was a wanted woman, but here, between Key and Gunner, she was simply a woman who was wanted, and that was something different altogether.

She wasn't sure how long she lay there. Gunner gave her a short break to drink a soda and eat a candy bar, assuring her she'd need both. There wasn't pain any longer—it had transcended pain and become something else. A feeling of light peace, even with Key glaring Gunner down.

She didn't bother talking during the process, and finally, Gunner rubbed a gloss of antibacterial gel onto his black-gloved hand and then rubbed it lightly on her newly tattooed side. "You're all done."

He helped her up, and she watched Key watch her in the mirror as she lifted her arm to reveal the beautiful slide of pink and white flowers that floated down her rib cage in a grand, graceful swirl that mirrored her curves perfectly.

"Gunner, I love it," she breathed.

"I know," he said, and Key snorted.

"Full of yourself much?"

"I'm damned good at what I do. Can you say the same thing?" Gunner asked, and before she knew what was happening, the two men were circling each other and yelling in what she assumed was Cajun French. She fully expected a punch to be thrown at any minute as they moved closer to each other, both gesturing wildly.

She couldn't understand a thing they were saying.

"Jem!" she called, but he came in from the kitchen, bottle in hand, unconcerned.

"They're big boys—they're fine," he said. "Let's see the tattoo."

She followed Jem's lead and ignored Gunner and Key as she and Jem gazed at her new skin art.

"Guy's good," Jem said grudgingly, and she agreed.

Life was so ugly most of the time. Something pretty etched onto her skin might help to balance that.

Chapter Twenty-three

Grace woke to Dare thrashing around in the bed.

He was so vulnerable, but he was still a warrior as he fought, completely caught up in the throes of his nightmare. She desperately wanted to help him. To heal him.

A part of her wanted to hate him for what he was doing to her, but she simply couldn't. He wasn't black or white, had so many gray spaces in him; she'd known that before she laid her hands on him.

She hadn't been born with a healing touch, but her gift allowed her to be open enough to learn Reiki. She used it now in an attempt to pull away the bad thoughts plaguing him.

But the bad was very, very strong. She closed her eyes and put her palms against his bare skin, breaking her rule of not touching anything that could harm her emotionally.

Mistake. In seconds, he was awake and uncoiled and on top of her, his body pinning hers to the mattress, his hands holding her wrists trapped over her head, and if she lived to be one hundred she'd never figure out how exactly he'd managed that in such a short span of time.

She'd been holding her breath, exhaled now in a soft, surprised gasp, realizing she was lucky that his hand hadn't ended up around her throat.

Surprising a man of his caliber was a very bad idea.

It took several moments before he actually focused on her, and when that realization hit, he still didn't roll off her—not immediately. And that attraction that had been there from the first jolted through her. His arousal was rock hard against her belly and her sex was wet for him.

If he'd rolled away first, she wasn't sure what she would've done, but he made the decision for both of them when he lowered his mouth to hers.

It was a hard, desperate kiss that left her wanting more immediately. It was as if they were in a fog, suspended between wake and sleep, confusion and clarity, where anything could happen. When they were at their most vulnerable.

She arched her back, pressed her hips up into him, and he responded in kind, grinding his pelvis into hers in a way that suggested nothing less than down-and-dirty sex that would leave them both breathless.

"Grace," he murmured as he kissed his way down her neck. Was he still dreaming? Did it matter?

How had she ended up a part of his dreams?

His hand released her wrists, and he thrust against her, his cock hard against her sex. She groaned and bucked up against him, and the sound seemed to rouse him.

He stopped, stared down at her. Looked confused, and then, "Ah, fuck. I'm sorry. Did I hurt you?"

"No. I should've known better than to touch you like that."

"Because you have nightmares too. Guess we're both all fucked-up," he muttered.

"Guess so." She smoothed the hair away from his forehead. "Do your dreams have to do with the scars on your hands?"

"Yeah." He glanced down at his hands, which were on either side of her. "I don't even remember it hurting when it happened."

"When you're in it, when it's actually happening, pain is the least of your worries."

He nodded his agreement. "Key saved my life. For a long time, I wished he'd left me to die, for both our sakes." He faltered for a long second, and then he told her what had happened. She was sure that for her sake he brushed over how horrific it actually was, but she knew. His eyes looked haunted.

She was also furious at Rip. At herself, for not finding a way to take him down, even if it meant hurting herself in the process. "I'm sorry, Dare."

"I'm still here. I'm not built to break."

She felt the flicker of a smile ghost across her face. "I think I'm not either."

"I know you're not."

Dare knew that lighting the fire at Grace's would come back to bite him in the ass during sleep, bring back memories of the jungle and a very different fire. He'd thought that just this once he might sleep a little longer, especially with Grace snuggled against him, but from the worried look on her face, he knew his nightmare had been full-fledged.

Part of him wanted to push her away, retreat. But he needed her. She was half on him, running her fingers through his hair, smoothing the sweat from his face and neck with a washcloth, like he'd done for her earlier.

His cock was as rigid as his posture. She ran a hand down his belly and wrapped a palm around the thick column, and he stilled his breathing.

"I haven't been touched in a long time," he said quietly.

"Do you like it?"

"Yes. Too fucking much, Grace. I don't want to goddamned care."

You can have this job, or you can have relationships, Dare's father had once told him. *To be successful at either, choose one and never look back.*

Still, Dare knew that leaving his mother had cost his father dearly. There was always a price with these jobs, and most of the time, it left a deep scar right down the middle of your life like a road map to hell.

Dare was headed down that same damned path, and it was already littered with mistakes and regrets.

"Will you tell me what happened?" she asked now.

"I lost everyone on my team. Those guys served as my family for ten-plus years." The grief in his eyes was as unmistakable as his expression was unreadable. "One minute we were in charge of the situation, and the next, everything exploded. Literally. They never found the bodies."

He choked those last words out. His lungs had tightened like he was breathing the thick smoke that got caught in the jungle air, unable to escape. Just like him.

Grace's hands were cool on his shoulders. They rubbed, kneaded the tension, worked his neck muscles; then she was kissing where her hands had touched.

Both had a background of pain—that alone was enough to bond them—but there was more there, and Dare would be a fool not to admit it. And he was no fool.

Chapter Twenty-four

Dare was playing games—like father, like son—but Rip would be damned if that mattered. His plans were moving along in the right direction, despite his missing man. Now, as Rip went over the encrypted e-mail his men had sent, he knew it was nearly time to tighten the noose he'd placed around all of them—Grace and Dare and Avery. He almost regretted having to include the brothers, Key and Jem, but they were too involved, too risky.

He didn't know how the man with the tattoo parlor played into all of this, but he was confident he would soon. In the end, he always got his way.

He wasn't going to be brought down by the group he'd created.

Rip had been given the chance of a lifetime when he got the offer to create an elite team made up of the craziest men and women the military ever had the pleasure of court-martialing.

They had the training—they'd had money spent on them—and they had the drive, the ambition, just didn't have the outlet any longer. He cultivated them from a pool of thousands, picked them because of their opposition to authority.

"You really want this?" his supervisor had asked. "Because you could be blowing your entire career on a bunch of fucked-up misfits."

Rip was a fucked-up misfit himself—he just hadn't let the CIA in on that entirely. "Yes, sir."

He'd taken the sealed envelope and left the office, and he'd never looked back.

Left in an orphanage in Belgrade, he'd been liberated by some goddamned American hippies and brought here at age ten. He'd spent the first few years hoarding food and trying desperately to lose that pathetic accent.

After three foster homes, they'd given up, mainly because he'd learned to fight and never let go of what was his, be it food or hand-me-down clothing or even something as simple as a school notebook. He'd had everything taken from him, and he couldn't— wouldn't—let that happen ever again.

He'd done institutional living until he'd left at age fifteen. By then, he'd come to the conclusion that he'd never let anyone be in the position to control him.

By then, he'd decided he was going to rule his own empire, and it was going to be big and dangerous.

At first, he lived on the streets in New York, and later, Miami, running drugs and guns and getting addicted to the latter rather than the former. He liked the power behind the guns, liked knowing different and even better ways to kill his opponents.

At nineteen, when he'd acquired just enough street

knowledge to be truly dangerous, he embraced the legitimacy of the Navy. Because he'd need that legitimacy to carry out his plans.

Behind every great fortune lay a great crime. His was still being committed daily.

Rip could've contented himself with simply being the best goddamned CIA spook he could be. Started out that way, trying to leave behind the stench of poverty and anger that had followed him from Belgrade.

He'd tried to be grateful. Humble.

Neither was part of his genetic makeup, though, and he'd stopped faulting himself for it a long time ago. Instead, he double-crossed the CIA, his friends—anyone and anything to make himself better at what he did. Studying the human condition became a second full-time job; it fucking fascinated him.

Because of it, he ended up heading one of the greatest secret teams of all time.

Teams of elite former soldiers were nothing new. Rip had made sure his team rose above by purposely picking men no one wanted and letting them work their magic.

After the Zaire mission, Section 8 had been officially disbanded. Although he knew they continued doing black ops on their own, by that point he was too far into his own assignments to worry. The lure of money and power strong-armed him.

And when he needed a team he trusted to work a personal mission for him, he called S8 together one last time. When that mission went wrong, Rip cut off all contact with them, but it didn't matter. Darius had discovered through mutual contacts at the CIA that it had been a personal mission for Rip . . . and he'd discovered Rip's identity as S8's handler.

Rip had had that mutual contact killed, but the damage had already been done.

Darius knew that S8 members had been killed doing Rip's personal business. And then Darius had taken Grace right out from under his nose.

Create a team that scares the hell out of you, and you know you're doing it right.

His pride and joy. His ego. His baby.

He'd created his own worst enemy, and they were the only ones worthy enough to be his adversaries. He smiled when he thought about the leverage in his basement and the intel that had been tortured out of him. Breaking a man you'd taught never to break was equal parts satisfying and heartbreaking.

It was only a matter of time before Grace was back on the island safely, and this time, he knew she'd never leave. She'd spit the name at him. Rip.

Rip. He rolled the name on his tongue out loud, but it never sounded right when he said it. That didn't stop him.

Grace had been the first one to call him Rip—she'd refused to call him Dad or Richard . . . and somehow she'd known that he'd see Rip as an insult, even though they were his initials.

But then he'd decided to embrace the nickname from her.

The fact that she was truly psychic was almost more of a hindrance to him than a help, although Esme always insisted that Grace was the best thing to happen to them. But when Grace had given false intel that could've cost him his life, he'd taken Esme away. Grace had been twelve then. For the next few years, she'd given him intel, and he'd made sure to check and double check, never relying solely on it.

When she was seventeen and she'd tried to kill him a second time, he'd known it was time to break her.

He also hadn't known if that was truly possible. Grace fascinated him in the way unbreakable people always had. He considered himself unbreakable, and the fact that Grace had never truly surrendered, no matter how much he tortured her, astounded him.

Her gift had been the first casualty when he'd attempted to break her—but not her spirit. Now, with the intel she'd learned from S8, she *could* take him down, gift or no gift. He had no choice but to kill her this time.

If at first you don't succeed . . .

"Try, try again. I'm coming for you, Gracie," he whispered quietly into the silence of his office. "And this time, there's no escape."

Chapter Twenty-five

It was just before first light when Gunner finished bringing the four of them through the bayou in the nearly silent Kodiak. Dare waited on the porch and watched them walk up toward the house, Key the last one in line.

The man had done that purposely. He waited until Avery, Gunner and the one Dare guessed to be Key's brother filed past him without a word.

Only then did Dare step down from the porch to meet Key where he'd stopped.

Key probably thought Dare wouldn't remember him, but Dare would never forget his face. That night in the jungle, it had been etched in an anguish that equaled Dare's, and Key's eyes still had a look of haunted pain that would never fade.

On that mission, Key had made the mistake of forging ahead against a direct order to save the single surviving member of not only the SEAL team but the entire village. Months later, Dare had been told that Key was still sitting in the brig. A year later, he'd been officially court-martialed and dishonorably discharged.

He'd lost everything because of Dare. Because of Dare's connections. Another person S8 and Powell had nearly ruined.

Rescuing Key from the trial and its aftermath would've put him right back in the line of fire. He'd hoped Key would do exactly what he did—disappear. S8's handler was no doubt still looking for him, or maybe he wasn't. Since Key had dropped it, didn't bring up what he knew about Dare and his background, he'd hoped that maybe Key was off the hook.

Dare hadn't wanted any more deaths on his hands. The guy was safer out of the service with a dishonorable discharge following him. It meant that he'd have to seek work outside the usual avenues, which kept him off the grid and, more than likely, using an alias.

It had meant that he'd first spend all his free time hunting Dare down like a dog.

Now Key was looking at him like he was seeing a ghost, reliving everything, the way Dare had in his earlier nightmare. And then he lunged, and Dare didn't bother fighting, let the soldier give him a solid punch and then tackle him to the ground.

Would he eventually let go of Dare's neck? Dare wasn't entirely sure.

"I gave you one shot. Next time, I fight back," Dare croaked.

"You can't think we're even." And yet Key eased up on his throat and, with a curse, stepped away from Dare.

Dare brushed himself off and motioned for Key to follow him.

He didn't. Avery came out and told them, "No fighting in the house."

"I'm not going in there," Key spat.

Dare turned to stare at him. "Your life's in danger because you saved me. You have to know I'm telling you the truth."

"I don't know anything anymore," Key told him.

"Come in and find out. You can't fucking believe I'd screw you over for saving my life."

"You didn't show at the trial."

"It was better for you that I didn't." *Fuck*. He looked at Key. "I'm sorry. I was in hell."

"So was I."

"I want to help you get out." He turned and found himself chest to chest with Jem. "You shouldn't get involved.

"You think I'm not involved already?" Jem snorted. "Now I want to know what we're up against."

He stepped aside to let Dare pass and then motioned for Key. Once they were all inside, Dare closed the door and put on the perimeter alarms and the cameras.

"Paranoid bastard," Jem said, but he nodded approvingly.

Grace was sleeping in the other room. Dare had explained whom he was meeting with, and she'd agreed it would go better if she wasn't present.

"I trust you," she told him.

Now they all sat around the scarred table Dare remembered his father making years ago. The whole house had memories. Land mines were everywhere; he wasn't sure how far back to begin.

Luckily, Key started by asking, "Did you know I was in danger at the trial?"

"I suspected."

"So you left me a sitting duck?"

"Coming close to you could've made it worse," Dare countered.

"And telling them that I disobeyed your order as well as my commanders really made things better," Key said, his voice steady, his eyes dark with anger.

Dare didn't know what else to say except, "I really thought it would."

Jem held up a hand. "Let's stop with the bullshit. Tell me what you know for sure about this saving-Key's-life crap, because I'm not buying it."

Dare eyed him. "CIA?"

"Former."

This could go so very badly. "You've heard of Section 8."

"That was a goddamned myth," Jem scoffed. Dare remained silent. "You're saying you—"

"I'm a legacy."

Jem stood and backed away, muttering under his breath. "This is bad, Key," he said.

"No shit," Key shot back, never taking his eyes off Dare.

"No, I mean, go underground for the rest of your life and don't come out." Jem lit a cigarette and remained standing. "We are fucked."

"You shouldn't have disobeyed that order," Dare told Key.

"You sorry I saved you?"

"Sometimes," Dare said. "I'm sure you feel the same."

Key muttered something under his breath and Gunner handed him a beer. He declined and asked for coffee instead. Jem sat back down and Dare told them, "My father discovered that Richard Powell was the handler in charge of S8. And he's trying to take out anyone with even a remote involvement with the original group. He's got men no more than ten miles away in each direction, and he's coming for us. There's a bounty on our heads—and no way to lift it."

Once Dare had laid it out for them, they remained silent for a while. Dare made the coffee Key had asked for; Avery played with her mug and tried to read the room.

There was no way out of this for any of them.

"So I'm supposed to die because I kept you alive," Key said slowly.

"Sadly, that's not the most fucked-up thing I've heard," Jem told them. "We're in this up to our necks, brother."

"Are you here just to state the obvious?" Key demanded.

"That's what family's for," Jem quipped. He lit another cigarette and winked at Avery, who realized she was a little bit in love with him because he was a general pain in the ass. "From what little I know, Section 8 turned out to be a fantastic cover for all Powell's side deals. Because the CIA was the prime spot for a double agent to work and thrive during S8's heyday. Now, with Homeland Security and ICE, things are tightening up. He'd never get away with that shit if he was starting out today. He went from handler to double agent and spy extraordinaire."

"So why can't we contact the CIA about this shit?" Key asked.

"Ah, my poor, naive brother," Jem started.

"Don't make me punch you," Key muttered, and Jem continued, "Look, the CIA lost control of him years ago and didn't seem to care, mainly because he made them a lot of deals, saved them money and, in the end, was too damned good at dealing with assets and double agents for them to let him go. Turned a blind eye and Powell took full advantage of it. He went from top-level CIA to international financier with top generals and other assorted politicians and alphabet agency higher-ups in his pocket. He makes them money; they keep him out of jail."

"Because he doesn't do his own dirty work."

"Not true—he does a lot of it. He likes to keep his hands dirty and his skills up," Jem said. "Can't blame him."

"Yeah, let's all give him a round of applause for never asking someone to do what he won't do himself," Dare said.

Jem ignored him. "He doesn't need technology—he needs people. And he gets them to do whatever he needs them to in terms of turning a blind eye or working for him. He convinces them that it's in their best interest, and his funds make it very worth their while."

"And you never ran across him?"

"He was high level when I went in. Retired before I

got to top level—just heard the rumors surrounding the legend. People typically either loved or hated him, most a mix of both. One thing for sure—he's not someone you want to try going up against alone, unless you have a death wish. And even I'm not that crazy." Jem sighed. "And now Rip's after Dare and Avery because you're kids of an original S8 member. Rip's after Key because he saved your sorry ass, and now Rip doesn't know if Key was hired by you or another S8 connection. So Key's effectively dead and I'm on the chopping block because I'm related to Key and CIA and probably because Rip knows I know of him. And Gunner?"

"No other reason than I let Avery walk inside my shop," Gunner said. "Nice recap, Jem. Makes me want to put that bullet in my head now instead of after a last meal."

Key stared at Dare now. "You're right—we have no choice but to work together."

"We're being hunted," Avery said quietly, and Key nodded in her direction.

"But if you have Powell's kid, that should solve all our problems," Jem said.

"You'd think," Dare said. "We're not using her."

"Makes sense—there's nothing to keep him from killing us once Powell gets her back," Key pointed out.

"She's leverage," Jem argued. "And I think I get a goddamned say in this."

Avery knew this would be the point of contention. Jem wasn't wholly wrong, but he didn't know what Grace had been through. She knew only the small amount Dare had shared before she'd left the house the last time, and it made her sick to her stomach.

Now she hoped to be the voice of reason.

"Grace started as leverage, but she's become more than that," Avery told them.

Dare continued: "I think she's an innocent, and that she can help us. More than that—she needs our help."

Jem stared at Dare. "You slept with her, didn't you?"

When Dare didn't answer, Jem continued. "I'll handle her from this point on."

"You'll do no such thing." In the blink of an eye, Dare was on Jem. They were evenly matched, so it could be a fight to the death.

"Stop them," Avery urged Key.

"Not my fight," he said mildly. She noted that Gunner remained strangely silent, taking it all in.

Avery thought about throwing water on them as though they were dogs, but in the end she left them to their fight and watched them intently, thinking of another time and place.

There was too much violence they needed to face. If they were already turning on one another, what hope did they have?

"Jem was gonna blow sooner or later," Key said.

"Dare too," she admitted. Gunner sighed and muttered something about being a lover, not a fighter, to which Key said, "I guess that's why you lost our fight last night."

"That, my friend, was a draw. We were too close to my tattoo equipment."

Key rolled his eyes. "Seriously?"

How they could stand there in the middle of this—the fighting, the death threats—and yet still somehow be light . . . "Do you think this is what the original Section 8 was like?" she asked them.

"It's not exactly how it started," Gunner said as he pulled Avery to the side as Jem and Dare slammed through the kitchen door out into the living room.

"From what Dare said, the operatives liked S8. It gave them an outlet," she said.

"They were . . . different. Doesn't mean they didn't have consciences. But their skills, their inability to follow traditional rules made them perfect for this opportunity."

"They had to follow some guidelines," Key said.

"They were told who to kill. That was the only rule in their playbook—kill the mark. How, when, where—that was all left to their creativity, and believe me, they got creative." Gunner shook his head. "We don't have to keep talking about this."

"I need to know. Want to, have to. Darius is a part of me. It might explain . . . me."

Gunner gave her a wry grin. "You think you can inherit that special brand of crazy?"

"Don't you?"

"Yes," Key said quietly. "Sounds like S8 was the CIA's version of *if you can't kill it, hire it.*"

She had to agree. "Look, according to Dare, Powell had no reason to go after S8. As their handler, he knew they did their jobs well. After the last mission went to hell, they were officially retired, with benefits and full immunity. There were never any leaks."

"So what happened to make Powell go after them?" Key asked.

Gunner shrugged. "When he went after S8, S8 turned right around and went after him. But I'll bet that when taking Grace became Darius's first priority, he signed his own death warrant."

She'd heard Dare's stories, absorbed them, turned them over in her mind, trying to think about what that must've been like to be a part of the original S8. There was George and Mad Dog Martin. But the king and queen of his team were Darius and Adele.

Adele had gone to war in a support position, as females did in the late seventies and early eighties, but she insisted on training along with the men. She continued to push for combat, and when she couldn't get it, she contented herself by blowing the enemy up as often and effectively as possible, albeit without any order, direct or otherwise.

They had new rules, a different set of standards, no boundaries to be seen and an oath to keep one another safe, no matter the cost to the mission. They knew how to lie and cheat and steal, deal with live ammo and find transport anywhere they were.

They kept people safe.

They functioned as a group, not alone.

"Dare's worked with a team. And you have too," she said to Key, who nodded, then pointed to Jem and said, "Obviously does not play well with others."

Jem and Dare had separated and were circling each other but somehow still managing to listen. "Ah, bite me. Gunner doesn't either."

"No, Gunner never has," Dare agreed before he lunged at Jem.

"Gunner is right in the fucking room, and I'm here with all of you, right? Fucking numbnuts." He continued muttering under his breath, during which time Avery learned several new creative combinations of curse words and committed them to memory for future reference.

She looked at Gunner and Key. Turned to watch Dare and Jem fighting. Thought about Grace, trying to take it all in. Of all of them, Grace was most used to this, had the closest connection to the original, maybe even closer than Dare, in some respects.

They functioned as a group. Not alone.

The yelling woke her. Grace peeked out the door and saw Dare rolling on the floor, punching another man. She saw Gunner and Avery and closed the door.

"Guess it's going well," she murmured to herself. Tried to shake off the sounds of shouting, but that always got to her. Brought her back even beyond living with Rip, to being so young and helpless, dragged around at her mother's whims.

Everything had changed when Esme met Rip. Grace had been nearly ten. Tired of the neighbors yelling at her. The neighboring moms looking down their noses at Esme even as they were jealous of her looks, and even more of the way their husbands looked at her.

And they did more than look. They came to her back door at night under the pretense of getting healing herbs or other potions or simply Esme's predictions for themselves or their kids, but really, they simply wanted Esme.

Richard Powell took them away from all of that. Esme met him one night at work. She waitressed at a bar that catered to the wealthy, and they all wanted her to tell their fortune, read their palm . . . kiss them silly.

Esme believed in love—wanted it with her whole being, despite her profession as a grifter. Grace's father had been someone Esme claimed to have loved, but he'd left her when he discovered she was pregnant.

At least that's what Esme had told her. She didn't believe in coddling Grace. Wanted her strong.

She had to believe Esme knew what Rip was really like from day one. Because Grace knew, sensed it, and it had nothing to do with her abilities.

What had Esme gotten out of it? The best Grace could figure was love and money. Esme had really and truly loved Richard. That love blinded her to everything bad there was inside him, no matter how insidious. And because Esme had spent a lifetime reading people and running her cons, she'd been able to help Rip with his business dealings easily.

She'd used Grace and her very real gift to aid that.

Grace had seen the evil inside the man clearly, had shrunk from Rip's hugs. Esme ignored it because she didn't want to see Grace as a barometer, didn't want to know how wrong she was.

Grace never told her. Instead, she cried silently in bed that last night they'd spent in the little blue house. She'd cried to leave a place she hated, because she knew what she was headed for was far worse.

It should've been every child's dream. She had huge rooms to herself, toys, anything and everything she could imagine. And it was all pure torture, one hundred percent pure torture, because she watched Esme lose herself completely to the darkness that lived inside Rip. Didn't happen all at once, but gradually, as Rip asked Esme to do more and more for him . . . she'd wilted. Only when it was too late did she even think about protesting.

Grace bided her time as her once budding gifts continued to wane under the pressure of helping a man who used them for personal gain. The more Esme pressured her, the worse it got, until finally, Esme seemed to understand what she'd done.

"I'll make it better for you, baby," she promised. And she'd tried, but it had been too late.

Once Esme was gone, all Rip's attention was focused on Grace, and he knew she'd seen through him from the start. Blamed her for her mother's gradual distrust.

If her mom hadn't fallen in love, it wouldn't have ended up like this. So Grace had gotten the message very early on that love equaled danger, and she'd promised herself that she'd never forget it.

She hadn't until Dare O'Rourke pressed against her and nearly made her forget her own name. She wasn't that stupid, that reckless, but in many respects, she was so much like Esme, no matter how long she'd tried to repress it. Esme gave away her heart too easily, while the only thing Grace gave up was her body. Because the more she numbed herself with sex, the better off she was. It was her insurance policy against love. If she could have cast a spell to ward it off, she would've. But she didn't mess with that, because spells could go awry.

She knew she couldn't alter the natural patterns of life. She could only hope to avoid them. Every once in a while, she had to revisit the past to reinforce that knowledge.

She had a single picture of Esme. Darius had let her keep it here, instead of at her place. And now she was glad she had.

Now she rooted around the top shelf of the closet to find the five-by-seven envelope, slid the picture out.

Esme was smiling, not wide, but the secret smile of happiness. The picture had been taken four days before she'd met Richard Powell. Grace felt the tears spring to her eyes, and she pushed them back with a fierceness she hadn't felt in a long time. Cursed herself for thinking she could deal with a weakness now.

"Sometimes, crying makes you stronger." Avery's voice came from behind her. Grace turned around, wiping her eyes with her fingers. "I lost my mom recently."

"Mine's been gone for years, but when I see her picture, it feels like yesterday," Grace admitted. It was refreshing to be able to talk with someone who understood.

"I'm sorry." Avery smiled a little when Grace showed her Esme's photo. "She's so beautiful. You look just like her."

"Do you look like your mom?"

"The hair used to, but my eyes . . ."

"Darius." It was Grace's turn to smile. "That's a nice memory for me."

"I'm glad. I never met him. And I'm trying really hard not to hate him for what he got my mom into. She spent her life protecting me from the things Darius got involved in."

Grace and Dare's sister were a lot alike. She could see the tight look of pain in Avery's eyes when she spoke of her parents. "Darius is a good man."

"You spoke in the present tense—you think he's still alive."

"I know what Dare told me, but I can't help but feel . . ." She trailed off, not wanting to say anything more.

"I really hope you're right, Grace," was all Avery said.

Chapter Twenty-six

Jem wiped the blood from his lip and went to find Key, who'd left sometime during his fight with Dare.

"Nice of you to stick around for backup."

"You didn't seem like you needed help," Key said. "Besides, I'd already softened him up for you."

"Thanks for that." Jem didn't sit down next to him, lit a cigarette instead and said, "There's no way around this."

"How the fuck can I work with him?" Key demanded.

"How can you not?" Jem countered. "Kill him once you've eradicated Powell and you're safe."

"Yeah, that's healthy," Key muttered. "Did they teach you that in therapy?"

"What were your plans when you met him face-to-face—a good, stern talking-to?"

Key had been so focused on simply finding Dare that he hadn't allowed himself to think about that. Because he'd been worried about what he might consider in the heat of all the anger and pain that still swirled around him like a massive hurricane that could've rivaled Katrina.

Fuck it all—would he have killed the guy? He'd lost everything to save Dare because he thought he was an innocent victim. He was—he still was.

Key sighed, dropped his head into his hands, elbows propped on the table.

"It's all right to want to kill him," was Jem's assurance.

"That makes me feel like all's right in the world."

"Stress will kill you, Key."

"So will Powell."

"True that." The Cajun cadence was heavy again in Jem's tone now that they were so close to home. Key was sure his sounded similar after only a week back.

"Gotta go check on the old place," Key said.

"Not a stop on my tour," Jem told him. No, Key hadn't thought it would be, but he hadn't thought it would be on his own either.

Life could screw you with surprises like that.

"Are things okay out there?" Grace asked her, swiftly changing the subject.

"Lots of pissed-off posturing," Avery said casually. She couldn't tell Grace that Dare and Jem were fighting over her. Grace would know soon enough, anyway. "I think they're pretty much agreeing that we need one another."

Agreeing because there was no other way out. There might not be any way out, but Avery gave Grace a smile and was grateful when she heard the fighting stop.

She excused herself from Grace and went out to the

kitchen to find Key and Jem sitting at the table. Jem had ice on his cheek, but he was still smiling.

She sat next to him, asked, "Why are you wanted?"

"Long-assed boring story," Jem told her. "Suffice it to say none of us are safe drawing attention to ourselves, and Powell knows it."

Key looked so miserable that Avery wondered if the original Section 8 members felt this way at first—isolated, looking for any way out of their current predicament.

The original S8's so-called miracle had ended up being a nightmare, but only at the end. Still, according to Darius, they'd ended up doing an awful lot of good. When she mentioned that, Jem snorted and Key asked, "You don't expect me to buy into that Robin Hood bullshit, right?"

"What do you buy into?" she demanded. "Because I need to believe in something."

Key stared at her, and for a second, she swore she saw that same warmth that had been there that first night. Just as quickly, it disappeared and his eyes held that stony gaze.

"What happened that night in the jungle?" she asked. Neither man said a word. "Fuck your code and that classified crap. Tell me now. Make me understand why my brother had a death wish and why you hate him so much."

Key slammed back his whiskey. "Little girl, don't ask for things you really don't want to have on your mind for the rest of your life."

"I shot two men, point-blank, because they raped

and killed my mother. I found her body. I was supposed to be with her, and if I was, what they did to her might not have happened, so I already live with shit in my mind I don't want. I think I can manage to fit in a little more, so tell me." She punctuated that by slamming her palms on the table, jarring the bottles and glasses.

"I saved your brother and caught hell for it. Is that what you want to hear?" Key asked.

"If it's the truth, yes," Avery said quietly. Jem swore an oath under his breath and shook his head as Key stormed out.

"This is going well," Jem commented. "This whole situation's insane."

"Yes," she agreed. "Are you, really?"

"Yep." Jem took a long drag from his cigarette and blew smoke rings in the air. "The deep, dark parts of the CIA that the American public likes to pretend don't exist loved that about me."

"I'll never understand these government agencies."

"You shouldn't even try—talk about making you crazy," Jem agreed.

"So crazy gives you license to do anything?"

"Basically, yes, and that was the premise for S8. I would've been a perfect candidate."

Jem and Key looked a lot alike once you got to know them. They had a similar crinkle to their eyes when they smiled, although Key did so a lot less than Jem. Their facial structure was similar, although Key was light and Jem was dark, much like her and Dare.

"Gunner said you grew up around here."

"In the next parish over," Jem said. "Most of it blew away with Katrina."

"That's a shame."

"No, that's karma." Jem sat forward. "Don't push him, pretty girl. My brother's got a whole lotta ugly inside and nowhere to put it. If you make him put it on you, he's gonna feel worse, *chère*."

"Dare won't tell me."

"Maybe you're not meant to know. You got your own burdens, true that?"

More than she'd ever thought she'd have at her age. She studied her fingers. Her nails were short; even so, her hands looked delicate, fingers long and tapered, like she should be playing a piano or doing something equally refined.

Instead, she was wanted for murder and about to become a member of something she felt an immediate kinship to. In the long run, she supposed it didn't matter how crazy she felt as long as she was doing something right.

After several long moments of silence, Jem said, "Maybe you can talk Key into this."

"Because it's our only choice?"

"Because it's our best choice," Jem said. "And I'm not your typical team player."

"Jem, you're not typical anything," she told him as she stood. She couldn't resist leaning down to give him a quick kiss on the cheek.

"What's that for, girlie? You gettin' sweet on me? 'Cause I can fight off those other two."

She wagged her finger at him before heading out

the door and off the back porch. She threaded her way through the tall grasses and down to the dock in her hastily pulled-on Keds and sat next to Key, crossing her legs instead of dangling them above the water the way Key was, even as he fished the murky waters.

She supposed that was what separated her from the native bayou dwellers. All she could think about were the alligators. After a few minutes he picked up a fishing rod and handed it to her. She cast the line, waited for it to make its soft plop into the water.

"Why do you hate Dare?" she asked finally, hoping he'd appreciate her not beating around the bush.

When he turned to look at her, his eyes intense, his face heartbreakingly handsome, she wanted to kiss him instead, to finish what they'd started the other night. Instead, Key started talking, telling her the story that Dare had refused to.

He started with, "Dare got me dishonorably discharged. I have a record. No one wants a vet with a record, and I wasn't ready to leave the Army."

"What happened?"

He glanced at her and back at the water. "If he didn't tell you, I'm guessing he doesn't want you to know."

"I'm guessing it's important I do know. Besides, maybe he didn't know how to tell me," she said, letting the line rest in the water. "I'm not catching anything."

"You didn't throw it out far enough." He took her line and showed her how to recast it. When they settled in again, she said, "It has something to do with the scars on his hands."

"Yes."

"You were there the night it happened?"

"I saved him," Key admitted after a long moment of silence. She let that sit between them for a while, until he pulled in a fish and recast his line. An alligator floated by like it didn't have a care in the world, and she watched it until it disappeared.

Key didn't bother pulling his feet up. "It won't get you."

"How can you be sure?"

He pulled a long knife out of his pocket and stuck it into the wood in between them. "I'll get it first. Wrestle it down and use the knife if that doesn't work."

"You wrestle alligators?"

"A summer job. Paid well. I come from a long line of alligator nuisance hunters. My daddy, his daddy before that . . ."

She tried to picture him wrestling down one of the big green reptiles—and winning. He smiled like he knew.

"I was on patrol with my Ranger team and a couple of Delta guys. A different job. The fire distracted me," he said. "I called it in and was told to stand down and ignore it."

But he'd seen too much in his short time in the Army to listen. A burning village. Something was happening and he needed to know what. So he broke away from his men and trailed the smoke to the fire—and he saw the hanging man with the spikes embedded in his hands.

"He was shirtless. Pants almost ripped off. He was choking. But still, he was fighting. At first, anyway.

And then it was like he gave up and let himself hang. The smoke and fire would burn him alive, and it was like, suddenly he didn't care."

"But you did."

He'd run through the fire and smoke and gotten Dare down. Carried him to the rest of his team. "I took the damned spikes out of his hands. Do you get that, Avery? I took the damned spikes out of his hands."

Key's voice shook a little when he spoke. Avery touched his arm, and Dare watched the whole scene from several feet away; he'd stopped, not wanting to walk into the middle of this discussion, and then looked down at his hands.

He remembered that well; Key hadn't wanted to cause him more pain. Dare had insisted, tried to pull them out himself. A teammate convinced Key it would be the best thing to take them out, since Dare would do himself more harm than good.

"He could've bled to damned death. Hell, maybe that's what he wanted. But I kept wondering— hoping—that I didn't ruin his hands completely," Key said.

Key had pulled them out fast—but carefully. Dare remembered screaming until he passed out. He hadn't seen Key again, not until tonight.

Dare turned away and walked back through the brush. Dare's connection to S8 had ruined Key's military career—his life. Key was an innocent, and he'd walked into Richard Powell's death trap for Dare that night in the jungle. And because Powell didn't know if

Dare had given Key any intel, and because Jem had tried to get intel to save Key's career, Jem was in danger as well. No way Rip would let a CIA man who had even a peripheral knowledge of S8 live.

No way would Rip let any man who had peripheral knowledge of S8 live.

If nothing else, Dare now had to get his life back as well—but at what cost? Their way in was Grace . . . and he'd promised not to use that one. Couldn't.

"We go back—regroup—and join you in a few days. I don't think we should stay together for now," Jem said when Dare got back to the porch, and Dare agreed.

"We've been lucky until now—remaining separate has fared us well, made it harder for Rip to track and catch us. But we're going to have to stick together when we leave New Orleans," Dare said. He wanted one last night alone with her. One last time to decide how he would move forward—with or without her. Because as much as he didn't want to let her go, helping her to disappear was their best bet and hers.

"We'll wait for your signal."

The two of them and Gunner did wait, until Key and Avery came up the path. It was time for them to head back, time to hear Key's decision.

"We go after him with everything we have," Key said. "That's what I know how to do—I fight. I have no problem fighting him."

"He's got too much lead time on us. He knows us way better than we know him," Dare said.

"Then we learn more about him," Jem said, pointed inside. "His daughter's the key."

For once, Dare agreed with that. He shook Jem's hand and Gunner's, hugged Avery, and they started down to the boat. Key lagged behind.

"You need to punch me again?" he asked, and Key stared at him like he was trying to read his mind.

"You wanted to die."

"Would've been a lot easier than the recovery."

"Did you ever really recover?" Key asked.

"Did you?"

"No, but I'm still hoping." When Key grinned, Dare could see that maybe, just maybe, there was hope for all of them.

They shook hands then. It would take longer to truly mend their fences, but they understood one another, and that was what was important.

Chapter Twenty-seven

When she heard everyone leaving, Grace came out of the room to say good-bye to Avery and Gunner and to meet the brothers.

Both looked at her with a mixture of kindness and suspicion, which she supposed came with the territory. Darius, Adele and Dare himself had looked at her the same way.

She didn't know exactly what kind of agreement they'd all come to, but it felt like a peaceful one, judging by the lack of tension that had flared earlier. And while Dare walked them out to the dock, she rustled in the refrigerator and found what she needed to make the dish Darius had taught her years earlier.

By the time Dare got back, the fan was blowing the delicious smells of meat and rice throughout the house.

"You're supposed to be resting."

"I rested the entire time you were meeting, and I'm all better," she told him. "I thought you might be hungry."

"Oh."

"You're suspicious."

He shrugged. "I'm always suspicious when someone does something nice for me."

"Because you think they want something from you."

He thought about that for a long second before answering. "Everyone's always wanted something from me. I can't remember a time when they didn't."

"That's sad," she told him. "Mainly because I feel exactly the same way."

"Don't we make a pair," he muttered.

"All I want to do is cook you dinner. I'm assuming you want it spicy?"

"There's no other option." He smiled then. She'd started to love when he smiled. She'd begun to grow love where she'd thought none could ever grow.

She hoped she wouldn't have to find out that she hated him for doing that. She wanted a single good memory from one man in her life.

"They're going to help," he told her, and she paused midstir and breathed a sigh of relief.

"There was some fighting. I'm guessing Jem and Key weren't completely happy with what they found out." She tried to keep her voice light but failed.

"Grace, no one blames you."

"Well, good for them. I blame me."

"You've done a lot of good. For yourself, with Marnie. You helped a lot of women, didn't you?"

She turned from the stove to face him. "I tried. I got them out of Louisiana," she said. "Whatever happened from there . . ."

"They had to take responsibility for," he finished.

"I don't think many of them knew how to. They

spent their lives being controlled by men, thinking they deserved it. And then they're supposed to move on by themselves and suddenly become independent?"

She realized she could've easily been talking about herself, quickly looked away, took a sip of her soda.

"You did it," he said quietly.

"You don't have to say that."

"I never say shit I don't mean. That's a waste of time and energy."

"She was the last one who was there for me," she said, and then she stopped as if she could hear Rip's *show no fear* speech. He'd taught her many useful things, and all of them would help her deal with him when the time came.

"I'm sorry, Grace. I really am. But you're not alone."

"It's better that way. People get hurt because of me."

"This wasn't your—"

"Don't say it, Dare. Don't."

He didn't press it, and she was grateful.

It was like waking up from a nightmare, and she'd done that too many times already. How much was one person supposed to bear before they broke?

Why wouldn't she just break? Crack. Cut from reality with a resounding crash and never, ever come back. It would be so easy to be crazy. Unattached. Uncaring.

She craved easy. Dare wasn't that, but as much as she tried to warn him away, she didn't think he'd go. And so she blurted out, "I never thought I'd live very long."

"That makes two of us. Guys like me aren't supposed to."

It wasn't a self-pitying statement or a self-deprecating one. It was an honest statement from an honest man.

An honest man she could love, if she didn't already. "Maybe together, we'll add it up to a little bit longer."

He didn't say anything, but he did give a slight nod.

"When are the others coming back?"

"Tomorrow night. They'll tie up loose ends, and then we decide how best to handle things from here."

"And you're not worried that they'll be followed?"

"No. They're careful." He took a taste of the gumbo directly from the pot, closed his eyes and smiled. "Woman, food like this is definitely the way to my heart."

"I'm glad," she said softly, met his gaze as a blush heated her cheeks.

She wasn't used to this kind of relationship—or any relationship, especially not without that edge of combativeness. She and Dare had sparred enough. He knew her hot buttons just enough to force her to drop the act.

Vulnerability with the right person wasn't bad at all, she decided. Especially when Dare turned the stove down to simmer and tugged her into his arms. He bent his head to kiss her, first on the neck, flicking his tongue down along her collarbone, giving her a pleasant shiver down her spine. When his lips met hers, she moaned softly against his mouth. Their tongues danced together, and she felt like she could kiss him like this forever.

Except they didn't have forever. They might not even have the next twenty-four hours, if Rip had anything to say about it.

*   *   *

Dare was in the goddamned gray, and he'd been there his entire life. Something had to be black-and-white one day, so clear-cut that he knew exactly what he was supposed to do.

It was never simple. He could sit here and bemoan his fate or sink into the beautiful woman offering herself and so much more to him. For right now, it would have to be enough.

"Stop thinking," he told her.

"I'm trying."

"Try harder. Stay in this moment with me."

To help her, he lifted her and brought her into the bedroom, laid her down, pulled down the borrowed shorts. Without tearing his eyes from her face, he fingered her clit, and she gasped, arched up off the bed. "How's that?"

"Good," she managed, and he rolled his thumb over the tight bundle of nerves again.

"Just good?"

"Very. Dare . . ."

He smiled then, loved watching her soften. He wasn't sure why she'd decided to give in, give herself up to him, but he wanted to show her it was the best decision she could've made.

He didn't want to let her go, wanted to wrap her up and keep her safe. If he thought he could run away with her, keep her from Rip and his revenge, he would.

But there was no sense trying to outrun the past.

Now who's thinking too much?

He laid down next to Grace, who began to move down his body. He wanted to stop her, to give her the pleasure, but instead, she bent her head to lick his cock.

Her tongue was warm, her palm cool against his skin, and he bit out a curse. She hummed around his shaft and continued to suck him, stroke him, work him the way she wanted to. He could come this way, wanted to . . . but wanted to be inside her even more.

"Grace, let me fuck you," he murmured, and she looked up at him under her long lashes and flushed, but she complied, moving up his body, pushing his back down to the bed.

She was warm against his skin, so inviting, and his dick had taken control. Dare was okay with that, especially when Grace wrapped a palm around his shaft and stroked as she eased it against her sex. Teased herself with it for a few seconds and then just said, "Please."

She didn't have to ask twice. He wrapped an arm around her back and flipped her gently so she was on her back. Then he took her. Put one of her legs over his shoulder so she was wide-open for him as he thrust, giving it to her the way she'd liked it the first time, varying between hard and gentle.

He was falling so deeply for her—told himself this was inevitable. That she felt it too. That no matter what, they were both in the right place at the right time.

Afterward, Dare insisted she remain in bed while he reheated the gumbo and brought it to her.

"So spoiling me's okay?" Grace teased him.

"Yes," he said seriously. "Deal with it."

She spooned the chicken, sausage and seafood mixture into her mouth and chased it with a sip of cold beer. This was so perfect, so different from the dire circumstances that had surrounded her days earlier.

But those same circumstances were all still there, hovering in the background like the proverbial other shoe waiting to drop. And it would always be that way, so for now, she'd simply stop and enjoy this time, because she'd never had anything like it before.

He polished off several bowls of her soup and sat back with a very satisfied look on his face.

"Is that for me—or for the gumbo?"

He pretended to think about it, and she gave him a playful shove. "This doing-nice-stuff thing isn't all it's cracked up to be."

"I like it." He pulled her to lie on top of him, the T-shirt of his she wore riding up.

The breeze from the open window settled over them, the night air cooling them down after their long bout of lovemaking. Round two or three—she'd lost count.

There would be more. She knew that. But for now, they rested, acted like two normal people who more than liked each other.

Except they weren't normal and this was so far from a date. Still, she liked it. "Darius always said you were tougher than he was."

At his father's name, Dare seemed to sober up. "Yeah, well, he tended to exaggerate."

"You talk about him in the past tense, even though you don't know if he's really dead."

"I have to. It's the only way to move forward," he admitted. "I've looked everywhere. Put out feelers.

Doing anything more would be dangerous if he is still alive. This way, if anyone's ever listening to me, they'll think he's definitely dead, and maybe they'll stop looking too."

A good plan, she had to admit, even though his face grew tight with emotion.

"I was twelve the first time he brought me here," he said. "I thought it was the greatest place on earth."

"Me too," she said.

"You really love it here."

She nodded. "I was hoping to stay here forever."

He didn't bother to tell her she couldn't. She knew it, and there was no reason to rub salt in what must already be burning wounds. So she continued, wondering if he'd answer her next question.

"Was there ever anyone special for you?"

Dare had learned over the years that the answer to that question most women wanted to hear was no. Luckily, it was also the truth in this case. "No. There were women, of course, but once I enlisted, there was barely time for anything but that."

"And keeping S8's secret," she said quietly.

"How did you—"

"They talked about you all the time. They loved you."

He didn't know if it hurt more or less to know that. "For Darius, there was someone special. And he ruined that—he ruined her."

"Avery's mom?"

"To name one. He wasn't a great husband to my mother, either."

"He's a good man."

"He's a good soldier. An even better merc. And if he just hadn't gotten involved in relationships when he had nothing to give, then I'd add on the *good man* part." Dare had never wanted to hurt anyone like that, never planned on it, and he wasn't about to start now.

"Darius and Adele always kept me at arm's length," she told him. "They were always kind. I didn't want for anything. But to get that close to having something normal and still not be allowed all the way in, it was almost . . ."

"Cruel," he finished for her. "I grew up in it. They didn't mean it to be, but it was. They didn't know any other way."

She'd forgotten how Dare must've grown up, how he would've been through some of the same stuff she had. Still, "I'd take them any day over Rip."

"Agreed. But hell, Grace, no child needs that shit." He'd been born into this lifestyle. So had Grace. He'd learned that you can't control the violence, that you could only take the punishment, control what's inside you so it doesn't kill you first.

It might be deemed abuse, but not in the typical fashion. But his childhood was spent learning about tactical errors and guns and knives. Close-quarters battles and hand-to-hand.

His father was a nonviolent man who worked in a violent world—used any means necessary to survive. He passed that lesson onto his son, and Dare learned it as a necessary part of life.

When he told her that, Grace said, "Doesn't seem fair to do to a kid."

He nodded. "I learned survival. Not always a bad thing."

"At what price?" she asked, and Dare told her, "There's always a price that comes with survival. Who's to say what it's worth?"

Chapter Twenty-eight

Jem took the stairs with Key up the four flights because Key still couldn't handle the enclosed space of the elevator. Jem knew exactly where that fear came from, knew his baby brother would white-knuckle it if he had to . . . but Jem wouldn't put Key through anything further. Hell, he owed him too much already.

When they got to the landing, they both stilled. Something was wrong—the door to their place was partially open, and it didn't look as if it had been kicked in.

"Fuck me," Jem said. He went in, gun drawn, with Key backing him up. Luckily, he'd taken his computer with him, because that would've been what they wanted. For the most part, it looked like a random robbery, their clothes strewn around, dishes slammed to the floor.

But Jem knew better.

"Part of the herding process?" Key asked. Jem nodded.

It was after midnight when Avery and Gunner arrived at the tattoo shop. Jem and Key had rejected the idea of staying there, and so they planned to meet up late the following night and head back to the bayou.

Now Avery used Gunner's washer and dryer as he drew on a sketchpad, shielding it from her view. She didn't know if he was drawing her or not, but she wasn't self-conscious about it.

"You and Key are getting closer," he noted, not looking up at her.

"You think?"

"Come on, Avery, who are you kidding?"

She shrugged. "I have more to worry about than my feelings."

"Now, that's the smartest thing I've heard you say all day."

"And I believe Dare about trusting Grace."

"And now you're back to square one," he told her. "Sometimes, men think with their dicks," Gunner pointed out.

She raised her brows. "Sometimes?"

Gunner muttered under his breath, then said, "Fine—we'll let Dare guide us through this one."

He put aside the sketchbook, said, "Come on, I'll show you the panic room."

She followed him downstairs—it was the same level as the garage, but she felt like she was on a different planet when she walked in and the security system slammed the two doors shut around them.

"This is very bare."

Gunner rolled his eyes. "Typically, people who hide here are grateful, not pissed at the lack of pretty."

No, pretty had left the building, probably scared

away by the cement-block walls and chilly atmosphere, despite the near hundred-degree temp outside. "This is worse than prison."

"Trust me—if you'd been there, you'd know better." He showed her the alarms, the codes.

"Why do I have the feeling we're sleeping down here tonight?"

"Trust those feelings," he said as he released the security. "You can bring a blankie."

"Asshole," she muttered as they went back upstairs. Instead of going for the sketchbook again, he opted for the laptop. He poured them each a whiskey, handed her one before he began typing.

"Seems my tracker is underwater," he told her. "Fuckin' TV shows are ruining my game by giving away all my tricks. Before *Burn Notice*, none of the bad guys thought to look for trackers. Now, forget it—you have to install it inside the door, and even then they have these scanner things . . . you're not even listening, are you?"

"Not really."

"Typical. No regard for technical genius," he grumbled.

She stared at the dot on the screen, which remained unmoving. "How long did it take him to find it?"

He smiled. "He wasn't that smart." He showed the path the man took, out of the bayou and into New Orleans, before he turned around and made a circle.

"So he's staying in the city."

"I'd bet on it."

She paused and then asked, "Do you think Powell killed Darius?"

He stopped typing. "It doesn't matter. Dare's already hell-bent on revenge. And that's a hell of a way to live and die, hear?" He took a sip of whiskey and then downed the rest of the brown liquid with a smooth chug.

"It matters to me," she said quietly.

"Drink," he told her, like that was the answer. Maybe it was.

She took a small sip and watched him carefully. He'd stilled a little. Typed more, read more, stilled.

She waited, even though patience certainly wasn't her strong suit. Finally, he told her, "I think we need to call Dare."

"What did you find?"

"We've got a problem. Grace's mother is alive and well."

"How did you find that out?" she asked, and he slid her a sideways glance that basically said, *I could tell you, but I'd have to kill you.*

What he actually said was, "I have my resources."

"You're all so brooding and mysterious. Do you cultivate that or does it just come naturally?"

"Everything about me is natural, *chère*." He drew out the last word and smiled, and yeah, she could totally see women standing in line to marry him. The fact that he'd actually done so three times was what surprised her. He didn't seem the type to be caught by anyone or anything.

Unless he lets himself.

Yes, Gunner was definitely an interesting one. "Grace told Dare that Rip took her mother away. You're saying she left the island—and Grace—behind voluntarily?"

"For a lot of money, and she appears to be suffering no twinge of a guilty conscience." Gunner cursed. "Grace said her mother was taken away when she was twelve, right? Said Rip killed her."

"Maybe that's what she thinks."

"Maybe. But hell, twelve years of programming from a grifter. Add in six more from Rip and we've got the makings of a perfect con."

"I know why I'm doing this—why Dare is. I can even understand Key and Jem, but you? You're not involved."

"You keep believing that," he muttered, and then, with his voice tight, he said, "We're being hunted. No one hunts me in my goddamned home."

Avery believed he could take on anything. All these men could.

The problem was Grace. Could they trust her? Her gut said yes, but there was so much evidence against her.

She dialed Dare's number, prepared to tell him the news while Gunner got their beds together in the panic room.

She was in no rush to go down there again. But when Jem and Key showed up at the door, she knew there was no longer a choice.

Chapter Twenty-nine

Dare gripped the phone as he walked quietly onto the back porch, Sig in hand. Grace slept soundly, a sleep fueled by good beer, good food and good sex. He wished he'd crawled in next to her and refused to answer his phone.

But the intel Avery and Gunner had discovered was something he definitely needed to know.

Now he told his sister, "I don't think Grace knows. If she does . . . shit, Avery, if she knows, she's playing me. And hell, knowing what Esme is, what Grace grew up with—"

"She was honest with you about Esme's grifting," Avery said. "She didn't try to deny that. Maybe she never knew. She's been led to believe her mother was killed. Maybe that was part of the deal—her mother didn't ever want Grace to know she'd abandoned her to that monster."

"She's a chameleon. She's learned to be exactly what people want her to be."

"Maybe she's never learned to be who she wants to

be. Or maybe you're meeting the real Grace," Avery suggested. "There's no one left from S8 to ask."

Dare wondered what Grace had really been doing the last two years since S8 fell apart. Adele had left her with money and resources to get false paperwork.

He also wondered what she'd learned from Darius and Adele.

"Darius put you on the path to Grace. Maybe he knew," Avery said now.

"Knew what?"

"That you'd fall in love with her."

Dare paused for a long moment, but he didn't deny anything. Couldn't. "Now Darius is psychic?"

"He knows you—and Grace. Sometimes, you just know when two people are going to connect."

"So this was his version of a blind date? Because I gotta tell ya, Match.com has nothing to worry about."

Avery gave a short laugh, and then he heard male voices in the background.

"Key and Jem staying with you?"

"They are now—someone broke into their apartment."

"I'll see you all tomorrow. Stick close to Gunner."

He waited until she promised before he hung up. Then he waited outside for a long while. Strummed the guitar and tried to process the news.

When to confront Grace? He still had so many questions for her—about Rip, about everything she knew . . . They needed her. And keeping her cooperating was most important, he decided.

He could find out more about her mother later. Feel

her out. And when he'd convinced himself that was the right thing to do, he went back inside to her.

He found Grace walking around the house, almost like she was making some kind of security sweep. When she got to the kitchen, she said, "Sorry—I just . . . I thought I smelled smoke."

"I'll take a look around outside," he told her. They'd washed their clothes from the night before, but maybe the smell lingered. He didn't smell anything outside or in. "I think we're all right," he told her, and although she nodded, she didn't look convinced at all.

She continued to walk around while he made dinner, able to sit down while they ate, but afterward she seemed to be unable to settle in.

"We could watch a movie," he suggested, but she didn't seem to hear him. Maybe they'd moved too fast the night before, but when he pulled her close, she melded to him, kissed his neck, murmured that he smelled nice.

She stayed against him for several minutes before abruptly pulling away. She was sitting up in bed, staring blankly into space.

"Grace?" he asked, but she didn't move. And then she moved from the bed and began to walk.

"Grace, answer me," he said, but she shook her head, put her hands out blindly like she'd lost her sight. She was murmuring something unintelligible, too low for him to make out anything but the small moans. Fear pulsed from her—tangible. He knew that smell, could taste it.

She was in pain, but it didn't seem to be physical.

The same thing had happened to her before they found Marnie dead, but not to this extreme.

"Come on, Grace—come back to me," he said, but she wasn't hearing him. She blinked rapidly, small moans of pain escaping her throat. And then she was sinking to the floor in his arms.

When he settled her down, she was half in his lap, her breathing shallow, her eyes staring at the ceiling but not seeing anything. She was semiconscious for about five minutes, and then she murmured something again and fell into a deep sleep.

He smelled the smoke about an hour later.

The house was on fire. Grace woke coughing. She was on the floor, not the bed, and she remembered getting up when the vision first came through. But at least down here she wasn't inhaling too much smoke.

In seconds, Dare was putting a wet towel over her face and guiding her through the house. She heard the flames crackling, felt the heat perilously close and was glad she didn't have to see it.

"I've got you," Dare said to urge her forward. Her feet hit wet earth. She kept moving even as Dare fired shots behind them. She wished she could do more, but she supposed that following directions was the most helpful thing of all.

Finally, after what felt like hours but what she guessed was mere minutes, he pulled the towel from her head and she realized they were on the shoreline in front of a decent-sized boat, with a small motor and plenty of room to make her feel safe. She had no idea where it had come from or how he'd gotten it here so easily, but she got in with Dare's help, and he got in behind her and paddled silently away from the shore.

She saw something sticking out of his shirt—the top of a brown envelope. Esme's picture.

"You okay?" he whispered, and she nodded, knitted her hands together so he wouldn't see them shaking. Alone, in the dark, the boat moved effortlessly—at times, when the moon shone through the thick cypress trees, she could see the soot on Dare's cheeks, the glint in his eyes.

She picked up the rifle and turned, stared into the darkness they'd come from, because Dare couldn't be expected to see coming and going.

"Good girl. You see anything, you shoot," he told her, his voice quieter than the noise of the bayou.

Why hadn't anyone come after them? Had Dare taken them out? Rip couldn't be here doing his own dirty work, although he was capable of it.

She forced her hands not to shake as she held the shotgun on her shoulder, continued peering into the dark waiting for someone to follow them. "Who did you shoot at?"

"Couldn't make him out—just a shadow pointing a gun at me. Probably the same guy who broke into your house," he told her.

"Did you kill him?"

"Yes. Got his ID too."

That made her feel better, but she still kept watch on their tail, because if he hadn't been working alone . . .

She forced her mind away from that, concentrated

on counting the minutes that passed as they moved farther from shore.

She heard the explosion when they'd been on the boat for maybe ten minutes, the sound shattering the still of the bayou and making her jump. "Was that—?"

"The house? Yes." Dare turned back to her, still paddling the small boat. There was an engine, but she understood why he wasn't using it. "It's only property. We're safe."

She nodded by rote. Maybe a part of her was still asleep and in shock. But it was warm here and she seemed calm enough and they were safe. The bayou enveloped them in a warm cloak.

But she'd miss that house. She'd risked her safety to come back here.

And you might've found it.

She had the clothes on her back and the picture of her mother—that was it.

She'd started over like this, when S8 first took her. She'd start again. But there was no promise that she wouldn't be doing it alone—again.

She glanced over toward Dare. She'd seen the bruises on his chest—entwined with the scars that marred his torso—and she wondered if he felt as strong on the inside as he looked on the outside. If he'd ever tell her if he didn't.

How could he not hold all of this against her? She was the catalyst for this event. It wasn't something she could see Dare getting past.

Maybe Dare was right, and it would be best for him

to go back to Rip and take a stand. She could go to the FBI, Interpol, turn herself in and help them catch Rip.

But she knew she'd never survive without Dare's help. What's more, she didn't want to.

In the cold semidarkness of the panic room, Avery woke to sudden movement and the flashing of the bank of computer screens, which had started to blink with silent red alarms. But the alarms weren't on the squares that showed the area surrounding Gunner's shops and garage.

No, what was blinking was Darius's house, where Dare and Grace were staying.

"Shit," she heard Jem mutter, smelled the cigarette smoke even after Gunner told him not to smoke down here. But they were beyond petty arguments now, sleeping on mattresses in the middle of the floor, huddled together, planning for most of the night. Avery felt like she was gaining ground with them.

There was a hand on her shoulder. She turned, expecting it to be Gunner, but found Key standing there instead.

"We have to do something," she said.

"They got out," he told her.

"How do you know?"

"I know Dare," he said. "So do you. They got out."

She couldn't tell if it was wish fulfillment or not, but she had to believe him. Which still meant Dare was in the middle of the bayou, running, being pursued by Powell's men. "We should've brought them back here."

"Too risky," Gunner said. "It's better that we're here to help."

"So let's go help," she said.

"We can't—not yet," Jem said.

"He knows what he's doing," Key told her as he shot a sharp glance Jem's way. "He can survive in the bayou for days."

"He's an easy target once daylight hits," she pointed out.

"Dare's always got an ace up his sleeve," Gunner said. "We wait to hear from him."

All Avery could do was drag the blanket around her and pray that Gunner was right.

Hours later, Dare stopped paddling and let the boat drift with the light current. They wouldn't go far, and soon he found a branch he could secure them to for the rest of the night.

"Where are we?" she asked.

"We're lost."

"You don't sound upset."

"We're right where we need to be." He pulled the netting over the T top of the boat, and it draped around them easily. In the bottom of the boat there were cushions, and another compartment held supplies, both medical and foodstuffs.

"Not bad."

"This is more comfortable than most missions I've been on," he admitted, handing her a bottle of water.

"I don't think I'd survive the military."

"Baby, you could survive anything." He took a

drink from his own water before saying, "I don't know how they found us."

"It was only a matter of time," she said. "That was Rip's motto, and I can see now that it holds true."

"He doesn't know what he's up against. No god-damned idea." Dare wasn't going down easily, if at all. He'd spend days in this bayou if that was what it took to shake their pursuers.

Gunner would know that something had happened. He wouldn't know if Dare and Grace were okay, but he would know not to come near the house.

They were now on red alert. And soon, Dare's suspicions would be confirmed.

He knew in his gut that the only way Rip's men could've found that house was through Darius—and he also knew that he needed to see if dumb luck struck twice. If his instincts were correct, the safe house he was taking them to wouldn't be that safe at all.

And that's exactly what he was counting on.

Was Darius? Or did he have no clue that Dare was actually here? Did he think his son was miles away, learning of the bayou house's destruction through the security warnings sent by computer?

Grace had nothing on her now that could send a message to Powell. If Powell's men didn't find the safe house, Grace was the leak.

If they did, Darius was. And he knew which option he wished for.

"You really know your way around here," she said.

When Darius had moved them here for a while, he'd insisted that Dare learn the bayou channels backward, forward, light and dark, and Dare had seen the benefits of it, so he did. He practiced then and he'd come here after Katrina to mark the changes, learn the new routes, find the barriers.

He was glad he'd done so, wasn't sure Powell's men had been that smart. But Grace had been here since well past Katrina, and Dare still couldn't get a handle on whether or not Powell had had recent—or any— contact with her.

He was so close to trusting her—and so close to freaking out. "Darius was big on planning for every eventuality. You grow up around that, and it becomes second nature."

"I guess I should be grateful for that." She leaned back along the pillow he'd given her, the mosquito netting keeping them comfortable, safe from the swarming bugs she heard buzzing around them. "Where do we go from here?"

"A second safe house."

"I'm so glad Darius was paranoid." But Grace didn't look sure of anything.

He grabbed some water, put it on a clean towel and moved closer to her to wipe the soot off her face and neck. She did the same for him, and his skin cooled under the moonlight. He stripped his shirt off and she continued to cool him down, rubbing the cloth against his chest.

He pulled her closer, to his lap. She grabbed on to him as the boat tipped hard.

"Easy, baby—I've got this."

She straddled him, and he tugged her hips so her

sex pressed his cock. They were both covered, but the sensation was still good. He rubbed her to him and she moaned, dropped the cloth. He pulled her T-shirt up and suckled a nipple. She arched to him, grabbed his shoulders, and he wanted to take down their pants, take her right here.

But this was just as hot. Making her come, watching the joy spread across her face, was his goal now. He sucked harder, let her move her hips against him. The boat rocked gently, her moans became a steady hum in the night and right before she came apart, she went so still . . . and then she whispered his name, over and over until her head dropped to his shoulder.

He wasn't sure how long they stayed like that, with her holding him as much as he was holding her. But eventually, he laid her down on some of the pillows and she curled up and slept—exhausted, yes, but some of the stress was alleviated for the moment.

He was still rock hard, but he'd deal with that. He ate, planned out their next moves. Made a quick call right before the sun came up and they got closer to shore, and then paddled them there.

Chapter Thirty

As dawn approached, Dare steered the boat toward shore and Grace realized they were only half a mile away from the shore and had been the entire night. No doubt Dare had been scoping it out to make sure it hadn't been compromised.

When they hit shore, Dare dragged the boat up and out with her still in it. He gently set her down, bare feet and all, while he hid the boat under some brush covering.

"Hop on," he told her, turning his back to her. She did so, her hands on his shoulders as he walked, weapon drawn. She wasn't sure how far he walked, but it seemed like miles. Finally, they approached a car parked to the side of a trailer. He let her down from his back, opened the car door for her.

"Stay down," he told her, and she did as he asked as he got into the driver's seat.

The car rolled silently down the road when he released the brake. When they were more than halfway down the dusty road, Dare bent down and pulled a plastic piece away from the bottom of the steering compartment. He stripped the plastic from the ends of the battery and starter wires and touched them together, and the car started.

"No way we'd be able to walk the rest of this," he told her. They drove for twenty minutes and then abandoned the car and walked for another ten. In front of her in the soft rising light loomed an old plantation house, still somehow stately despite the disrepair. She wasn't even sure the porch could hold her.

The flooring creaked, and Dare held her close until they got inside.

There was spare furniture, old and dusty. No one had been here for a long while. But there was electricity, at least, and it was better than spending another night on the bayou.

Although that wasn't all that bad. She blushed thinking about the things Dare had done to her in the dark on that boat, and her body hummed with the memory.

"If there's a broom, I can sweep up some of this dust," she said, but he was motioning to her to follow him.

"Don't bother," he said, pointing to the inside of the closet. When she looked in, she saw an open door and stairs leading down.

She wanted to back away. Felt her throat tighten up. Secret rooms hadn't been kind to her.

"I promise, it's okay. You'll like it much better than the cabin. And I'll give you the combination—you can come up here at any time."

"I don't know, Dare . . . I don't know if I can do this."

"Go halfway down—look for yourself."

She did, slowly. *Breathe, Grace, breathe*, she told herself. She ducked her head and saw the modern conveniences surrounding her. Carpet. Hardwood floor. Stainless steel appliances, a bed and tons of light, none of it very fluorescent looking. And a wall of computers, full color, that showed the outside of the house.

If she stared at it long enough, it could give her the illusion of being outside. "I think I can do this," she said out loud, more to herself than to Dare, and she went down the stairs all the way and looked around.

It was clean down here. She noted that it was steel reinforced along the ceiling and the back of the door when Dare closed it.

"How is this possible in the bayou?"

"All these houses are raised off the ground. This is built into that space, but you'd never know it. It's concrete and steel, double reinforced," he told her, then warned, "I'm going to activate the locks—it's going to be loud."

She nodded, and it was loud, with steel slamming down. She drew a deep breath and stared at the cameras, her link to the outside, as Dare said, "We're completely safe."

There was the slightly dank smell of the bayou down here, but he put on some kind of air circulation system, and the smell was alleviated almost immediately.

He went to the computers and pulled out a sat phone to call Gunner, told him where they were. Then she listened while they talked for a while about their next step.

When they hung up, she asked, "Do you think Rip knows where we are?"

He wanted to be honest with her, to share that maybe Darius was alive. But he couldn't, and instead told her, "No idea. But Jem and Key are coming to get us and bring us to Gunner's. And if Powell's men are out there, we'll grab them too. Maybe one of them will talk."

He knew that was wishful thinking.

"And then what?"

"Jem and Key's apartment was searched. Someone tried to break into Gunner's too, but the alarm scared them away before they could do anything. We're sticking together and we're all getting the hell out of town."

After he spoke with Dare, Gunner pulled up a camera feed that focused on another bayou house, this one a dilapidated plantation house. It didn't look like it could stand up to any assault, until Gunner explained about the secret room built into the foundation.

Key had gone upstairs for surveillance, to make sure that nothing had been touched. Even though they'd monitored the cameras all night, they couldn't be too careful.

"They're okay, Avery," Gunner repeated to her.

"I know."

"You look like you're going to faint." His words weren't unkind, but they were a reminder that she needed to pull herself together. Put up or shut up—this was the time to prove she could be a part of this mission.

Key looked off when he came back downstairs. He sat heavily in one of the chairs and stared at the computer screens, which showed the heavy rain that had just started to pour down, while Avery helped Gunner clean some weapons and check other equipment. She needed to do something to get through the day, until they could finally take some action against Richard Powell and his men.

Key and Jem were planning on hiding in the bayou with sniper rifles, because they had the edge, knew the land like they knew themselves. Avery watched the brothers outfit themselves in what would look like hunting gear to the average bayou dweller before they left the relative safety of the tattoo shop.

Avery and Gunner would be right behind them. But they wouldn't go into the bayou. They'd stay in a tricked-out van and scope out the scene from the security feed set up long ago by Darius so they could survey the safe house, direct the brothers and back them up if necessary.

"The house is completely isolated," Gunner told her as she stepped into borrowed camouflage gear. "The safe-house part is impenetrable."

"Not if they throw grenades."

"Place is steel reinforced. It's a bomb shelter. Ground is set to blow around it too."

"So Dare and Grace will be fine. It's Key and Jem who'll be in major danger."

"Yes, but they love this shit," Gunner told her.

"Jem does, not Key," she said, too softly for Gunner to hear.

"Dare won't let you get involved beyond this," Gunner said, handed her the mic. "I think I'm going to need your help. So don't screw this up and prove me wrong."

She wouldn't. She'd been weapons trained, knew self-defense. She knew thugs, wife beaters and thieves. But strategy like this . . . military grade . . . lives depended on it. "Gunner, I'm—"

"I'm here—go with your gut. We're looking to get their voices on tape first and then finish them. Powell needs to think they're all alive and we need enough of their voices—and their equipment—to fake that. Jem and Key can do this."

In less than an hour, Jem and Key would be in place. She scrubbed her hands together and refused to take her eyes from the screen. "What now?"

"Now we take a nice ride into the Bayou Teche, *chère*."

Key and Jem took a cab to the edge of the bayou and walked the rest of the way in. Their guns were hidden in their fishing bags, with poles hanging out the ends of them. Wearing the camouflage of fishermen and poachers alike, they looked no different from any other Cajun in the bayou.

It wasn't the first time Jem had been in a combat situation with his brother, but it was definitely the most serious. Both men were sufficiently tense for battle, didn't talk as they wound their way close to Dare's safe house.

Once they were within half a mile, they slowed their

roll, walked carefully so as not to make noise. For the last leg, they crawled along on their bellies.

"We are not alone," Jem muttered.

"Are you seeing aliens again, or are there guys in the woods?" Key asked. "Because with you, I'm never sure."

Jem snorted. "Two guys in the trees. Snipers. Here long before us."

Key took a quick look through the binoculars and spotted the men, their rifles aimed at the plantation house. "We could take them down and question them, and let Gunner grab Dare and Grace."

"It'll take them too long to get here. We'll have to knock them out, grab Grace and Dare and bring everyone back to Gunner's."

Key scanned the area and shook his head. "Something doesn't feel right."

"Like the fact that this guy is always several steps ahead of us."

"I don't think the snipers are the only muscle." Key looked at him. "We can take them."

Jem didn't need to hear another word, was prepared to move forward; then the snipers left the safety of the trees, dropped to the ground and headed toward the road. Jem and Key followed, saw them preparing to get on an ATV.

"That's not a great sign," Jem said, and Key agreed.

"We best get Dare and Grace outta there now, before we lose the chance."

"I say we get them first." Jem pointed his rifle, but it was Key who fired first, hitting one man in the chest. "How're we going to talk to a dead man?"

"I'm guessing the other one will spill to keep his life," Key told Jem.

He raised his gun and called, "Drop your weapon," to the other man, who held up his hands in a show of surrender, but then bullets rang out over their heads. Key and Jem ducked behind the trees and the guy took the opportunity to run.

"Where're they coming from?" Jem called over the firing.

Key pointed to the other side of the house, and they headed that way to take on the newest threat.

While Dare watched through the cameras, Jem and Key killed one man and stalked the others firing on them, and Grace began that incessant pacing again, the way she had at the house before the fire. He didn't bother to tell her to relax, because he knew he couldn't preach what he couldn't practice.

Jem texted him about the snipers. They'd already been set up in the trees. Because they were out of camera range, Dare hadn't seen them set up, but in his mind, there was only one way they'd known about this place.

Darius. His father was alive. He was sure of it.

But it didn't matter how Powell's men had found this place. Dare and his team still had to execute the rest of their plan. And even though he'd been prepared for the shooting to begin, he still started with the violence of it. He hadn't heard that much fire power since the night in the jungle, and this was not bringing back any fond memories. Key and Jem were firing. They took out two of the three men Dare could see and were advancing on the third one, in the hope of keeping him alive for intel.

He had faith in Key and Jem for this mission, but Grace was tugging at his arm, her face pale. "We've got to get Key and Jem in here."

"The plan is—"

"Rip's plan is bigger than bullets." She was panicked, and he tried to reassure her with, "They know what they're doing," because he knew how intense it looked out there. How violent it had sounded. But it was quiet now, save for Key yelling at the final man to stand down.

But she persisted. "They know what they're doing in any situation but this. Something bad's going to happen out there—they're not prepared. They need to come inside or they'll die."

Dare lived by his gut, but he wasn't used to trusting someone else's. This could be the moment they'd discover everything.

"Key and Jem—come inside now," Dare ordered.

"We're clear," Jem argued. "Come out while you can."

"No," Grace told Dare, her tone still urgent.

"Bomb," she whispered.

He wanted to ask how she knew, but there was no time to waste. Especially because, as she spoke, the lone man Key and Jem had their weapons trained on turned the gun on his own head and shot himself.

Grace turned away from the screen, and Jem and Key stopped arguing. Within minutes, the two men, in black gear and guns, were down the steps and the security perimeters were set behind them. As the lock-down measures clicked in around them, they heard the *whomp-whomp* of the chopper blades. And then the earth shook from the bomb that Dare and the others hadn't known about.

"You knew—motherfucker," Jem muttered at Dare. "You knew the bastard was going to try to wipe us out."

"I didn't, no," Dare said, his gaze locked on Grace now. She was holding her hand over her mouth, star-ing at the blank computer screens as the comms were wiped out by the explosions. The shelter shook a little, and she looked up as if expecting it all to come down on their heads.

It wouldn't, even with a bomb like that. But if Pow-ell knew about the bomb shelter, he wouldn't have tried to kill them aboveground. He would've sent men in to get them.

"Then who knew?" Jem demanded, his gaze set-tling on Grace.

"I knew."

"How? Because you were in contact with Powell?"

"No."

"Whose side are you on?" Jem demanded, and Dare found himself wondering the same thing.

"Yours," she told Dare.

"She just saved our lives," Key reminded them. "Why do that if she's not on our side?"

"I wouldn't betray all of you, not after what I've been through."

"Then tell us how you knew his plan," Jem de-manded. "Because it sure as shit feels like a setup, all around. You save us, we trust you. And then boom, we're dead."

Grace shoved away from Dare. "I will never be on Richard Powell's side. Never."

"Guys, let's discuss this later," Key urged.

"We'll discuss it now," Jem said.

"While you guys talk, I'll head out and take out the men who are, no doubt, coming this way to check for bodies," Key told them as he slung his gun over his shoulder.

Dare glanced at the nonworking cameras and then the glint in Key's eyes. "Forget it. They don't know we're here—and you going out there is a death wish."

"Even better—we'll surprise the hell out of them and focus on our original plan," Jem argued.

"They gotta come now, before the police get here."

"That means we stay put for a while," Dare said.

"I'll make a call to the police, tell them it's a false alarm—or a CIA matter. Buy us some time," Jem told them, grabbed the sat phone.

"Gunner can take care of it," Dare said.

Grace looked over at Dare. "Gunner's outside. With Avery."

They'd gotten there just in time. They'd seen the bomb go off in the distance, and by the time they'd gotten to the house, it was leveled. As Dare had promised, no one could tell there was a bunker built into it, and the bomb hadn't been nearly strong enough to take out the foundation of the house, which still stood.

"The men who did this won't wait for the fire to be

out before they search for bodies," Gunner told her as they sped along the bayou in his nearly silent boat, climbing out along the slippery banks as the smell of smoke invaded her nose and mouth.

Gunner wet a bandana with bottled water and tied it over her nose and mouth, did the same for himself. They moved quickly through the brush toward the smoke, her heart pounding and her weapon at the ready. She might've been nervous before. Now all she had on her mind was keeping her brother safe, no matter the cost. Her body was on autopilot, her mind surveying the distance between herself and the house. She was born for this—until this moment, she hadn't realized the truth in that statement.

Gunner pulled her next to him. There were men rifling through the wreckage, picking their way along it carefully, no doubt looking for bodies. She didn't hear any sirens in the distance. This part of the bayou seemed pretty deserted—but still, someone should've come.

Gunner moved close to her ear. "They probably called in to the police station and told them to ignore calls. Powell could have someone in his pocket there."

That would explain it.

"So what now?" she whispered back.

"We can't take any of them alive," Gunner said. "Let's just get rid of all of them."

"Got it."

Gunner stared at her for a long moment; then his eyes went first to the rifle and back to her face. "You can live with this?"

She nodded without hesitation. He placed plugs in her ears and in his, then moved so they were shoulder to shoulder. She lifted her rifle when he did the same, leveled it, and began to fire in time with Gunner, letting his powerful body and stance guide hers. She and Gunner were the perfect wild cards. She felt like living up to that name.

When the weapon discharged fast and furious, she fought hard to keep her stance against the kickback. She had a few practice rounds under her belt, but nothing like the sustained fire this promised to be.

They were severely undermanned, but Gunner was taking down men left and right, and she was too. They'd given up on plan A but had gotten here as fast as they could and were now working a Hail Mary situation.

She was shaking. Sweating. Watching the men go down, until finally her clip ran empty. But she couldn't let go of the gun.

Her ears rang, despite the earplugs. And then Gunner was next to her, his heavy hand on her gun, pushing it down to face the ground, touching her cheek, bringing her back.

She turned against him and pressed her cheek to his chest for a long moment, and then she pushed against him and walked away, not at all sure where she was going.

Chapter Thirty-one

It grew silent outside. Dare stared at the sat phone as if willing it to ring, and then he grabbed for his phone and Grace saw the look of relief on his face.

"They're okay. They'll sit tight and then go back to Gunner's and wait for us," he said, and Jem and Key nodded in agreement.

Grace sat there with her belly twisting. She knew the time for questioning her had come.

You should've told Dare before this, she rebuked herself. But it was too late for that kind of hindsight. She'd done what she needed to in order to survive.

But she'd trusted him enough to let him in, more than any man she'd ever known. It was time to tell him the whole truth and pray that he understood why she'd been reluctant to do so before.

"Rip must've known where I was the entire time." She looked up to see the three men watching her. "The entire time I was back in New Orleans—I think he knew. God, I can't go back to him."

Her last words were a plea to Dare, but Jem told her

harshly, "You don't get to make those decisions. We can't trust you."

She needed to prove she could be trusted, but how? All these men—and Avery—their lives were on the line like hers . . . because of her. "I'm not. I haven't had contact with Rip in six years."

"Then how did you know his plan?" Dare asked finally, and she told him the truth she'd been holding back from him, from Darius and Adele.

"Because I'm psychic—I know things before they happen. At least that's what I was able to do at one point in time," she admitted.

There was dead silence for a long minute as Dare stared at her, brow furrowed. Key was expressionless as Jem pulled up a chair and said, "I think we're in for a long explanation."

Dare came up behind him, grabbed him before he could sit. "I'll talk to Grace alone. You and Key take shifts at the door, just in case."

"Sweetheart, if you can predict the future, why didn't you know about Powell coming for you before this?" Jem continued as if he hadn't heard a word Dare said. "Or maybe you did and decided to play both sides of the fence."

"I haven't been able to predict anything for a long time." And that was the truth. It had all started with that sudden, unexpected burst of knowledge that Dare was coming for her, and continued into the situation with Marnie . . . then predicting the fire.

But was that first a premonition or wishful thinking? She'd been thinking of S8 and Darius and Adele

during recent months, surprised she'd heard nothing
from them.

"You've had one before—at the house, right before
Marnie called and we went to her house."

She wanted to deny it but knew they were past that
point, both on her end and because of the trust they'd
built between them.

Would he believe her? Or would he believe her and
decide she was too much of a liability to him . . . or
worse, an asset to Rip?

None of the options were very good. She hated this
moment, because once again, her whole life hung in
the balance. She twisted her hands together hard as she
answered, "Yes. It's my third this week. Before that . . .
it's been a while."

"How long?"

"They're not like they were before, when I was much
younger. Now they all seem to come when there's danger near—they only come to me when there's trouble. In
truth, that's the way it is for most predictions—the
stronger the danger or the joy or the sadness that's coming, the easier it is to feel them."

When she said that, Dare moved away from her,
and she got up to follow him. Touched his shoulder.
Spoke his name.

Fell right into his trap. He turned to her, said, "If
you're really psychic, you'd know we were coming for
you." He pressed her against the wall. Her breath came
in quick gasps. "Did you know? Can you predict the
future . . . or did Rip predict it for you?"

"I'm not lying about Rip. I'm not," she swore. "I

haven't been able to predict the future for a long time. That's the truth."

"Why now?"

Because I'm healing . . . falling in love. Trusting someone.
"I don't know," she lied.

"Did you set me up?" he demanded.

"I didn't know who was coming first, the white knight or the black one," she whispered. "I didn't know until you touched me."

Dare ground his jaw so hard he was surprised nothing cracked. His head throbbed as he ran back all the intel he'd memorized about Richard Powell over the past weeks—it all amounted to shit.

Grace could be pulling the greatest ruse ever. He had to be the one to pick apart the truth from the lies.

How was he supposed to build on a foundation that had never been solid or stable to start with? And yet, everything about Grace Powell begged him to.

Darius took her in.

Then again, his father had done a lot of questionable things in his time. And as much as he hated to admit it, Jem had a point about everything. Trusting a woman after kissing her in this kind of situation bordered on something close to suicide.

Like any man in his situation, asking for help was out of the question. He would figure it out himself and would make sure it didn't come back to bite Avery in the ass.

He needed to hear more. Apparently, so did Jem and Key—and he couldn't blame them—but they'd moved

off to the side so Grace wouldn't feel so threatened.
Dare moved away from her, led her back to the table.
She sat, looked up at him so earnestly when he told her
to tell him everything.

*You knew the whole time that she was holding something
back.* And this was a hell of a thing to hide—but she'd
done it for her survival. He understood that.

Still, her survival could mean the rest of their down-
fall.

"Tell me about this psychic thing."

"I'm a broken psychic who grew up with a grifter
for a mother and a psycho stepfather," she said angrily.

"And your psychic gift just happens to work now?"

"It's broken. It's a fragile gift to start with. If I'd
known Marnie was going to die, do you think I'd have
let that happen?"

No, he didn't believe that she'd do that—you didn't
fake grief like that.

"It's brought me nothing but trouble. I have no idea
why it's called a gift." She ran a fingertip across the
surface of the table, following a crack. "My first vision . . ." She laughed, but there were tears in her eyes
as she remembered. "When I was little, I told my mom
she was going to marry a rich man who would ruin us
both," she said haltingly. "Esme slapped me and sent
me to bed without supper. She said it was for me trying
to fool her with her own scam."

Dare flinched for her. His face and fists tightened,
but his voice was calm when he asked, "When did she
finally realize you were seeing something real?"

"I kept everything to myself from that point on. I

knew when her scams would work and when they wouldn't, so we moved a lot, because I refused to warn her. That was in the beginning, and then she got better."

"Because you helped her."

"She didn't know, but I'd give her hints. She didn't realize they were coming from my visions—she thought it was stuff I picked up from the other kids talking." She took a drink of the tea. "But one night, there was a fire. Later, we found out a wife of one of Esme's conquests lit it. But hours before, I smelled smoke. That was the strongest prediction I'd ever had, and I guess that's always been the case for me. I told her, but she told me it was nothing. So I . . ."

"Stayed up all night, waiting for the fire to start," he finished for her.

"I woke her up and got her outside. She believed me after that." She paused. "She was far from perfect, but she was all I had. She didn't know any other way. She'd come from a long line of grifters. But even though she wasn't honest, I didn't get the feeling of pure evil I did when I met Rip."

She shuddered, remembering that day.

"And your mother recalled your visions."

"It was always meant to be. I don't think she could've escaped him if she'd wanted to. He was a better grifter than she ever was."

He looked surprised, and she asked, "You don't know Rip's background?"

"No. Look, I didn't even know the guy existed until last month."

"Right, and Darius wouldn't have left any information about Rip for you. He said he always preferred firsthand info, and I'm betting you're the same." She got up and began to pace a little. She imagined watching Adele and Darius plan in their war room, as they'd called the living room during those times. Occasionally she'd take notes for them, a lot of terms she didn't understand.

Sometimes she'd ask for an explanation. Sometimes she was sorry she did.

"I didn't want you to think I was crazy. Sometimes the visions made me feel crazy."

"And Powell used you because you could predict things."

She glanced up at Dare, admitting, "I kept him alive for a long time. Esme would sit me down at dinner with her and Rip and then, after, question me if I had gotten any feelings about him. And typically, I would. I would see danger—or death—and later, I realized that she'd have me come into the room before Rip was about to go to a dangerous meeting, for instance. I would know if Rip was walking into traps and was telling her that without realizing she was using me. Not at first, anyway. The thing is, Rip knew whether or not he was in danger before I said a word—his intuition, his survival skills, were strong enough to rival any psychic's. But Rip's really into the psychic stuff."

"I don't see that."

"You'd be surprised. He's a man who wants total control, and he didn't like that I might know things he didn't. For a long time after he let his men torture me,

I couldn't see anything but what was directly in front of me, with my own eyes. I liked it that way. But I think he was also always studying me—waiting for me to break. I think . . . I think he liked it that I wouldn't. If I had broken, I don't think he would've kept me alive."

"Tell me about Esme."

"You know she was a fake. A grifter." She spat the words like they tasted bad on her tongue. "As soon as she knew I was the real thing, she started to use me in her schemes."

"And Powell was the biggest scheme of all."

"At first I didn't think so. I think she liked him and thought he'd take care of us. I mean, he was handsome and rich and she was young and pretty. And they were actually a lot alike."

"How's that?"

"They both like control and power."

"Who doesn't?" Dare muttered.

"The problem is, I can't control it. And it doesn't happen constantly. It's just . . . a feeling. Like the night your house burned, I started to feel warm, smelled smoke hours before it happened. I couldn't be sure and I didn't want you to think I was crazy. So I tried to wait up."

"You were trying to save me."

"Trying, yes."

"Hey, come on, Grace—I don't blame you."

"Maybe you should."

Chapter Thirty-two

Avery and Gunner waited for a long while in the woods after the explosion leveled the house. Even though Gunner's bike was well hidden, he wasn't taking any chances.

Avery remained as quiet as he did. She felt strong. Vindicated. But she knew that she'd chosen a life of living off the grid, above the law . . . she'd done that from the moment she'd avenged her mother. But this solidified it.

She had no remorse for killing killers. But she did need to mourn her mother and the life she'd tried to save Avery from. And sitting here quietly in the middle of the bayou, which teemed with life, she mourned. Let the tears stream down her face; she'd never let herself cry for her mom until now, didn't bother to wipe them away.

Gunner didn't ask what was wrong, try to stop her. Instead, he sat close enough to her that their shoulders touched, two soldiers in the aftermath of battle trying to absorb what had gone down. Trying to let it all settle in.

As it started to grow dark, Gunner stood and helped her up, led her toward his bike. She stared over his shoulder for most of the ride, not really taking anything in. Trees whizzed by and finally they were back in the city. Gunner looped around, checked the shop and entered from the garage three doors down.

"What now?" she asked.

He showed her the string of texts he must've written when she'd been having her quiet mini-breakdown.

Basically, staying clear of the place had been the very best thing they could've done.

"Wait a second—you agreed with this?"

Gunner stared at her. "Yes."

"Dare is going to call Rip?"

"The guy's going to know the boy's not dead, and he'll keep coming for you. Dare won't let you live like that."

"You think Rip's going to listen to that?"

"For the right price, any man will listen."

She had the distinct feeling they weren't talking about money any longer.

Dare asked Grace to draw the compound as she remembered it. She bent her head over the paper and drew furiously as Jem watched and Key remained with an ear pressed to the door in an attempt to hear anything.

Dare could understand Key's hatred of being cut off from the outside world. Knowing they were safe here helped moderately. Grace's confession, more so. She'd finally admitted what she'd been holding back, and

Dare could understand exactly why. It was a good tactical move. She had no idea if he would've tried to use her, the way Powell had. He wouldn't have—but it changed nothing. Powell still wanted her dead, along with the rest of them.

"Here you go," she told him. He glanced at it, but Jem held out his hand and Dare passed it along to him, for him and his brother to study. It appeared for now that they were going into Powell's sanctuary at some point, to hunt him in his home the way he'd hunted them.

"If you don't believe me, Dare . . . after everything we've been through . . . I don't know what I'll do," she told him quietly. "You have to understand why I didn't tell you."

He put his hand over hers. "Yeah, I get it. I wish you'd told me—all of us—but in the end . . ."

"You saved our asses," Key interjected. Grace turned to him and gave a small smile.

"Thanks," she said softly, and he nodded. She turned back to Dare, asked, "How did Rip find me?"

"I don't know if he found you so much as Darius told Powell where you were to try to pass a message on to me," Dare admitted. "He's been missing for a year. And I've been thinking about how long a man could deal with torture and not break."

Key gave him a hard look. "Forever, if he wants."

"Right. Especially someone like him. But if he pretended that Powell broke him—if he gave away intel to Powell that I know he never would've, beyond purposely . . ."

"Darius is sending us a message about Powell," Jem said.

"I thought about it when the house caught fire. After that, and the fact that Powell's men found the house but didn't know about the shelter below convinced me."

"Darius didn't know we'd be here, though," Key said.

"Didn't matter. He knew I'd find out it'd been bombed," Dare pointed out. He looked at Grace. "You're supposed to not be in New Orleans, right?"

"I was never supposed to come back here," she agreed.

"Darius disappeared right after I was almost killed on my last SEAL mission. He never came to the hospital. I assumed he was MIA or KIA. Now I think he might've been searching for Powell. And if I'm right and Darius is being held and tortured by Powell . . . he might've assumed that Grace was gone or that I was with her. Either way, message received, loud and clear. Darius gave away this locale—and the house— purposely because it was the only way to tip his hand."

"Even if it meant giving me away?" she asked.

"You had a number to call, right?"

She nodded reluctantly. "Darius and Adele gave it to me."

"I'd be the one on the receiving end of it. Luckily, Avery got me up and moving before you ended up in Powell's hands." Dare looked troubled.

"And we're . . . dead?" Key asked. "Because if he doesn't find traces of a body, he's going to keep searching for proof of life."

"No way Powell's going to stop now. But at least

we've got a secure place to plan. You need to keep Avery and Gunner away," Jem said.

"I'll call Gunner," Dare agreed, motioning for Grace to follow him. She did, to the corner, where one of the cots was set up. "You okay?"

"He's got Darius—and if you're right, he's had him for a year. And I never thought to call you. I was upset that I didn't hear from him. Selfish."

"Did he tell you he'd call?"

"He never made any promises like that."

Typical. So fucking typical. "None of this is your fault."

"You look like you think it's yours," she countered. "Can we just agree to share the burden of guilt and figure out how to move forward?"

"Yes."

"Darius believed in me when I didn't. So do you. I never want you to think I'd do anything disloyal to you."

"Trust doesn't come easily to either of us. I think we've come far in a little less than a week."

It was the best he could give her. And it was what he wanted to believe. She touched his cheek because she knew, and said, "I'll make something to eat for you guys while you plan the next steps."

"Why don't you sleep, Grace? You need to, and this is the best time." Dare didn't have to ask twice. She looked exhausted, and even though she protested a little, she fell asleep almost as soon as her head hit the pillow. He pulled the covers over her and she curled into a ball.

He went back over to Jem, who was still looking over the plans. Key had moved to the corner, pulled out a sleeping bag and laid himself down across the door, his back to them.

Jem looked up at him. "The fact that she can't see things on command goes a long way toward proving she's not a fake," Jem offered. "The fakes, they work their shows all day, seeing future after future. The real thing, their gift is way more temperamental. Makes it difficult to use them in any law enforcement capacity."

"Psychic, Jem?"

"Worked with some of them at the CIA. I guess they think all crazy is the same."

"Grace doesn't seem crazy."

"Unlike you, I don't think crazy's a bad thing," Jem said. "Her mother was a con, but not a great one. She was two-bit. So I don't think she hooked Powell. I think it was the other way around."

"If Grace was the real deal . . ." Dare trailed off.

"Now, that's a secret worth keeping."

"But if she can't see the future—"

"Doesn't matter to him now. She's a game to him. He set it up so that, no matter what, he can get to her. We think she's guilty, she bolts from us, he picks her up—or off. Or we do."

"She's as fucked as we are," Dare muttered. "Unless she's good enough to play all of us."

"No one's that good," Jem said.

"Except Powell," Dare pointed out. "He's played us like puppets, and it took me too damned long to see Darius's hand in all of this. Powell's men found us too easily."

"You really think your father did this on purpose?"

"Yeah, I do. I know how S8's brand of crazy works."

"You're sure?"

"Darius would've blown this place up himself if anyone knew about it before this. He's done it before when he claimed a location was compromised. I just never knew who was compromising it."

"So Powell's been after him for years and now he's got him. Do you think Powell could've truly broken him and all the intel he gave Powell wasn't on purpose? Honestly, Dare, he's not a young one anymore."

Dare shook his head. "There are a lot of things I can say about my father. Him surrendering isn't one of them." Instead of commenting further, he glanced at Key, sleeping across the doorway. "What's his deal?"

"He hasn't killed you yet, so I'm taking that as a good sign." Jem stared down at the map Grace had drawn for them. "She's missing something here."

"What do you mean?"

Jem slid the paper toward him and pointed to the lower floor. "She drew this tunnel—these doors. And she started to draw more. Paused. Erased it."

"She made a mistake."

"You know, I read people. Before I did it for a living, I did it for sport and survival. I knew when my daddy was over the edge, when he wasn't. I know what I saw in Grace's eyes, her face, when she drew that line. She started thinking about something, then realized she didn't want to take that walk down memory lane."

"Okay, even if you're right, why should she have to?"

"Because if I'm right, the rooms she doesn't want to draw will have the best point of entry and exit."

"And you know this because . . . ?" Dare pressed.

"She had a way out and she didn't take it." Jem shrugged. "I see that look in my brother's eyes all the time. I've got to live with that. So does he. Don't make Grace."

Key lay on the floor, listening to every word of Dare and Jem's conversation. He wished he could call Jem a liar, but he wasn't.

Key could've left. Found Jem. Done anything but stay in that house and deal with enough abuse for two boys.

He closed his eyes, rested briefly but couldn't escape from the dreams that circled his mind, the old house, seeing Dare hanging in the jungle.

No man lived through that without scars. No one lived through anything they had lived through without them.

Finally, he shifted, stood. Jem was in the kitchen area, Dare resting next to Grace.

"She's good," Key said.

"Avery's fine, too," Jem responded. "I know you didn't want to say much in front of Dare."

"Nothing to say." Key wiped crumbs from his mouth and grabbed for more muffins. Jem snorted and Key went to study the plans on the table.

"You know she's not sharing shit if we're here," he told Jem. His brother didn't seem surprised that he'd listened in on the conversation.

"Think they torched the old place?"

"Could've only improved it." Key stared at Jem. "Bet that old Jeep in the shed would work with some rigging."

"The old man sure took care of it."

"Better than us," Key agreed. "Guess that actually works in our favor now."

"You ready to check it out?"

"Never," Key told him, even as he readied his weapon and prepared to open the door to let them out into the bayou.

Chapter Thirty-three

Grace woke to Dare rubbing her back lightly. "Sorry. Didn't want to wake you, but we need to talk while we have some time alone."

He handed her a soda and she sat up, blinked. "Where are they?"

"Scoping out transport. They'll be all right," Dare assured her. "When they're done, we'll all get out of here together."

"Where to?"

"Gunner's shop. And then we'll figure out what else to do."

She nodded, played with the tab on the can. "Jem was looking at the map a lot. Does he think I'm still trying to screw him over?"

"He wanted you to finish it."

She stared at him, a flush on her cheeks. Fear in her eyes. "I don't want to."

"I know. But it will help end things once and for all." He drew her close. "What happened in that room?"

She got up, paper under her fingers. With Dare next to her, she redrew the line she'd started to, picturing it in her mind. The large room with the single light hanging overhead and the cinder-block walls that kept the screams from traveling, made them echo in her own ears, its own form of torture.

"I spent a long time down here," she whispered. "At first, I was drugged and tied. After a while, they didn't need either. I just obeyed."

"You did what you needed to."

"There's a window—here." She pointed and he made a small x. "Through here, a corridor to a service exit."

Another larger X. "I'm guessing this leads down a private drive."

She nodded. "I knew that, but instead, I stayed. Got myself all steeled up inside. I put up my own walls."

"So no one could ever use this against you."

"So no one could ever get in again." The fact that he understood allowed her to finally breathe. "It was several weeks after he'd killed my mother. I wasn't cooperating. My mother always warned me not to, and honestly, I couldn't have if I'd tried. My gifts were frozen, in a way. But Rip didn't stand for anyone disobeying him, and I was going to pay for my insubordination."

Dare's face hardened. His body was filled with scars too, some of them because of Powell.

"If I'd killed him when I had the chance, you'd never have gotten hurt," she told him.

"And you might not be here. I'd much rather it worked out this way."

His reassurance rang so true, it gave her the strength to go on. "I confronted Rip about what he'd done to my mother."

She'd been fifteen, in the throes of a rebellion a thousand times worse and more warranted than the average teenage girl's. And her adopted father had not prepared her well for that eventuality. She'd barely gotten the question out before he'd smacked her hard, the back of his hand slamming her cheekbone.

She'd seen stars, tasted blood, and she didn't know if things would be better if she'd stopped while she was ahead, but she hadn't. Instead, she'd slapped him back as hard as she could. He might've drawn first blood, but it was just as satisfying watching it drip from his nose.

It made his smile that much more chilling. He'd looked satanic with blood dripping down his lips, staining his teeth.

She figured that was fitting, because she spent the next several months in hell. Some of it was foggy, some way too clear, and as much as she tried never to relive it, that time would break back insidiously into her dreams.

"They hit me," she started quietly. "Whipped me. It was never him, although I know he watched."

"Fucking bastard."

"He had three men he trusted. Three bodyguards. They all had their turn. One of them was the man who wrecked my house—Gunner showed me his picture. I don't know if Rip told them to or if he just told them to torture me any way they wanted. There were no cameras in that room. He never wanted anything on tape."

Dare looked at her like he didn't want to believe what she was saying. But he had to know—to understand how far she'd come, how different things were now between them.

"When your father tried to recruit me, I resisted because I thought they'd do the same thing. I used to sleep with a knife under my pillow. Your dad gave it to me."

"I will find those men and take them apart, piece by piece, for what they did to you," he promised.

Those men had taken the last of her innocence, her dignity. Since then, she'd slept with many men, all of her choosing. Then she'd walk away, satisfied that she still felt nothing.

When Rip's bodyguards had raped her, over and over, she would tell herself, *I feel nothing*. Told herself there was no difference between what they did and the beatings.

Whoever controlled the sex held the power. She could never be controlled again. She'd give herself orgasms, but sex was the place for power, not pleasure. But Dare had changed that. She'd tried to stop it, to fight it, but her body turned traitor, refused to let that happen.

She'd let him in and now hoped she wouldn't pay the price. With him, she responded in a way she'd never be able to control . . . his fingers skimmed her hot, begging flesh and he chuckled against her neck when she gasped.

She was a virgin in so many ways. And most thankful she'd waited for Dare.

Rip had tortured her with a single purpose in mind—to break her. He was intrigued by the fact that she wouldn't surrender. The fact that she couldn't read the future any longer—and he'd tested her in subtle ways—was a secondary pleasure for him, something he no doubt assumed could happen. And it had. He'd taken her last safe refuge, or so he'd thought.

Dare's fists were clenched on the table. She told him all the things she'd kept inside forever—that she'd been hit. Starved. Beaten down, mentally and physically.

He watched her like it all showed in her eyes. It probably did.

"I get the drugging thing now," he told her.

"You were only trying to help." She sounded raw, even to her own ears. But sometimes wounds needed to open again, get cleaned properly, before they'd heal.

Maybe it was finally time to let that happen.

"I won't live in fear. If he did his worst to me, I was living through it, not hiding from it. The night I left, I watched Rip murder a high-level CIA agent. I'm the only witness. I recorded it. They had a disagreement about the way Rip was doing business. Rip lost it." She poured it all out now. "And the recording is hidden somewhere only your father knew about."

"Did Rip know what you did?"

"Not at the time."

God, it had been horrible watching it. She'd forced herself to stay still, to record, because she couldn't have saved the man if she'd tried. When she'd walked in, Rip was holding the knife at an angle in the man's chest, and the man's eyes were starting to go blank.

She'd recorded it because she'd had the cell phone

in hand already. She'd been handed it by one of the men who was pretending to be a caterer for one of Rip's parties but who, in reality, was working for Darius. She'd been told to capture what she could on Rip's desk, to be prepared to make up an excuse if she'd gotten caught. It was well planned on Darius's part—and that plan included her.

"Grace, if you don't want to do this, we'll still take you," the man who'd handed her the phone had said.

"I want to help."

She had, but she would've much preferred to deal with the documents than this. Thankfully, Rip was on some sort of killing high, not processing anyone else in the room with him.

She hadn't worn perfume of any sort for that very reason. She never liked to draw attention to herself. Somehow, still, she was always on the receiving end of much of the unwanted kind. Her skin was good, her eyes and hair pretty and her lips full—she looked like her mother, and no matter how she tried to make herself look plain, it didn't happen.

She'd quickly dropped behind the couch in the corner once Rip let the man's body sink down. Only then did Rip pull the knife out of the prone body. She recorded him cleaning it with a calculated effort before he placed a call to his men to come in, wrap the dead man in the carpet and dump the whole thing— weighted—into the ocean.

Once he'd left, so did she, not waiting to watch the removal of the body. The risk of her getting caught was far too great. An hour later, she was on a chopper fly-

ing far away from the private island where she'd lived
for the past eight years.

"Where's the recording now?" Dare asked.

"Darius said he kept it someplace safe. He didn't
think it would matter in the long run—not to the CIA.
He said it might even make the CIA come after him
and Adele."

It was unfortunately true—there was no predicting
how the CIA would act, but taking down a valuable
asset like Powell wasn't typically something they'd be
in a rush to do.

"They'd rather cover it up," she said when he told
her that. "So me making that recording was more insurance on me for Darius than for me."

"I hate to say it, but yes, it was. It's probably in one
of the safe deposit boxes he keeps, but it's not going to
help us now."

At his words, Grace smiled tightly, and maybe she'd
realized that from the beginning. Not being trusted
was a state she'd lived in for so long, she was used to
it, and that made Dare's gut clench. Mainly because he
hadn't trusted her either. Not until today.

He'd watched her twisting her hands together as
she told the story. She'd been to hell and back. Held on
to her secret like it was the only thing that could save
her. Whether it would or wouldn't hadn't mattered as
much as her belief that it could.

"I know how hard it must've been to keep all this
from me—from Darius and Adele," he told her.

"My mom used to say that everyone had a secret

persona—she just gave hers a name . . . and a pay-check." Grace shrugged. "I'm beginning to think she was right."

"You were scared. For good reason."

"It's not a perfect science. It's not something I want. I like the practical magic aspect, the healing, but the other stuff—I never want to be so vulnerable and used."

Dare could understand that because his urge to use her gift to save both her and Avery and Darius was undeniable.

His desire for her safety was a larger entity, and he contented himself with the knowledge that he hadn't turned into a total monster.

"You believe me that it just started coming back. That I haven't been in contact with him."

"I believe that you haven't been in contact with Powell. But I don't think it just started coming back."

She looked so frustrated. "I can't explain it. I don't want it. It's gotten me in trouble my entire life."

He could believe it.

"I felt a twinge right before you came here," she admitted. "But it was dread—and I don't have to fear you, right?"

"You did," Dare said. "But I think you were feeling something else. Someone else."

She didn't deny it, asked, "Where do we go from here? Do you want me to tell you what I know about Rip? What Darius and Adele and I discussed?"

"We could start there."

"Rip's deals were bad for the U.S.—he was selling

secrets. After some of S8's agents got killed on a personal mission for Rip, S8's mission became discovering
the identity of and destroying the man who'd created
them. I was collateral damage . . . but Darius told me
that they decided they couldn't leave me behind. At
first they thought I might be working with Rip. That I
escaped with them purposely to spy on them."

"And then they saw your scars."

"Yes. They were still pretty fresh. It was the way he
kept me in line. He kept trying to break me, but I
wouldn't break. And that made him try all the more,
because that interested him. He told me I was a lot like
him." She shook her head, then drew in a deep breath
and pushed forward. "Rip knew they'd discovered
him, but he couldn't take out the whole team at once.
Even for a top-level agent, it would draw suspicion. S8
had been squeaky-clean until that point, Rip's pride
and joy."

"He was a double agent, just like Jem said."

"Is," she corrected. "Jem's right. His cover's always
been international wealthy financier. Which means his
deals wouldn't always be on the up-and-up—part of
his cover. Makes things really convenient for his dirty
games. He's gotten the CIA some of their best intel in
forever. Darius believed it was probably less than a
quarter of what he actually knows. To be alive, he's
got to be smart and play both sides of the fence. His
CIA background check shows he's a distant cousin of
a rich Boston family," she said. "But that's the biggest
lie of all."

"You're sure?"

"I had a lot of time on my hands as a young girl. I got into more places than I should've because security thought I was just playing."

"You got into his safe?"

"I watched him do it a million times," she admitted. "At the time, his security cameras weren't what they are now. He felt more secure in his own home with a lot of muscle. It changed as I got older, but by then, I knew all about him. He hated that I knew where he really came from—the fact that he was a poor orphan was information he'd managed to bury. From everyone but me."

"Did Darius know this?" Dare wanted to know.

"I told him, yes. We discussed Rip in the beginning. He wanted me to tell him everything, and then he let me try to forget." She shook her head at the irony of that. "For Rip, the thrill of the hunt, of anything new, is what he loves. He looks at all of it as a game. People are like animals to him. Pawns. He's got a great job that allows him to quietly collect power."

Dare was getting a better picture of Powell, a better idea of his motivation. But none of that mattered, because both he and Grace were the pawns. The game was already in motion.

"I can't believe I didn't see it before," he said.

"You couldn't have known," she offered.

Maybe, but now he had the real enemy in his sights, and he was locked in and ready to move.

"I feel so goddamned guilty, Dare," she spit out.

"You didn't start this."

"Rip tried to destroy S8 because they threatened to

destroy him—they discovered he was their handler, and they were never supposed to know that, which you already know. They didn't play their hand right away, though. They got me out first, and he suspected they had something to do with it. That's what made all of it personal."

"Darius doesn't blame you. Darius set this in motion—it's the only explanation. When he realized Rip was going after me . . . he knew it was time to take Rip down, even if it meant dying. Darius pulled us all together. He knew how powerful a group working together could be," Dare said.

"I could've tried to escape earlier, and on my own. I didn't have to drag S8 into it."

"S8 never lets themselves be dragged into things like that. You did it to keep yourself alive, and then you left as soon as you could."

"Yes, that's true. Freedom always comes with a price. I told myself I could do more good alive than dead. And I've been trying. I feel like it will never be enough."

"I know that feeling." He paused. "But it might."

She ran a hand along his shoulder, along the back of his neck, like she was drawing strength from his skin. Her touch was fire to his cold—he wanted, needed more.

"Let's make this right for all of us," she told him. "Let me go back to him and finish this."

"Grace, you know he'll kill you. You have too much intel on him. Even if he's still intrigued by the fact that you didn't break, even if you pretend you can use your gift for him, what makes you think he'll suddenly believe—or trust—you?"

"It's worth a try. I learned everything from my mother. The key isn't reading cards—it's reading people," she explained. "Once you center in on their needs, it's easy. And Rip had a lot of them."

"You betrayed him once before."

"He's always been fascinated with people he thinks are as strong as he is. Wants to know more about them. He'd rather keep me underground and torture me, push my limits rather than kill me fast. He'll learn more that way."

"Yeah, that's really going to convince me to let you go," Dare said angrily.

"I have so much to make up for. Don't you understand? I'm the reason my mother was killed. I fed her bad information, she gave it to Rip and he believed we were in on it together."

"But you weren't."

She shook her head. "No, Esme believed me. She loved him. She wouldn't have wanted him dead. That's all on me, and she paid the price. He must've been suspicious, or maybe he was regularly testing me all the time I was using my gift and I didn't realize it. But he knew, that night, that I was sending him to his death. I saw death and danger and I told Esme that he would be fine, that there was no danger. He knew I'd lied because he'd known that the meeting was a setup, that there was someone planning on killing him that night, so he wasn't going to go to the meeting. He killed my mother because I lied."

"That's not what happened," Dare said. "He made you think that so you'd believe you had nothing."

"Wait—you're saying my mother's alive?"

"Alive and well and living in luxury," Dare said, hating the look of utter betrayal in her eyes. Hated having to be the one to tell her. But she had a right to know, and he'd only wished she'd known earlier.

"Why? Why would she leave me behind like that?"

"I don't know."

She stared at her hands for several minutes, then met his eyes. "I don't ever want to know. And if she and Rip planned it all to break me, they were wrong."

"*That* I believe."

After he spoke, Dare pulled her to him in that way that always made her feel whole. She wanted to make him feel the same way. She wanted not to be scared of all of this.

But with him, her gift could grow. Flourish. Whether she used it or not, Dare wouldn't make her feel abnormal.

But there was no turning back.

"What's going on in there?" He tapped the side of her head.

"You don't know how often I've thought of getting revenge against Rip," she admitted. "It's not healthy, I know. But I couldn't help it."

When Rip had first let her out of the basement, she'd made tons of sketches of his property. She'd mapped out the ways she'd get off the island. How she'd kill him, make him suffer. She continued after she was rescued. Decided she would go back in there and take the revenge herself, because hiring someone to do it would be too easy—and also ineffective.

Darius and Adele both advised her to forget it. They would get revenge for their group and for her.

"They were right," he told her now. "You're way too close to this. It's too personal."

"As opposed to how close you are to the situation?" she asked wryly. "I know—you're going to give me the *I'm a professional* speech. But we both know that's bullshit too. Personal is personal—you can't just turn it off."

"I have to. If I don't, I'll get all of us killed."

Just by trusting her, he'd put himself in a tough position—she got that. She was lucky that Key and Jem seemed to believe her. That Dare did.

"Now tell me what you're really thinking about."

She gave him a tight smile at being caught. "This ability. It's something that might not come back fully. But it might . . . and I'll know things. At its height, I could feel everything. See things about people they might not have wanted me to see. And you . . . you have so many secrets, so much pain. And it's invading you. I don't want you to have to deal with that."

"I don't care if you see everything, that you'll feel my pain. Big fucking deal. Everyone has pain, so don't put that shit on me. You're the one who doesn't want to know."

She took a step back from the sheer force of his words. From the truth of them too.

How could she answer the truth?

"I've sensed it since the beginning. You told me

about it, confirmed it, but I knew that the black king was inside of you as much as the white knight was. You're both."

Now it was his turn to look as if he'd been slapped. He looked exposed, and she knew he hated that, but there was no rancor in his eyes.

No one ever liked what she had to say.

He stood then, managed, "You've known how fucked-up I am, and you still . . . you still . . ."

She embraced him, put her cheek to his chest to hear his heart beating. "I still."

Chapter Thirty-four

It was an hours-long hike through the bayou to the house. Key and Jem didn't find any bodies around the bomb shelter, figured those men had gotten away.

"They'll be back since they didn't find any of our bodies either," Jem said, like he was reading Key's mind.

The rest of the walk had been silent, both of them on high alert, guns drawn, taking the back routes they knew so well.

The bayou looked desolate and Key might've felt badly, but in his mind's eye it had always looked like this. Black-and-white. Sad. Never like the lush beauty tourists described seeing in this area.

No, the bayou had been hell personified for him.

Jem would always say, *Everything can't be protected or preserved. Some things are just shit and they'll always be shit, no excuses.*

He hadn't lived the childhood Jem had, but he wasn't sure Jem had lived it either, at least not anywhere but in his mind.

Jem was like their father's side, the one with the

crazy gene passed down from father to son. Key had heard about it for as long as he could remember, grew up like a ticking time bomb, waiting to go as nuts as everyone else. He still remained guarded. Ashamed of his family, which had been so damned poor they'd relied on the kindness of others to keep them going.

Jem was bent to excess, but he didn't seem to have taken up the constant drinking their father had. Key felt like somehow they'd both partially escaped the curse, and he wondered if now they were punishing themselves for that. Because the CIA and the military were extremely punishing jobs—and neither of them was in any hurry to have a family and pass along their genes.

Key wasn't an idiot, had known what Jem was for a long time. But he also knew the crazy streak that ran in their family was as much a gift as a curse, though it was one that all too often took people before their time. Jem had made better use of it than most, although the CIA would've wrecked him if he'd stayed in longer.

Key had been twelve the night Jem left for good.

He watched his sixteen-year-old brother get into the boat along the shore of the bayou and zoom off. Key waited and watched until morning for Jem to come back, but he never did.

Key survived five more years and did the same. Worked odd jobs around New Orleans until he could enlist; he paid an uncle to vouch for his age so he could get into the military at seventeen.

It was in the jungles of South America that he saw Jem again for the first time. To that point, Jem had offered no explanation for why he'd left.

"Couldn't take care of a twelve-year-old. Couldn't take care of myself," Jem finally told him later at the FOB.

Key stared at the man his brother had become. Jem did the same to him. "Damned proud of you, Key. I always knew you'd get out. You're different."

Key couldn't argue—he did feel different, but he knew the blood that ran through him, that it might be simply a matter of time before the family curse reared its ugly head for him.

"You're pissed."

Key didn't answer the man with the dark beard and the darker eyes, with the deep, easy laugh, instead asked, "How did you get involved in the CIA?"

"Long story."

"Always is." Key gave up, as he often did with Jem. Having his brother in his life meant asking no questions. Instead, Key did some research in order to piece together some of Jem's life.

He could never find the answers he sought.

One day, Jem might sit down and tell him, or maybe he'd die with all that knowledge inside him.

"Looks different," Jem said now as they stared at the old house, and yeah, there was that perception problem again.

"Yes," Key said hollowly.

"Looks just like I remember," Jem continued, and when Key looked at him, Jem said, "I'm not that fucked-up that I didn't know. I just had to pretend it was all right, Key."

"Good," Key told him finally, because he didn't know what else to say. His skin ached being this close to the old house, like it could still feel the sting of the whip. The bite of the belt buckle that did enough damage for teachers to notice—but Child Protective Services never came.

No one rescued him, so he'd rescued himself. No doubt he was better off for it.

But he'd always be angry at Jem, didn't know how to rid himself of that.

"Do you know what happened to them?" Jem asked.

"Assuming they drank themselves to death. Maybe they died in Katrina. Never heard, never really cared," Key said tightly, hated that this place could still be such a weakness for him; he didn't do weak anymore.

Jem clapped a hand on his shoulder. "You ever want to know, just ask."

"Will do." Key turned his back on the land that for all he knew still belonged to his family and went back to the shed where the old Jeep was covered as though it was the most special treasure.

Right now, it sure damned was.

"Why'd you even come back here?" Jem asked as he clambered into the Jeep and hot-wired it. The engine started to turn, then sputter.

Key held up a hand and went under the hood to poke around. "Why'd you?"

"Couldn't leave you alone again."

"I've done just fine."

"Yeah, you have. But you don't believe that yet."

"Try now," Key directed, refusing to answer his question. The Jeep purred. Gas tank was full. He got into the passenger's side as Jem let the Jeep idle for a moment.

"Don't you know by now that there are no coincidences?" Jem said finally. "Everything goes according to a greater plan."

"They're not my plans," Key said, and Jem stared at his brother.

"You saved Dare—that wasn't according to plan."

"And look where it got me."

"Where you're supposed to be."

"Looking after you again?" Key shot back harshly.

Key's words cut Jem like a knife. Key had never thrown that in his face. And Jem was well aware he might've pushed it too far this time.

"Where would you go if you didn't have to worry about me full-time?" Jem asked finally.

"I have no fucking idea." Key sounded more furious about that than anything.

Key had had the weight of the entire family on him for so long, while Jem had easily slipped out of the noose of responsibility.

Key had been through hell, according to Jem's sources, and Jem figured he was as good as anyone to lead him out. "How about you let me worry about you for a while, then?"

"You're going to keep me out of trouble."

"Now, don't go putting words in my mouth." Jem lit up a Cuban cigar he'd lifted from the head shrink. "I'll get you into enough trouble so that you forget yours."

Key didn't say anything for a long time, and then, "Let's go pick up Dare and Grace."

Darius could barely stand, let alone fight, but all he had to do now was hang on. He'd sent the message he'd needed to, hoped Dare was on the bayou, ready and willing to receive it. Either way, his boy would get notice of the safe house blowing up.

He had to pretend that the man standing in front of him had broken him, and that galled him most of all. He had searched for this man nonstop for nearly a year, had finally found him, had taken his daughter from him, but the guy refused to give up. He'd disappeared for five years as he killed off members of S8 operatives' families, but finally, Darius was able to track him again.

Now, after two months of living in this goddamned cell, Darius refused to give up.

"Thanks for the intel, Darius. It was a big help."

"Fuck. You." Finally he got to his feet, swore he heard the crunch of his own ribs as he did so. He refused to give in to the pain. It had always been there. Always would be.

"If you'd just given up looking for me, this never would've happened."

"Fight me," he demanded.

"I'm not stupid, Darius."

"Which means you're an old man now. Just like me."

"Just like you, I never stopped fighting. I just do it differently."

"Does this"—Darius looked down at his bruised and battered body and finished—"look different to you?"

The man in front of him smirked a little. "My time— our time—is over. I just want to live out my life."

"You'd never be satisfied with that," Darius told him. "Old warriors are a fucking pathetic thing. All the drive, a failing mind and body. Warriors need to die young."

"There is nothing on me that's failing."

Darius raised his chin and asked the question he hadn't ever wanted answered, not since he'd taken Grace and finally seen pictures of the notoriously private Richard Powell. But suddenly, he needed to know. "Tell me how you managed to survive the fight and get out of the jungle."

When they'd left the house on the bayou, Dare had managed to grab only the fire safe along with Esme's picture. Now he watched Grace sift through the contents of the small box, looking for anything that could possibly help them.

She was sticking her hand inside the broken plastic band on the inside of the box. She stuck two fingers in there and winced as she pulled them out. Before he could ask if she was okay, she opened what looked like an old photo. It was folded in half, practically crackled when she opened it.

She stared down at it, engrossed. Her head cocked, eyes widened, and a flush broke out along her face and neck.

Before he could stop her, she had the gun pointed at him. "Stay back."

"Did you have another vision?"

"Stay. Back."

He did. Arms up. "Grace, talk to me."

"Why? So you can lie to me more, just like your father did?"

The picture fluttered to the floor—an old S8 picture, maybe the only one that existed. He didn't think Darius was particularly sentimental, didn't know why he would've kept such a memory.

"I'm leaving. Give me the keys to the truck."

"You can't leave. You're in—"

"Danger? With or without you, it seems. Keys, or I will shoot you, and you know I'll hit you. I've made it this far. I'm not letting that happen again. Do you understand?"

"No, I don't. Fuck." He ran a frustrated hand through his hair but tossed her the keys anyway.

She should've known it was too easy. When she raised her arms to get the keys, he was on her. She got off a shot into the floor, but he had her, against the wall, gun facing down. Useless.

"You promised you were telling the truth."

"I am."

"How can you look at me and lie like that?"

He leaned his forehead against hers. "What did you see in that picture that upset you?"

"You're serious?"

"Dead serious."

She closed her eyes and wished, for the first time, that her gift wasn't broken, but she knew Dare wasn't lying. "Rip is standing next to Darius."

He jerked back, stunned. Grabbed the photo from the floor. "Powell?"

She nodded, pointed. "Right there."

"That's Simon—he's dead."

"That's Rip, and he's alive," she insisted, and he paled, and oh God, he hadn't known. "I've never seen that before. If Darius had ever shown it to me . . ."

But Dare wasn't exactly listening. He was half clutching the table like it was the only thing holding him up. Simon. Rip. One and the same, which meant that Darius had worked and trained side by side with the man who'd ended up killing the team members and their families.

"It doesn't make sense," he whispered, but they both knew it did. Rip had inserted himself into his own creation, worked side by side with the group he'd ended up killing.

Grace realized she still held the gun. She placed it on the table and went to Dare, to apologize, offer comfort, but he literally held her at arm's length, putting out his hand so she couldn't get close.

"I'm sorry. My sense of self-preservation is strong."

"Mine too," he managed, his voice like gravel, his expression battered.

"Does it bother you that I thought you were a certain kind of man, like Rip? Or is it worse that you are that certain kind of man when it's called for?"

"Honestly, I don't know."

Tell me how you managed to survive the fight and get out of the jungle.

"When you run toward something instead of running from it, you'd be surprised how that forces people to let their resistance down. Confuses them."

"There were over twenty soldiers."

Rip shrugged. "I'd dealt with worse."

"I trusted you, *Simon*."

"That's what made you so easy to use." He paused, only because he hadn't heard that name in forever. Hadn't been able to come down here and face Darius either. Just had his security personnel keeping an eye on him, which meant they'd had to stop Darius from escaping and beating the shit out of them as well.

By going back to being Simon, using his given name, and inserting himself into S8, he'd finally had people in his life he cared about—and who cared about him. He couldn't decide if he'd ruined it or if Darius had by going back on the promise they'd made.

We don't try to find out who's behind S8. No matter what.

Because that would be deadly and stupid and would solve nothing. Would make everything worse, in fact. But once Darius realized that their handler had brought them back together on that final job for the handler's own personal gain, all bets were off.

Besides, it had only been him and Adele left to break the promise. Or so they'd thought . . .

"You broke the promise," Rip said, as if that explained it all. And maybe, for him, it did. Growing up as Simon, everything was always extremes—black or white. That's why he'd moved through life and his jobs so easily, how he'd slid into the persona of Richard Powell. When you didn't have gray areas, you knew exactly how to operate.

"And you lied to us the entire time!" Darius pointed out with a roar.

"Necessity," Rip dismissed. "Didn't mean I didn't put my life on the line, same as you."

Darius couldn't argue that—Simon had been on every mission, with them every step of the way. Until . . . "You should never have called on us again. Not under the official S8 moniker."

Would Rip ever admit his fault?

"I was in a bind. S8 was the only thing that could help me. I didn't think that men would die. I didn't do that on purpose.

"And then you turned around and broke your promise. I suggested that rule to protect you. If you'd never gone looking for me . . ."

"No one from S8 would've died. Beyond the men who'd already died for you," Darius said through gritted teeth. "You broke the promise long before we did. And what about Grace?"

"She was mine. And no one takes what's mine."

"S8 was yours too. So no one takes what's yours . . . except you."

"Except me."

Chapter Thirty-five

The ride through the bayou back to New Orleans was tense at best, but going during the daylight ensured that Powell's men couldn't make any major moves. Jem and Key both knew the bayou roads as well as, if not better than, Dare, and the brothers took them on a wild ride until they ended up in Gunner's garage.

From there, Gunner guided them into his shop through the panic room. When Grace looked inside, she paused and moved backward quickly into Dare's chest.

"I can't," she told him, and when he looked inside he saw exactly why. For a long moment, they all stood there, and then Jem said, "Can you just go through to the upstairs, Grace? We'll all be with you."

"God, I feel stupid," she said.

"You shouldn't," Dare assured her. He took her hand, and Jem led the way in, looking around as if clearing the place. The door at the top creaked open and they could see Gunner at the top of the stairs.

"We're coming up," Jem told Gunner, who waved them through.

"Come on, baby—better to get inside fast while we haven't been spotted," Dare said, and that was the impetus Grace needed to get moving. Holding tight to his hand, she walked in front of him, almost at a march, with her head held forward. Key was the last in, securing things behind them.

Once they were all on the stairs, Gunner shut the big door leading to the garage. She jumped when it closed with a decisive bang, but she kept going. Finally, they were at the top of the stairs, and she breathed a small sigh of relief as Avery hugged her, and then Dare.

"Didn't mean to scare you," he told her while her arms were around his neck.

"I know." She pulled back. "Grace, I've got some clothes for you."

Grace followed Avery up another flight of stairs.

"They okay up there?" Dare asked Gunner, who nodded.

"It's all bulletproof and tinted windows, but Avery knows not to take too long. We'll sleep in the panic room, if you think Grace can handle it."

"She'll have to," Dare said. "I'm going to go up and check on them."

"Don't blame you." Gunner went back to scanning the monitors that showed the surrounding streets.

He heard them talking as he went up the stairs. They were talking about Darius, Grace sharing with Avery things she knew about him.

He tended to forget that Avery didn't know the man she was risking her life for. It couldn't be easy for her to know that Darius was the one who'd gotten her mother killed and put Avery's back to the wall.

But Grace . . . she spoke highly of Darius. She was telling Avery how he played the guitar so loud, the neighbors would complain. And that whenever he tried to cook he'd start small fires in the kitchen.

She told Avery that she had his eyes. His smile. His laugh.

To hear Darius talked about in that way, a way he'd never known his father, was cool. Because his dad had always been rough, gruff, no-nonsense. But with Grace, Darius had obviously been different, no doubt treating her as he would've treated Avery.

The closest Dare had ever come to seeing his father's softer side was when he played guitar. Sometimes he'd find the phone next to him while he played his music, and now, listening to Avery talk, he realized what Darius had been doing.

He would call Avery's mom, not say anything, but rather, just play his guitar so she could hear him over the phone line. An *I'm thinking of you* thing, which was romantic and heartbreaking all at once . . . hell, it made Dare finger the pick around his neck and wonder how much a love like that might've changed Darius if he'd let it.

Dare's whole life might've been different, no matter how often Darius told Dare that he'd been born ready for the military. There was truth in that.

Now he stood against the doorjamb, listening to Grace's memories, watching Avery smile, knowing this was all the calm before the storm.

Avery would take care of Grace, would keep her safe. They would become friends—Dare knew that for certain.

It made the rest of his choices that much easier.

Jem and Gunner cooked, and by midafternoon, they were all eating in the back room with the monitors surrounding them. The mood was surprisingly upbeat, which tended to happen when everyone lived through a mission, no matter what other obstacles abounded. There was laughing and teasing and plenty of food to satisfy them.

Even Grace smiled a few times, seemed to feel as if the group trusted her.

Dare was as worried as hell about her. Held her hand under the table. Wanted to take her into his arms and tell her everything would be okay.

Wanted her to be able to see the future and know that it would. But she didn't want that gift. Claimed he was the one bringing it out in her.

He finished his gumbo, drank his beer and switched to water. After dessert, which Gunner got from the restaurant he owned, it was time for business. Dare could tell by the way the men got restless and Avery fidgeted. Grace became quiet.

"You really think Darius is with Powell? That he's the one feeding Powell the intel?" Avery asked finally. Jem pushed his plate away, and Key took a long drink from his beer.

"Yes—he's doing it purposely," Dare said after a long moment. "I don't think he got captured on purpose, and I think he held out as long as he could."

"What's Powell's next move?" Key asked.

"He's going to ask for a trade," Gunner said, and Grace paled.

"He's not getting it," Dare assured her.

"What *is* he getting?" Grace asked. Before anyone could answer her, Gunner's shop phone rang.

"I think that's for you," Gunner said to Dare, who braced himself before picking up the phone.

"How does he know where we are if no one followed us?" Grace asked.

"I left the number where he could find it in the underground room," Dare told her before he spoke into the phone. "Dare speaking."

"Why don't you put me on speakerphone so you can all listen?" Richard Powell suggested, and Dare did as he asked, Powell's voice filling the room. "Hello, everyone. Hi, Gracie—I've missed you. I hear you've been doing well."

Grace held tightly to the bottle of beer she'd been drinking—it was slightly raised, as if she was ready to smash it against the phone.

"What's your endgame?" Dare asked.

"Grace."

"Forget it."

"There's someone I think you'll be interested in hearing from," Powell said. "Say hello, Darius."

Dare's gut tightened. Avery put a hand over her mouth, and Grace cried silently when Darius's voice came over the line.

"Dare, I'm fine—"

"He won't be," Powell broke in. "And I wouldn't

call the shape he's in fine, although I know he can handle more than the average man."

"Don't hurt him," Grace said, even as Dare attempted to stop her from talking.

"Grace, you know how I've been worried about you."

"I'll bet you've been," she said fiercely.

"You come back and it'll all go away. Dare gets his father back and Dare gets to live, as do the rest of your new friends."

"I need proof of life," Dare cut in. "You could've taped his voice." He gave Powell the number to a throwaway cell, and a minute later, Powell said, "Check your phone."

Darius, holding today's *New York Times*. Gunner pulled up the front page on the computer—a match.

Darius looked horrible, but Dare ignored Grace's gasp of surprise behind him.

"Speak to me, Powell," Dare told him. "Let's keep it short and simple."

"Short and simple? Fine. Grace for Darius. A fair trade."

Grace shook her head at the impossible decision her stepfather had put out there.

"What's fair about it?"

"Normally, I'd just take them both. It's a onetime offer."

"And what about me?"

"What about you?"

"You keep trying to kill me. And others around me."

"You want me to call off the dogs? That's not part of the deal." Powell said. "Darius for Grace. You have twenty-four hours to decide. Feel free not to take that long—and I'll feel free to proceed as I've been with Darius and hope he holds up."

The last thing they heard over the line before it cut out was Darius's screams.

Grace didn't realize she'd dropped the bottle until she heard the crash and tinkle of broken glass on the floor. There was a long pause, and until Avery put a hand on her shoulder, she hadn't realized she'd been holding her breath.

She exhaled, held on to the chair; her legs felt shaky.

"I'll do it," she said, and they all started talking at once. She put up her hand and told them, "I'm the reason you're involved in all of this. I'm the problem. I'll go to him and he'll free Darius."

"First of all, I don't trust him to make that trade. Even if I did, I already told you, I'm not letting you go back there. It's a death sentence, no matter how much you think otherwise. Manipulation only works to a certain point with Powell," Dare told her.

"I'll do better this time," she said. "Look, if I can prove to him that not only did I survive, but my gift is fine, he'll want to keep me alive, at least to test me. Sometimes a fake psychic's better than a real one. People only want to hear good things—everyone says, 'I really want to know,' but no one does. So when you tell them something they want to believe, it's perfect. Deal's done—I'm a magician."

"And when it doesn't happen?"

"I always say, there's no time limit."

"Powell's never going to buy that, Grace. He hasn't even mentioned your gift as a reason to get you back. I won't make the trade, even in the short term while we plan a rescue to get you back. You have enough nightmares."

"So do you. So will Darius. So do all of us. You've done everything you could to protect me. Let me make this sacrifice for all of you. I trust you'll save me." Grace looked around wildly, hoping that one of them would be nodding. Instead, they all looked at her solemnly, with Jem shaking his head.

"Grace, honey, look—if I thought you had something to do with Powell, I wouldn't let you do it because that would be suicide for us. But I do trust you and it's still suicide for all of us, and even I'm not that crazy," Jem said.

"Maybe that's the problem—maybe we're not acting crazy enough. I'm willing to do this—you all need to let me," Grace insisted. "You have no right to tell me what I can't do with my own life. For Darius. He saved me—it's time for me to return the favor."

They were all still arguing an hour later. It was exactly what Dare had been hoping for.

He'd remained quiet, watching Grace argue with Jem and Avery and Gunner. That was expected of him after hearing and seeing the condition Darius was in. He hated to see Grace and Avery so upset about it, but it was necessary.

Finally, he muttered, "I need some time alone to think," and went into another room.

The arguing didn't stop when he left. He just hoped Key would stop Grace from attempting to follow him.

He dialed the number, waited to hear Powell's voice. "About time—I was just getting ready to kill your father."

"Thanks for holding off on that."

"You've thought about my proposal. I hope you understand that saying no won't change anything you're currently experiencing. In fact, I'm having a good time, so I might not want to stop at all."

"Listen good, Powell, because I don't repeat myself. Instead of the trade you proposed, here's my proposal—me and Key for Darius and Grace."

He forced himself silent, screwed his eyes tight and prayed Gunner would keep Grace away from him long enough for him to complete this deal. Lying to her was bad enough—having her know about it beforehand would break his damned heart.

Finally, Powell spoke. "None of you will ever discuss S8. Especially Grace."

"Right," Dare agreed.

"And I believe that because?"

"Grace hasn't spoken about it yet, and she's had the opportunity. They all know I'd be the first to die if they do. They know you won't stop coming for them. All they want is to live out their lives with some semblance of normalcy."

"What kind of life will you and Key be living?"

"Whatever kind you decide."

Chapter Thirty-six

When Dare came back into the room, Grace came right over to him.

"I'm sorry, Dare. So sorry it's come down to this," she murmured into his neck.

"We'll figure it out," he told her.

"It's time to lock down for the night. We're vulnerable until we make a decision," Gunner told them, pointed to the panic room.

When Dare looked at Grace, he saw her blanch at the thought of spending an extended amount of time down there. She'd barely made it walking through, and that had been a by-the-skin-of-her-teeth experience.

He already had other plans for her, so when she looked at him and pleaded, "I can't stay down there," he conceded easily.

"Tonight, we don't have to. After that . . ."

"Okay, yes, after that, I'll be okay."

It was a lie, but he allowed it because she really believed it. It was one of the many reasons he'd fallen for her. She was as strong as anything. He believed she would turn herself over to Powell if given the whisper of a chance, which was why he'd moved so quickly.

He didn't need to be psychic to know her plans. Now he had to hope her gift remained faulty for the next twelve hours. She'd told him that stress made it harder to pick apart the feelings, and she was wrapped up in her own stress and fear.

Gunner wasn't happy with Dare's decision to stay outside the panic room with Grace, gave Dare the side eye, but didn't say anything except, "Keep the walkie-talkie close—we'll be monitoring the cameras all night. Windows stay closed."

"Yes, Mom," Dare told him dryly, and Jem snorted.

He led Grace upstairs to one of the bedrooms, shut the door behind them and waited for the alarms to lock into place. "Come on—come to bed with me."

She did that, fit into his arms. "I won't make you choose between us, Dare—I won't."

"I'm not."

"You are. This is my decision. You'll never forgive yourself for letting your father die."

"Darius is more than capable of taking care of himself."

"He sacrificed for me."

"He did that so you wouldn't have to," Dare told her.

There was no easy decision here, only heartbreak. She refused to let him take a single ounce of guilt. "Please, we can figure this out, but you have to get Darius out. Promise me that."

"Promise." His hand wound around the back of her

neck, pulled her close, and she managed a smile, the first he'd seen in hours.

"Promise you won't make a decision without me."

He kissed her, and it felt like a promise, especially when he dragged her toward the bed.

"Promise," she insisted, and he murmured, "Promise." She ignored the nagging voice in the back of her head, choosing instead to revel in the pleasure of his mouth on her belly, her breasts, moving down between her legs to lick her core.

He took her over and over, even when she begged for mercy. She lost track of everything except the complete wash of pleasure.

And when he climbed up her body, kissing her breasts and neck, nuzzling her, she wrapped her arms around him and he did the same, didn't try to make love to her, despite the fact that she felt his hardness press against her.

"We both have scars," she whispered. "Lots of them."

"Yeah." He pushed off her and moved away, sat on the edge of the bed. Everything was weighing heavily on him, she knew. It was the same for her.

When he finally turned to look at her over his shoulder, he looked as haunted as she felt. "Grace, I won't lose you."

"It's the best thing for you."

"What's best for you?"

"I don't know if that's ever mattered. Not even sure it's supposed to."

"It should—it *is* supposed to," he told her. "I'm not letting you do what you're thinking of."

"Just don't let me go tonight, Dare." She put her arms around him, nuzzled her face against the back of his neck before kissing it, working slowly down his back, along his shoulders.

Finally, he lifted his head and turned to look at her over his shoulder. "Thank you."

"You're the one who saved me."

"Somehow, you're saving me," Dare told her. "Come over here."

She moved to straddle him, still wearing just a T-shirt and nothing underneath. His hands moved along her thighs, around to cup her ass and pull her closer. Her sex brushed his erection and she shifted while he groaned.

She kissed him until she couldn't wait any longer, lowered herself along the length of him. For a long moment, they just breathed, and then she began to take him, moving up and down. Running the show.

When he kissed her, it was full of an aching hunger, like he couldn't get enough of her. She rocked against him, taking him in deeply, bringing them both to the inevitable end.

He groaned her name against her neck, then the word *love* . . . it was the only promise she hadn't asked for and the one she'd wanted the most.

Key and Avery monitored the computers together for the first shift, an arrangement Avery was pretty sure Jem had orchestrated. As he and Gunner slept across the room, she helped Key keep track of the surrounding activity.

She couldn't count this as being alone with him, but it was the best she'd get. She wondered if he thought about their time in the bar, or her tattoo.

Her skin tingled whenever she was close to him. She wondered if she should've kissed him on the dock, if he'd have pushed her away. Then she told herself this wasn't the time to be thinking about her personal life.

Then again, her personal and professional lives had collided, and she'd never be able to pick them apart again. "It's really quiet out there."

"Almost too quiet," he agreed. "I'd say it's not normal, but I don't know what the hell is anymore."

"You don't think that Grace should allow herself to be the bait, do you? Powell will see that coming from a million miles away. He wants her dead."

Key nodded, turned his gaze to her. "What would you do?"

"I'd do anything for my family. For the person I love," she said, and suddenly, without a doubt, she knew Key was telling her what was going to happen. She'd suspected that since Dare had moved away from the group, but she didn't want to believe it.

She knew better than to ask outright. All she could do was let Dare do what he needed to for the people he loved.

"So, the pickpocketing," he said, changing the subject quickly, before she could think too much or ask questions. "That's a handy skill."

"My mom used to hire former inmates to help her on bounties. They were all reformed, but they had a lot of skills, and I was eager to learn. Pickpocket, car thief, safecracking—for a kid, it was better than Disneyland. But martial arts were always my favorite. Mom was big on being able to defend yourself. So I picked up different kinds of life skills."

"What about technology?" he asked, and she shook her head.

"I can get around the Web, but we never had a hacker come in to help us with bounties," she admitted. "Are you good at that?"

"Not me—Jem is. I'm a better hitter," he said.

"I guess we do make a good team."

He grunted in reply, and she took that as a yes.

"Maybe you can show me some of your self-defense tricks sometime."

"Girls shouldn't fight—they break too easily," he said finally.

"Good thing I'm not a girl," she told him coolly, and yes, he remembered those kisses. She was all woman, and he still dreamt about her at night. She made him all hot and bothered, but she was still too young, too innocent, despite all the tricks she could pull.

Then again, she'd also seen far too much in her life, and he knew all about that.

He stared at her again. "I think you know how to take care of yourself pretty well already."

"There's always more to learn. Are you willing to teach me?"

They weren't talking about self-defense any longer—at least she wasn't. She felt a hundred degrees hotter despite the chilly room. Wanted to touch his skin, breathe him in. Surrender to him in a way she'd never done with anyone.

"I don't know if I can," he said honestly. "I don't know if I'm ready to teach anyone anything."

"I think you are."

"I think you're giving me too much credit, Avery." He turned back to the computer monitor, and she knew she'd gotten as much as she was going to get that night.

Jem paced the floor, not looking at Key. He hadn't been told any more than Grace or Avery or Gunner, but obviously, Key and Dare had decided to move forward with a plan without consulting anyone.

"I know you're pissed—," Key started, but Jem waved him off in favor of talking to Dare.

"Maybe vengeance isn't the answer," Jem said.

"It's the only answer," Dare countered.

"It's going to burn you out and leave you with nothing. You've got to have more driving you. More than pure, white-hot revenge. Think about karma."

Dare leveled a gaze at Jem. "Karma hasn't exactly worked."

"You're living and breathing and you've got the one thing Powell wants most in the world."

"And you want me to use her as leverage."

"She wants that too. Don't let your dick get in the way."

"And then what?" Dare demanded. "He's not going to let us live once he has her. He's not going to let her live. And even if he was—"

"I'm not saying he keeps her forever—I'm saying use her as bait, letting her fake her way through the psychic bullshit. There's no way he's not coming after her while you and Key are off doing his bidding."

"I'm counting on it—and you and Gunner and Avery—to keep Grace safe."

Jem ran a hand through his hair and muttered something about doing it but not liking it. Then he grabbed Key and hugged him. Held out his hand to Dare and said, "You take care of him or I'm coming after you."

"Consider it done," Dare said.

"Avery and Grace will be safe if it's the last damned thing I do."

The men nodded, and Jem let them out the front door, relocked the place and prepared for the fallout that would soon follow.

Chapter Thirty-seven

Grace slept hard. She blamed the stress of the day, the impatient and then slow lovemaking . . . Her dreams had all been good ones.

At some point when she was drifting off, Dare had told her he loved her. She wasn't sure if she said it back to him in her dreams or out loud, but she knew she would tell him now.

When her eyes opened, she knew what she had to do. She would call Rip herself. Go to him. Force the group's hand to come get her.

She turned over, saw the bed empty next to her, the pillow still dented from where Dare had slept. The light was on in the bathroom, the door cracked open.

"Dare?" she asked softly, got no response. It was too quiet.

With a growing dread, she kicked the covers off and headed to the bathroom. The empty bathroom.

No. *No no no no no.*

She wouldn't realize she'd been screaming that out loud until later, when her voice was hoarse. She wanted to run out the door, tried to, but Jem was there, and then Avery and Gunner. Avery held her tightly, forced her to sit down and breathe.

Grace crumpled. For the first several minutes, she could do nothing but cry. *You should've known.*

Maybe she had and just pushed it aside, the way she'd been doing to her gift since it had started returning.

If she'd used it, maybe she could've stopped him.

But she knew that was a lie.

"Tactically, it was the right move for Dare—you have to know that," Jem told her when she looked up at him, wiped the tears from her cheeks with her palms.

"I don't know anything, obviously."

"He and Key went together. They did it for us," Avery said softly, and Grace realized she hadn't known what the men were up to either. Her expression held that slightly stunned and betrayed look Grace knew she wore as her own. She squeezed Avery's hand.

"It's a huge sacrifice," she whispered hollowly. "I would never have asked them to do that."

"Me neither," Avery said. "Which is exactly why they did. It's who they are."

"You can't let them do this—you have to bring them back," Grace insisted. "Rip is . . . he's a monster."

"Dare did this for you most of all. I can't—won't—take that away from him," Jem said. "All a man's got is his word, his honor, and you and Avery will be safe now."

"You can't be sure of that," she protested weakly.

"I'm sure of my brother and I'm sure of Dare. You

are too," he said quietly. She wanted to shake him, to scream until her throat went raw and silent. Break everything in the house.

But none of it would bring the man she loved back to her.

"I'll go get him myself," she threatened.

"And make his sacrifice mean nothing? Darlin', you will get him killed," Jem broke in. "Dare wants you safe. Happy. Give him that."

Could she? It wasn't fair that he'd shown her such happiness only to have it taken away by one of the cruelest choices of all. "I'm supposed to rebuild again—without him—knowing what I've brought on him?"

"He's a big boy—he chose it."

"He's selfish," she spat.

"Maybe, Grace. But they didn't see another option to keep us free," Avery said.

"Maybe we didn't mind not being free," Grace argued.

"We didn't make that clear enough, then," Avery agreed. "Or else he knew we weren't making the decisions for the right reasons."

Grace couldn't argue with that, not completely. Fear-based decisions were never good, never right. She'd been planning on taking danger for the freedom, and maybe that hadn't been the right price. Maybe the trade-off wouldn't have been worth it.

"I don't trust Rip," she said tiredly.

"Neither do Dare and Key," Jem said. "One of

them's going to die—and I guarantee it will be Powell."

She wished she could be as sure.

Avery wasn't sure if she was angrier at Key for not telling her or at herself for not getting it. He'd hinted. She'd suspected what Dare would do, but to have the two of them sacrificing themselves for this newfound team . . .

It didn't matter whom she was angry at—the fact was that it was there, balled up, tense and coiled. She knew it could rise up at any moment and she'd lash out at whoever was closest.

Dare and Key must've discussed it beforehand, but when? They'd always all been together—she would've noticed the two of them with their heads together for a plan like this.

She'd seen no signs of distress on Key's face, but with his training, she supposed she wouldn't have.

Did you really think you'd be the one to break through his emotions?

"You all right?" Gunner asked now. He handed her a plate—eggs, bacon, toast. Slid coffee next to her. "Eat."

She didn't want to, but Gunner watched her like a hawk. She forked some eggs, ate a strip of bacon, wished Gunner didn't know anything about her feelings for Key.

"I don't understand the plan—Powell will kill them," she said finally.

Gunner poured himself more coffee. "That's the point."

"He was never going to let any of us go."

"*Never* is the key word." He looked up at her. "They'll have to jump through some hoops to get there."

"Powell's hoping one of them kills the other."

"He's hoping no one's watching Grace carefully." As he spoke, Grace was downstairs in the cement-block room, trying to avoid a panic attack.

Avery had offered to stay with Grace, but Grace said she'd rather be by herself. Before Avery had left her alone, she'd asked Grace, "Can you see . . . everything?"

"Sadly, no. Only when it's about me."

"So if someone's coming to get you—"

"I should know." She rubbed her arms. "Maybe."

"Reassuring," Avery had said, but she'd done so with a smile, and Grace had laughed a little.

"You're more pissed at Key than Dare," Gunner said now. "You should stay away from him. Like Jem told you, he's not good for anyone."

"I guess you've all had a blast discussing my love life." She paused. "What about you—are you good for anyone?"

"Me? *Chère*, I'm worse. Way worse."

"So I shouldn't be with anyone, then?"

"Never a good idea to fall for your team members," Gunner advised.

"I never said I fell for you," she told him.

"True—you didn't."

"What if I did?"

"Don't bullshit me—you fell for Key the second you saw him."

"How do you know?"

"I was there, Avery—watching to make sure you didn't get yourself killed."

"Do you always warn women away from you?"

"Only the ones I like," he told her.

Chapter Thirty-eight

Dare and Key headed out to the airport while they waited for Powell's call. Dare knew they would be tested. There was no way Powell would trust them right off the bat to come directly to his private island.

There was no way he was ever going to trust them at all, but he and Key were prepared for that eventuality. Welcomed it as part of their plan, conceived quietly enough by Key, who'd of course foreseen the obvious but came up with a way to attack Powell that he might not suspect.

And even if he did, well, Dare and Key together could be unstoppable.

A day earlier, when he'd come into the bunker to get them into the car, Key had told Dare about it quickly. He'd let Grace into the back of the Jeep, and as the two men walked around the side of the car, Key had spoken quickly and quietly, laying out what he was willing to do if push came to shove, Grace never knowing that they'd had that conversation.

Now they sat in the car, watching the planes ascend

over them. When Powell finally called, it was close to three in the morning.

"I've got a job for you two," he told them. "I want to see how well you'll perform. Consider this your test."

"Test us if you have to, but leave the others out of it," Dare said.

"I'm a man of my word," Powell said, and Key mouthed *bullshit*. "It's too late for me to get the jet out now. You'll have to fly commercial. Go to the airport hotel. You'll find a package addressed to you, Dare, waiting for you at the front desk. Check in and you'll know what to do."

Powell hung up without saying anything further, and Dare drove the car toward the hotel. While Key waited in the car, Dare picked up the package, checked in, went up in the elevator as he read the directive.

They were headed out to Belgrade in the morning. But he was as sure as hell not staying in the hotel that night.

He was just as sure Powell would never have expected him to. He left his key, TV on, stuff from the minibar taken. He ordered room service for two, accepted it and then took off out the balcony of the empty room next door. Key had moved into the driver's seat, headed down the back road, and they stayed in the car until it was time for the flight, mapping out plans.

After consulting with Jem on the new phones Gunner had given them, they finally had a course of action that would be perfect.

Grace had spent the first twenty-four hours without Dare pacing. She knew she was driving the others crazy, but they were either too kind or too stressed to say anything to her.

Avery kept offering her decaf tea. Gunner offered to give her a tattoo. Jem offered her cigarettes and whiskey, and those she accepted. But it didn't stop her from the steady, restless pacing, as though there was a destination she was attempting to reach.

"Grace, are you, ah, you know?" Jem touched his head.

"Trying to get a vision? I'm not trying. I think it's trying to get through to me."

"Have more whiskey," he suggested.

She knew he was just as worried as she was, could see in his eyes that he could think of nothing but his younger brother. He'd told her earlier that he'd offered to trade places with Key, but that Key and Dare had decided that taking down Rip together was the way it was meant to be.

She also knew that more whiskey would make it easier to get her into the panic room tonight. It had taken several shots, Avery holding her hand and Jem distracting her with mindless television to make her forget that *panic room* could easily equal *panic attack*.

She'd fallen asleep and dreamt of Dare kidnapping her. She supposed it could've been worse.

She took two shots in a row to calm down and startled when Gunner's shop phone rang. Gunner went for it but Grace stopped him.

"Don't. It's for me."

"It's him, isn't it?"

"Yes."

The three of them gathered around her as she picked up the phone. There would be no speakerphone for this conversation, even though Grace would tell them everything.

She picked up the phone and said hello. Her heart raced when Rip said, "You knew I'd call."

She ignored that. "Why are you calling? I thought you got what you wanted."

"Ah, Gracie, you knew Dare and Key were my second choices."

"Is Darius freed yet?"

"Unfortunately, no. Not until Dare and Key are done with their test period, which, from the reports trickling in, isn't going all that well."

She fisted her hand around the receiver and fought the urge to scream at him. Remaining as icy as he was had always been the right way to handle him. He appreciated that, and in his sick world, that was the way to get through to him. "You're rethinking your offer, then?"

"Yes. I tossed and turned. And you know how I hate to lose sleep. But I've decided to reach out to you once more, for old times' sake. For our family."

She couldn't believe he could say that with any kind of straight face. He was deliberately baiting her, but she wasn't biting.

Finally he laid it out for her. "If you come back, I'll get Dare, Key and Darius back in one piece."

"You promised Dare already."

"You're compromised beyond saving, and I'm going to get you, one way or another. And if Dare's willing to risk his life for you, he's thinking with more than his brain, which means he isn't thinking. Which makes him a liability to me."

She closed her eyes, leaned against the wall to hold herself up. "What do you want me to do?"

"I'll send someone for you."

"I want to come to you on my own steam," she said firmly. "And you won't kill my escort."

"No one walks onto the island but you."

"Fine. And how do I know you'll keep your end of the bargain?"

A long pause and then, "Grace, I thought you knew everything."

But Rip doesn't. And she had to walk a tightrope very carefully to stay interesting enough for Rip to keep her alive. "Dare and Key aren't on the island, so keep them off. And Darius can leave with my escort."

She was met with silence, and she prayed she'd gotten it right. Finally he said, "Consider it done. Darius can go when you get here. I'll let you have a heartfelt reunion so you can convince him you want to be here. I don't want any further rescue efforts. They're starting to bore the hell out of me."

She echoed his words. "Consider it done."

Rip cut the line. She hung up the phone with a shaking hand and turned to Jem and Gunner. "Can either of you fly a chopper?"

Dare and Key deplaned after midnight Belgrade time and weren't surprised to find themselves surrounded in the parking lot when they went to grab the rental car that Powell had reserved for them.

There were sixteen men. Key muttered the information to Dare before they'd even gotten close.

Key's specialty was hand-to-hand. According to Jem, there was no one better. Now the former soldier's casual posture belied his ability to do significant damage to his opponents.

A gun clicked and the tallest man told them, "Come with us."

"Afraid those aren't my orders," Dare said almost apologetically to him. "But thanks for the nice offer."

"We're your new orders."

"I'm afraid we'll have to decline coming with you," Dare told them. "If you try to force us, we'll kill all of you."

The men laughed, the tall one telling him, "You can't take all of us down."

Dare studied them—he could do it alone if he had to. Luckily, he didn't have to. He waited until one of the men approached Key, gun drawn.

Classic mistake—he'd held the gun too close to Key. Key grabbed it, slammed the man to the ground, and emptied the clip before throwing the gun at the head of attacker number two. It distracted him enough for Key to jump him, while Dare went for the tall guy, disarming him by slamming his wrist against the hood of the nearest car.

Even as they fought, Dare knew what was coming, knew they'd have to surrender at some point. Until then, they took out their aggression on these men as they waited for the inevitable.

When the hood went over his head, Dare flashed back to Hell Week during BUD/S training and SERE—weeks he didn't know if he'd survive. But he did and he would again, and if he played this endgame well, Powell would be the only one who didn't.

Chapter Thirty-nine

Jem was convinced it was the worst plan in the world, if not the most difficult, far-fetched one, which was exactly why he was on board with it.

"He won't kill me on sight," Grace had insisted.

"That a psychic thing or a wishful-thinking thing?" Jem asked, and Grace had said honestly, "A little of both."

Now, with Gunner and Avery hidden in the back, the helo rose over the ocean stretch that would deliver them to Rip's mysterious island. None of them had let Dare or Key in on the plan, in case they'd already been compromised. They hadn't heard from either man in twenty-four hours, and they were all trying not to believe Powell's party line.

Grace had paced all night, but she hadn't gotten a single lead on either man. Or Powell, for that matter.

"This is not good," Gunner muttered over and over as they mapped out the water surrounding the island.

Avery barely said anything. She was stoic and serious. She'd told Grace she was terrified of heights, but with Gunner's help she was holding it together well.

She had something else to focus on—getting Dare and Darius back safely—and that would go a long way in keeping her fears quashed.

"We're sixty miles out," Jem called back.

Grace sat next to him, hands clasped tightly in her lap.

"You know, one of your visions would be most helpful right about now," he joked.

She gave a thin smile, trying not to look nervous and failing spectacularly. "I wish."

"He's fine," he repeated for the millionth time. "You'd know if he wasn't. You would."

"Yes, I believe that," she said into the miked headphones they all wore to block out the noise in the helo.

Gunner would drop out of the helo over the ocean, then wait until the right moment to surface on the island and hide. Jem and Avery would drop Grace on the island, then land the helo back on the mainland and travel by boat back to the island under the cover of darkness. Because this wasn't about a stealth escape. No, this was about killing Powell and anyone else on the goddamned island who worked for him so their lives weren't a total goatfuck.

Granted, they could be totally goatfucked for so many other reasons, but why dwell on that now when they were facing sudden death?

He hadn't been on a mission this shit-in-your-pants in years. He was back.

"ETA?" Gunner asked.

"You'd better start getting ready. Got to drop you well out of binocular range."

Gunner was trained like a SEAL for the UDT. He'd needed no convincing to take part in the mission and had assumed this role with no arguments.

"He'll swim in after the dust has cleared. Powell will be convinced you're alone, as promised."

"Dare's going to kill you for this," she murmured.

"Hoping you can convince him differently, sweetheart," Jem muttered back, and this time she gave him a real smile.

"I'll put in a good word."

Good, she was feeling confident about the plan—an excellent sign, which meant she was ready to tangle with this Powell bastard.

Grace watched Jem pilot the chopper with an ease she hadn't seen before. She had mixed feelings about the birds in general, remembered her first trip in one to Rip's magical island when she'd just turned ten.

"Richard's having a birthday party for you, to welcome us into his life," Esme had told her, pointed out the sights through the window as Grace tried not to throw up. Her nausea had nothing to do with the flight or the altitude, but rather with knowing that life as she knew it was over.

Years later she'd watched the chopper rise with her mother inside it. The woman she'd been told was dead and now knew lived somewhere on another island in luxury, no doubt funded by Rip. She'd be finding out more about that on this trip.

The last time she'd been on a helo, she'd come out of

the trunk she'd been hiding in, helped by the two caterers/black ops operators hired by Section 8 to take her out.

And now . . . she was doing this last trip here for herself as much as to save Dare and Key and Darius. As angry as she wanted to be at Dare for tricking her, she understood he'd done it for her. A declaration of love couldn't have been more beautiful.

She couldn't wait to see him again and tell him that feeling was reciprocal. But first things first—she had to prepare for Rip. To get back into cold, calculating mode. To play the role of the grifter, in case her gift decided to remain unpredictable.

"I know I said I didn't want you back, but I'd welcome you with open arms," she whispered to herself, not caring if Jem heard. "I'd take you every day for the rest of my life if you'd help us with this."

No answer, no sign from above. But Jem reached out and gave her a squeeze on her shoulder. For now, that would have to be enough.

Dare wasn't sure where the hell he was when he woke. Last he remembered, he and Key had fought through sixteen men and won. Stolen a car and gotten to the hotel, where they were ambushed by stun guns and tranquilizer darts, enough to take down a goddamned elephant.

He listened carefully, heard the rush of ocean waves, and he knew exactly where he was.

"Powell's island of fun," Key muttered from the cell

next to him, his voice coming through the small opening in the cement wall. "About time you woke up from your beauty sleep."

"You all right?"

"Fine, except for the bonds."

Dare felt the chains weighting his wrists and ankles. A nice, sadistic touch. He'd expected nothing less.

"They're coming for us," Key said. "There are ten of them. I bet I can take mine down first."

"Bastard," he muttered. "You've got a bet."

The chains wound around his limbs would take too long to unwind. He'd use them to his advantage. When the first guy came in, he backed up to get him close. And then Dare slammed the man's nose with both fists together, next opening his forearms to slip the man's head inside.

He checked the man and let him drop.

He glanced at the dead man on the floor. Ten men—nine to go.

Chapter Forty

Grace stepped off the chopper without a backward look at either Jem or the hidden Avery. Eyes would be on her, and she knew if she showed the least bit of interest in the pilot, Rip would have no compunction about shooting the helo down.

She ducked and walked along the small landing strip, saw Rip waiting by a car for her. He was alone.

He could kill her on sight—she knew that. But she had to hope there was a small part of Rip that was still curious about her gift. He might test her before he killed her.

"Where's Darius?" she called over the whir of the chopper blades.

"I'll take you to see him. I don't think he's well enough for travel." Rip stared at her. Somehow, he hadn't aged at all. She supposed evil did that to a person, because his dark-haired, olive-skinned good looks were still perfect, save for a few more lines around his eyes.

She hated to admit it, but they only added to his

mystique. She also hated to send Jem away without Darius, but she knew better than to push.

"I'm not happy about this—you're already breaking your promise," she said.

"For Darius's best interest, Grace. I also want to make sure you kept your end and there won't be anyone following you."

She turned and waved Jem off. The chopper rose and in minutes was back out over the ocean. She fought off the panic as she turned back to Rip and held out her hands. "Unless someone's hiding under my jacket, I'm quite alone, as promised."

Rip furrowed his brow a little, then motioned to the car. "Get in. We'll go to the house so you can see your precious Darius."

She did as she was told, and the car wound along the familiar single-lane roads up to the main house. Everything looked the way she remembered it, a paradise in hell. How it could be so beautiful and terrifying at the same time defied explanation.

He pulled into the circular drive in front of the house, and she waited until he came around to open her door. The perfect gentleman, as always.

She burned to ask him about Esme, but it was too soon. She needed to buy time, for Gunner to swim to shore in the dusk. For Jem and Avery to follow.

But if she saw a gun and an opportunity, she would take it. The time for playing it safe was long past.

"Where's the staff?" she asked casually as they walked into the house.

"They're preparing for a party I'm having next week,"

he said. "It seemed like the perfect time to let them have their meeting, so you wouldn't be overwhelmed."

There were no bodyguards around either. None that she could see, anyway, but she doubted they were too far away. Surveillance cameras had been added since the last time she'd been here. They were small and Grace noticed them only because Gunner and Avery had given her a quick lesson in the hours before they'd begun to execute their plan. They wanted her to know what to look for, showed her how to disable cameras here and there without causing too much suspicion.

"Don't do it if he's close," Gunner had warned. "I'd rather get around them than you get hurt."

She kept her hands in her pockets now as they walked toward the small elevator that led to the basement.

The basement. She froze, but only for a second, because a sudden, strong image of Rip being killed flashed in front of her eyes. She caught herself before he noticed and walked into the elevator with him.

She stood, facing the door, nearly shoulder to shoulder with him in the small space. If he noticed she was nervous, he didn't say anything, not even when she hesitated before she walked out of the elevator and into the cold cement hallway.

You'll be okay down here . . . you survived the first time.

She moved ahead on her tour down memory lane. It was meant to break her, she knew. Rip had no idea that instead it was making her stronger.

"Keep moving—I know you remember the way," Rip said.

"Yes, I do." She turned to face him confidently. "I know you do as well."

His smile faltered slightly, but only someone who knew him as well as she did would notice. Eight years of living with him had taught her something—she just had to free herself to remember.

"Darius is this way." He motioned for her to follow him instead of her leading again. She watched the broad expanse of his shoulders as he marched down the small hallway and opened the third door on the left. He let her go inside and slammed the door behind her.

"Darius—oh, my God." She moved forward to the man lying prone on the floor, chained to the wall.

He rolled over and opened his eyes. "How did he get you back here?"

She had to lie to him, get him to believe that she did this purposely, or else Rip would kill them both. "I came back on my own. It's better this way, Darius. Always looking over my shoulder . . . moving around . . . I couldn't live like that. All I have to do is tell him what I see, and that's it."

"Grace—"

"Please—don't make this harder. I appreciate what you did, but I'm fine with my decision." She touched the side of his face. "You can go. I'm going to stay of my own free will."

"I don't believe you."

"You should. I'm too stubborn not to make my own decisions. You know that as well as anyone." She paused. "He said he was going to free you when I got here. Then he said you couldn't be moved."

"He's right about that." Darius moved the towel covering his abdomen and she saw the blood seeping through it. "He shot me about half an hour ago. Going to be a slow bleed out."

"I won't let that happen. Rip, you need to get him help, right now!" she called out. The door slammed open. Rip looked as enraged as he had those times he'd come to visit her in the basement.

"I'll do nothing of the sort. Not until you come with me," he told her.

"Go, Grace. Do what he says," Darius told her. She wanted to tell him to hang on, that help was on the way, but she didn't dare.

Instead, she followed Rip out of the room and back into the elevator.

Ground level. Not the basement. She wanted to breathe a sigh of relief, but she knew that torture could happen anywhere. Hell was just a state of mind.

Six down. Dare crouched against the wall. His nose was broken, along with two fingers and a knuckle. Maybe even a wrist and definitely a few ribs.

It didn't matter. He and Key were the only ones in this fight getting out of here alive.

"I've got seven down," Key called through the window. Dare heard the crack of bone as Key's fists hit a nose or a neck and another body dropped. "Make that eight."

The bastard was enjoying himself. Dare understood the sentiment. Sometimes, there was no enemy to fight, but this time, Key was fighting back against the man who took his job, his livelihood . . . his pride. Key was taking it back, and Dare was more than glad to help.

Grace followed Rip into his massive office with its view of the beach. She forced herself not to look out, in case she spotted and gave away Gunner.

No one's going to see me, chère, he'd assured her. She wanted to believe him, but he didn't know Rip. Not like she did.

She sat in a chair, took the scotch he offered, because she couldn't afford to piss him off more. He could order his goons to take her to the basement. She could handle that—she could handle anything—but if she could avoid it, so much the better for all of them.

God, Dare, where are you?

As she thought it, a white-hot spike went through her skull, knocking her out of her chair and onto her knees. The dizziness and pain were worse than they'd been before, and she wondered why these visions were becoming similar to near-death experiences. They hadn't been nearly as painful when she was younger.

Nothing had been as bad. She supposed it was all relative. She brought her hands to her head, held it tightly as if that could lessen the throbbing. Tried to open her eyes to see through the pain, but she couldn't. She could only see what was flashing before her closed eyes, tried to make sense of it as quickly as she could.

She didn't know how long she was out. When she

came to, she noted that Rip had kindly thrown cold water over her head. She'd barely noticed at the time, remembered feeling for a moment like she'd been drowning, but it hadn't been enough to make her come to.

Now Rip stood over her, arms crossed, face demanding as he spoke.

"I knew a gift like yours wouldn't stay away forever. You were always so strong. You could've easily been my daughter."

"Thank God I'm not."

"Tell me what you saw, Gracie. Tell me or I'll shoot Darius again right in front of you."

He went to drag her up roughly by the arm, and even if she hadn't wanted to tell him anything, she couldn't have helped it. Blurted out, "You're going to be killed by your own men," but kept the other thing she'd sensed to herself, because it was too ugly to deal with.

Rip laughed long and loud as he released her arm and shoved her back down to the floor. "Not with the money I'm paying them. Every man has a price, and I've hit theirs many times over."

But she knew what she saw—Rip being beaten to death by some of the very men who'd hurt her once. Neither Darius nor Dare was among them. "You think Dare is responsible, but he's not."

"That's where you're definitely wrong. I don't fear Dare, just like I didn't fear S8. Good competitors— allowed me to keep my skills up. But did I think they could take down what I'd worked for? No."

He had the confidence only a man in his position could. It had been honed on years of experience—he was good, she knew that.

But her feelings, while admittedly few and far between, had never been wrong. Why would they start now? "I've done what you asked."

"Right—just when I needed you to. Because you've always been so cooperative."

"That wasn't my fault." She heard a growl come out of her mouth, despite the fact that she could barely lift her head, and he actually smiled at that.

"Finally, some backbone."

"I had plenty in your basement."

"I didn't have your mother killed, you know."

That had been a blow to her, far worse than any physical one could be. He was finally telling the truth, and she was glad she'd prepared for it. Still, she played dumb. "Then where did she go? Did you send her away somewhere and keep her from me?"

"I let her go away, but I never kept her from you. That was her choice."

"Why would she do that?" She spoke more to herself than to Rip, but he answered, telling her, "I paid her well. That's all she ever cared about. Money."

"I don't believe you."

"I think you knew your mom as well as I did—she was a grifter, and a good one. And she lived to deceive many more people. Now, I don't know if someone else killed her. I know there were times I wanted to."

If her mother had truly left her here, knowing what would happen . . . her own mother . . .

"You're more like me than you could ever realize, Grace. We were both abandoned and we both survived. We didn't need weak people around us—you should look on your mother leaving you behind as a blessing."

"I am nothing like you," she bit out, even as a small part of her saw the partial truth in that comparison.

Rip simply laughed like he knew better.

Chapter Forty-one

Powell slammed into the basement area, his eyes snapping with anger. He was big, still in shape from his SEAL and S8 days. He wouldn't go down easily, but Dare was primed for this fight.

The last guy Dare had taken out had managed to stick a hypodermic into his side first. Dare had gotten it out before the guy had been able to push all the medicine through, but at least a quarter was in Dare's system. It made him unsteady, but he had adrenaline and anger fueling him.

"I'm taking Grace and my father off this island, Powell," he said.

"On this island, only my fantasies come true," Powell told him. "And Grace is doing well upstairs. I think the island's really bringing out her gift again. Or maybe it's just spending time with me that's helping. And feel free to call me Rip, just like Grace."

"I'm not calling you shit, and this isn't exactly my idea of fantasy island," Dare spat. The chains were cutting into his wrists, but he'd managed to get the ones off his legs before Powell walked in.

Key was gone on his own steam, disappeared into the wildness of the island, prepared to disable some alarm systems.

They both knew Powell wasn't worried about finding Key, really only cared about Dare—about pitting father against son, maybe . . . or just shooting both to watch them bleed out. The clock was ticking. Powell just didn't realize that Dare was the ticking time bomb in this case.

Dare watched Powell carefully. The man was doing the same to him, checking for weaknesses, cracks in the system.

"Fight me like a goddamned man," Dare said through clenched teeth. "Or did you forget how to fight?"

Powell smiled then. "I've never forgotten how to fight, Dare. Never will. And when you go down, I'm going to put this hood on you and leave you here. My men have their orders to kill you once that happens."

They began to circle each other. The bulb sputtered, dimmed for a second, and Powell chose that moment to charge. The man still had the young foster child inside of him, remembered what it was like to fight for his food, his pride, his life.

Dare went at him like he was fighting the goddamned devil and didn't want to give him the chance to get the upper hand. Powell was on him, trying to pin him to the ground, and Dare used the chains to press against his neck.

Powell grunted and Dare was able to get him off

balance. Powell stumbled to the side, didn't fall down completely, but it gave Dare enough time to get to his feet, despite the pain.

Powell got to his feet then and shoved Dare. He was off balance, the goddamned drugs wreaking havoc on his system, the chains weighing him down. But he was taking Powell down, no matter what it took.

Just as the lights went off completely, he hauled off and slammed Powell in the cheek, knocking him senseless for a moment. And just when he prepared to grab him by the neck and demand to see Grace, generator power kicked in and a hand gripped his arm and hauled him to his feet.

He was unsteady, but the hold was strong, basically held him up. When he glanced behind him to assess where to place the blow, he stilled.

Gunner. Still damp from having swum to the island.

Gunner. This was good. Except the hold tightened as Powell got to his feet and smiled at them.

It was a hold Dare would have a problem breaking at the moment, which normally wouldn't be an issue. But the way Gunner looked at Powell and Powell looked at Gunner . . .

What the fuck was going on?

"Last I heard, you were dead," Powell said.

"You heard wrong," Gunner told him.

"Well, it's still nice to see you, James," Powell said.

"You too, Dad."

Dad.

Dare whipped his head to stare between Gunner

and Powell. The men didn't look at all alike—Gunner had that cool Nordic coloring, while Powell was darker. "You're . . ."

"You didn't know," Powell answered for Gunner. He looked amused, and Gunner wasn't making eye contact with Dare any longer. Dare swallowed hard and fucking prayed this was going to somehow work out in his favor.

He didn't see how, though. Because if they truly had been herded toward Gunner, Dare had been focusing on the wrong sibling being the problem. While he was watching Grace . . . it was really Gunner he should've been watching.

Tied up and gagged, Grace watched the security cameras helplessly. Darius lay so still in one cell. Another was bloody but bare—Key.

And the third . . . my God, the third showed Dare, in chains. And Rip was in front of him.

She couldn't hear a word they were saying, but she saw the fighting. She swore she could hear bones crunching, saw the blood. She wanted to turn away but couldn't. She willed Dare to take Rip down, once and for all.

But Dare wouldn't be the one to kill him, not according to her visions. And those same visions hadn't told her shit about what kind of outcome Dare had in all of this.

Please, no . . . let Dare win this one. Let me be wrong if that's necessary.

But she'd promised she'd trust what she saw. And when she saw Gunner, her heart beat faster. The cavalry was there . . .

Until she watched as Gunner pointed the gun at Dare's head instead of Rip's.

No—that couldn't be. How could all of them have been so wrong about Gunner? Had he been working for Rip the entire time?

She fought to keep the tears from her eyes as she strained to see what was happening. She tried to move the chair forward as the lights went out. When the generator kicked on maybe two minutes later, all she saw on the monitor was Dare, with a hood over his head, being dragged away by Rip's men.

They were beating him. She broke out in a cold sweat . . . and then she breathed deeply as the gag was taken off and Dare was behind her.

She looked back at the camera—saw the man struggling as Dare untied her.

"Dare." She let him gather her in his arms. "I knew it wasn't you. I knew it."

Her gift had worked just when she'd needed it most.

"I'm sorry if you had to think it for a single goddamned second," he told her. "Come on, we're getting the hell off fantasy island."

The helo was waiting on the landing pad. Grace and Avery ran as Gunner and Dare carried Darius on the stretcher and Key covered them with the rifle.

He herded them inside, ready to cover them with

fire, but none came. It wouldn't, until the bodyguards realized they'd killed their own boss.

Grace could think of nothing but the pure poetic justice in that act.

"Hang on," Jem called, and the chopper rose, fast and furious, and left behind the island Grace never wanted to see again.

But Darius, he was dying, even as Dare and Gunner furiously worked on him. She didn't have the horrible, painful vision the way she'd had it in Rip's office, but a peaceful feeling settled over her, like Darius was going to pass into a good place.

She bit her bottom lip as Avery clutched her hand. And then the chopper started to descend and she realized that Jem was landing on another island in order to allow them to work on Darius, to talk to him.

He cut the motor, and there was silence, except for Darius's harsh breaths.

"Go to him," she urged Avery. "Go now—hold his hand."

There was something in Grace's tone . . . and after a long moment, Avery uncurled her hand from Grace's and did just that.

Avery sank to her knees next to Dare, who was holding a towel to try to stop the bleeding. Gunner was running blood, but it seemed to be going out as fast as it was going in, and Darius was breathing fast, but his eyes were wide open.

Maybe he was in shock, she thought. *How could any-*

one be this close to death and still be awake and trying to talk?

She grabbed his hand, held it up to her heart.

"I'm your . . ." Darius didn't finish his sentence. Didn't have to. The dying man saw eyes that were a mirror image of his. "Guess . . . there's no . . . getting around it."

She smiled. "I'm Avery."

"I know . . . baby. Your eyes . . . much prettier . . . than mine," Darius told her, his words slow and labored. "You're . . . spitting image . . . of your mother."

"She's—"

"I know . . . I'm sorry." He turned his head then, coughed hard, and she saw him spit out blood before taking a breath and turning back to her.

Almost superhuman. *This is your legacy.*

"I'm glad you . . . Dare found each other. You . . . take care of him. I know . . . a lot to ask."

"I will." No hesitation. She wouldn't lose any more family. "I understand why you left us."

"Forgive . . . me?"

She couldn't find her voice, and so she nodded, because she could forgive him, even though it would take more time. But Darius had done the best he could, tried to save Dare. Had saved Grace and countless other people during his S8 tenure.

He smiled at that. Looked up at Dare and seemed to be asking the same of him.

"I already did," Dare told his father quietly. Darius smiled at that. Looked at the group gathered around him. "Family . . . born . . . and . . . chosen."

He closed his eyes and took a last shuddering breath. Avery felt like she lost hers, found Dare holding her, and she cried her eyes out on her brother's shoulder until the helo started up again to take them away.

Chapter Forty-two

Dare hadn't spoken to Gunner about what had happened at Powell's, hadn't had the chance once the power went out and Gunner slipped him the keys to his chains.

It had all happened in a blur, Gunner shoving him out of the room in the dark. He stripped his clothes, passed them to Gunner. When the lights came on, Gunner had Powell on the ground, dressed in Dare's clothes, a gun to his head. He'd knocked Powell out after whispering something to him that Dare hadn't been able to make out.

And then Gunner had tossed him Powell's pants, which Dare yanked on. Gunner had pushed Dare to hide in Darius's cell and disappeared himself when the bodyguards Gunner must've called for came charging in. He heard the orders come over their walkie-talkies. Powell's voice—or Gunner's best imitation of it.

"Kill him. Don't call me again until there's no pulse," came the order, and at that moment, a high-pitched wail came from under Powell's hood.

Dare snuck out just as the beating started. Untied Grace and got her to the helo.

Now, they all stood together on the tarmac from where Jem had taken off. The ride had been quiet and tense, with no one speaking much.

They'd all seen what happened between Gunner and Powell from one camera or another. Now they all stared at him, until Dare breathed, "Gunner . . . fuck."

"Yeah, that about sums it up," Gunner said. "Thanks for taking care of that for me."

He sounded calm, but he looked shaken as he referenced Dare getting Powell alone so Gunner could have him killed.

"Gunner, what the hell?" Jem asked, but Gunner shook his head.

"Can't get into that now," he told them. He got no argument. Whatever the story was, it would be huge.

Grace stepped forward and hugged Gunner hard. Gunner hugged her back, and Dare assured him, "It's over."

"Not for me, no," Gunner said. "But this—this was necessary before I could fix everything. I was going to leave it alone, be content with what I had."

"And now?"

"I'm done with the status quo."

"What about the team?" Avery asked him, and he shrugged noncommittally.

"Some things I have to do first. I'm not ruling it out."

"So we've got a broken psychic, Powell's son, a

bounty hunter turned murderer, a discharged Ranger, and fucked-up SEAL," Jem said.

"Former," Dare said. "And a mental patient."

"Not a bad start for a team," Jem said.

"This isn't a team," Dare muttered.

"Smells like one to me," Key said with a smile. "And pay up, because I won our bet."

Dare held Grace back while the others climbed into the waiting truck. Darius's body would be transported back from the private airport separately, to be cremated in the bayou that he'd loved so much.

It was an ending—and a beginning.

"You saved me," she said.

"And you saved me," he told her. "I can't believe you went there, put yourself in that kind of danger for me."

"That's what you do when you love somebody, Dare."

"I want to strangle you for doing it, so you're damned lucky I love you too."

She smiled at that, and he tried not to worry about the bruise on her cheek or the cut on her arm. Even though Darius didn't make it through, he'd helped put them all together, and Dare couldn't ever properly thank the man for that as long as he lived.

He figured the best way to do so would be to live up to Darius's legacy—and surpass it. Because they wouldn't work for anyone but themselves—they'd need to trust only one another.

"Dare, I have something to tell you," she murmured.

"You already did."

"No, there's more." She looked troubled. "I knew . . .

about Darius. I knew he would die today. And when I see things like that, I can't change them. There was nothing I could do."

"Ah, baby, I know. There's nothing you could've done. I hate that you have to see things like that sometimes."

She gave a small, wan smile. "I wish I could see good things."

"Maybe you don't need to be psychic to see the good. It's all right here," he told her, and she gave him a fierce hug.

"To fresh starts."

"That's the best offer I've heard all damned day." He paused. "When I think of what we almost lost . . ."

"Sometimes, maybe you have to lose everything to gain anything," she said.

"I think you're a very smart woman, Grace O'Rourke."

"I don't remember getting married."

"Small detail. You've been mine from the moment I met you."

She wouldn't have had it any other way.

Acknowledgments

Writing a book is never a solitary venture. I have to thank my editor, Danielle Perez, for her patience and help. For Kara Welsh and Claire Zion, for their support. For the art department and their simply amazing cover.

For the wonderful readers who buy my books, chat about them on Facebook and Twitter and send me terrific e-mails. I couldn't do this job without your support.

And as always, I have to thank my family—Zoo, Lily, Chance and Gus—for their constant, unwavering faith in me.

Please look for *Unbreakable*,
the second novel in the Section 8 series,
coming in November 2013 from Signet Eclipse
Please read on for an excerpt from

LONELY IS THE NIGHT: A SHADOW FORCE NOVELLA,

on sale in e-book now.

Chapter One

"He's all yours."

U.S. Marshal Grier Vanderhall looked at the sullen, dark-haired eighteen-year-old named Benji Warner and wanted to give a sarcastic "Yay."

Instead, she nodded to the district attorney, a tall, mirthless woman, and motioned to Benji to follow her. Maybe spending time with that woman had sucked all the fun from the kid. Or maybe it had to do with being a reluctant witness with a bounty on his head.

It was broad daylight and she walked Benji out to the truck, which was directly behind the back door with her partner parked behind it. Jack nodded at her as she escorted Benji into the waiting truck. She preferred using her own car for transfers, but the marshal's truck was appropriately bulletproofed, with tinted windows, an unfortunate necessity for this case.

Mr. Sullen was in the backseat, where there were no door handles. This wasn't her first rodeo, and there were plenty of instances of a witness scared and running like a rabbit. She also cuffed one of his hands to the metal loops on the floor using a long chain. He couldn't get to her in the front seat that way, but he wasn't completely constrained.

He complained bitterly about it under his breath but he didn't try to resist.

He was both a witness and a criminal—the reluctance of the first made the latter more of an issue than it might normally be.

She was looking at a minimum five-hour drive to get to the safe house. She fired the truck up, opened the window and waved for Jack to pull up.

"The place is all set—I vetted it myself this morning and Al will check on it right before you get there. Call him when you're half an hour out. I'll be there tomorrow night," he told her. His dark hair was hidden under a Cabela's baseball hat, his dark eyes hidden by the Ray-Bans he always wore. He would finish out their old case, handing off the witness to her new handler tonight. Watching Benji was their new twenty-four-seven gig for the next two months. This was without a doubt her most high-profile witness—Jack's as well.

"Do what you have to. We'll be fine," she said.

"Watch yourself," he mouthed before pulling away, and she took the truck in the opposite direction, heading down toward the freeway. She looked in the rearview mirror. "We'll stop for lunch in a few hours."

"Whatever."

Awesome. She turned up the radio and zoomed along, determined to get there before nightfall. There had been ugly threats during this case aimed at Benji, the DA and anyone else involved, including the marshal's office. The men who led the illegal fighting ring were both currently out on bail and purported to be trying to leave the country. The only evidence against them was Benji, and that had come late in the game.

Either way, it was going to get ugly.

She got them half an hour from their destination—this inconspicuous diner was the perfect place for a quick bite before they made it into town. Benji followed her, ordered an obscene amount of food and then stared out the window.

She didn't press him. Didn't say anything until the food came—she was hoping that made him semihuman.

After she finished half her own burger, she told him, "You're going to be all right. You're young. You can start over."

He blinked. Frowned. And finally, he spoke more than a one-word answer. "They're never going to just let me go like that. These guys . . . you don't understand."

"I hate to tell you this, Benji, but all my witnesses say that. It's okay to be scared, but you have to not let it rule your life. That's *my* job."

"That's not much of a life."

She wagged a fry at him. "You're smart—for someone so young."

"Eighteen isn't young."

No, it wasn't. And he was facing jail time for causing the inadvertent death of a sixteen-year-old during one of the cage fights. The dead man's parents were the ones who had started the ball rolling on this, and even though this case was growing so big and threatening to

378   *Excerpt from* LONELY IS THE NIGHT

topple everyone in its path, they were pushing forward.

For Benji, it was testify or go to jail. And even then, he'd picked jail. It was only at the DA's insistence—and no doubt the scare tactics of a minimum twenty-five years to life versus freedom and WITSEC—that he'd reluctantly agreed. She didn't want to know the specifics he'd been threatened with.

"You sure you don't want to contact your parents?" she asked, and he shook his head.

"No. It'll put them in danger and I've put them through enough hell not being in contact with them for the last two years. You protect me, I'll protect them." He looked her right in the eye as he spoke those last words. He was older, wiser than his years. His sense of honor could very well get him killed. He reminded her of a young Reid.

She bit into her burger viciously, her teeth gnashing together the way they always did when she thought about him. She didn't know why—he was the one who had every right to be mad, not her.

The boy pushed his plate back, finally satiated. He'd been living on his own for two years, making more money than he'd make at any other job in such a short amount of time. Even after a doctor told him that another concussion like the recent ones he'd suffered could either kill him or cause permanent brain damage, he still wanted to fight. Told the DA, "It doesn't matter. It's what I'm good at."

It wasn't her job to counsel him. She was supposed to find him a safe place to live, give him money and ensure he kept a low profile until the trial, which already had constant continuances.

Three months, minimum. She took money from her wallet and put it down on the table. "Come on, if you're finished. Let's get you settled."

"Gotta use the john."

She nodded. Couldn't exactly follow him in there but she did go in first to check. No windows. Perfect. She made her call to Al while waiting in the hallway leading to and not outside the door to be less conspicuous, and he rolled his eyes at the whole thing.

Once they were back in the truck and moving, there was silence for most of the trip. But when they pulled up outside the motel, where the marshals had a block of four adjoining rooms on the second floor, he leaned forward and put a hand on her shoulder.

"Are you going to give me a weapon? Because when these guys come after me, I'm not going to be able to fight them with my fists."

She turned to face him. "No weapons. You won't need them. You have me."

She didn't know if that answer satisfied him or not.

Grier secured the doors from the inside and alarmed them so Benji couldn't leave. Those same alarms would alert her if someone tried to get in by buzzing the button she wore around her neck.

She was supposed to handcuff one of his wrists to something at all times.

He's a dangerous kid, Grier. He kills with his hands, Jack had warned her. And she wasn't stupid.

"Come on, settle in somewhere so I can put this on." She held up the cuffs, was surprised when he offered no resistance. Maybe he was tired. She locked a wrist to the metal of the bed, the chain long enough for him to sit up, lie down and generally get comfortable. "Just yell if you need anything or want to move."

There was a table with two chairs. She put the remote near him, and a bottle of water. The rooms were already stocked with snacks and there were take-out menus and clothes.

Once in, they weren't coming out until trial. She and Jack would relieve each other, but they'd each be sleeping here, hence all the rooms. Plus, it was a good way to keep surveilling the street.

"You're not scared of me, are you?" Benji asked suddenly.

"No," she answered truthfully. "Should I be?"

"I only fight in the ring. For money. And I didn't mean to hurt that kid."

She wanted to correct him when he said *hurt*, but didn't. It was in his eyes—he knew what he'd done. The only reason he'd gotten caught was through a routine traffic stop—but the police had an APB out on him, thanks to a video one of the members of the audience had filmed and put up on YouTube. It had been damaging enough to force Benji to admit what he'd done to the DA. But until he got in front of a jury—and even when he did—all bets were off. He could recant everything.

Grier didn't want to know exactly how. "You're doing the right thing now. Fighting for money the way you're doing it isn't legal for a reason. People get hurt."

"Boxers get hurt all the time. Football players too," he pointed out.

"Yeah, well, they're trying to regulate all that now, aren't they?"

"Never happen." He was staring down at his cuffed wrist. His hand was fisted and she saw the scars on his knuckles, courtesy of the skin being broken open time and time again. "I miss it."

"Fighting?"

"Training. It's a release for me. You wouldn't understand."

"You'd be surprised at what I understand." She watched him for a long moment. "I can't let you leave here, but I could let you work out. I won't be able to get much—some weights. A jump rope."

His face brightened a little. "Yeah, that would be good. Thanks."

"Get some rest."

In return, the TV blasted behind her. When she turned back, his eyes were closed.

Kids today.

By the time she settled in, it was after midnight. She was holding the phone, the way she always did around this hour, because she was thinking about Reid. She'd taken his number off her phone to avoid temptation or misdialing but she'd memorized it. Repeated it over and over in her head, thought about his blue eyes and handsome face, the rub of his hands on her body.

She put the phone back into her pocket and blew out a frustrated breath. Things were so complicated between them. When they'd met, she'd been chasing down a missing witness named Teddie, and Reid had been protecting Teddie by running interference. Grier and Reid had a brief affair, during which she'd bandaged his wounds—and he'd paid her back by saving her life. It culminated in her being targeted by the very dangerous man hunting Reid and WITSEC's plan to fake her death to help her escape.

That's where everything went terribly wrong between them. He'd watched her get shot, and then he'd figured out what she'd done, but she could only imagine how he'd felt. He'd been so angry—rightfully so—and then he'd come through and saved her ass again, not once, but twice after that.

Maybe that was the problem—she wasn't ready to admit she'd been wrong. That had never been her strong point. She'd also convinced herself that it was better—safer—that he didn't know the plan. And she was right about that, but Reid wasn't just anyone. He was a Delta Force Operator, worked black ops jobs and knew the inherent dangers of her situation. And then she'd let a year go by—a lifetime for a man like that. He'd probably been to a different country a month, started a war, found different women to seduce.

She was so tense. Needed a long run. Maybe when Jack got here tomorrow, she'd sneak out and run until she stopped thinking.

She heard the clinking of Benji's chain. When she looked in, she noted he'd turned on his side, his arm dangling down. The TV seemed to be louder than it had been, but it kept him asleep.

Witnesses were generally happiest when asleep.

Her phone rang. Unknown number, but that wasn't odd for her. "Vanderhall."

"I've got information on the fighting ring." It was a low, gruff voice with a heavy East Coast accent. New York, for sure.

"I'm listening."

If she held him on the line for thirty seconds, she'd get a trace. But the entire world knew that trick now. "I need to see you in person."

"Not possible," she said.

"It is."

She whirled around, because the voice had come from behind her. A tall man stood there, his face uncovered.

He's not bothering to cover his face.

She fought for her life—it was the only way she could save herself and her witness.

He was too close, too big and he pinned her arms. She fought. Scratched, clawed and punched and she might've actually gotten to her gun in her pocket if another man hadn't come up from behind her and squeezed the pressure point in her neck.

Before she lost consciousness, she heard one of them say, "We've got ourselves a fighter."

Then she dropped with a thud that echoed in her ears. Woke in a moving car—the trunk—and fought to keep her eyes open. There was duct tape around her arms and legs. Across her mouth. She tried to move around, to find a weapon, anything.

Before she could stop herself, she passed out again.

The next time she woke, everything was wavy and

she fought the urge to laugh. Everything was funny. Everything was wonderful, especially because the duct tape was gone. She stood, stared at the wavy lines again and realized they were iron bars that reinforced the heavy metal door from the inside.

And she laughed again.

The next time she opened her eyes, her head throbbed and she definitely wasn't laughing. She lay there for a few minutes, looking around, noting the camera mounted in the far right corner. She couldn't get up to look out the square window, but saw nothing but darkness.

Her hands were tied above her head, ankles lashed together and her head throbbing. She'd been drugged— she knew that for sure—and they'd hit her over the head for good measure, the bastards.

She swallowed—her throat was so dry, it burned. She'd been put into a short-sleeved T-shirt and she searched her arms, looking for track marks. She finally found them, in between her fingers.

"You're as smart as I thought you'd be."

She glanced up to see a big man watching her. She blinked, stared at his face. He was handsome, despite the craggy pockmarks that cratered the skin on his cheeks. "Where am I?"

"The place you and your people were trying to keep Benji from. And now you've got a job here."

She stared back down at the track marks, her mind working overtime. They were drugging her with addictive narcotics. She'd go into withdrawal without them if they kept injecting her at this rate. She'd have to beg them for drugs, would have to fight for them.

She'd always felt that it was safer to work within the law, and she wasn't so sure that was going to save her this time.

She closed her eyes and thought about Reid, what he'd do in a situation like this.

He'd fight, any way he had to. He'd always been dangerous. When she'd told him she thought he was one of the good guys, he'd told her she was wrong.

Wrong or not, she wished he was here to help her, but she'd used up all her get-out-of-jail-free cards with him.

She shouldn't be using this time to think about regrets, shouldn't be seeing her life flash before her eyes. That meant she was giving up and she couldn't do that yet. "I never thought women would be such a big draw. But some of their fights actually outperform the men's for money."

She committed the face to memory. This wasn't the man on trial for illegal cage fighting. And this operation was bigger than any one conviction could touch. It had sprawled, spawned leagues and the like.

"Where's Benji?"

He smiled. "Right back where he wanted to be. Fighting."

"I want to see him."

"You're not in a position to give orders, Grier. You're just another fighter, struggling up the ranks."

"I hope there's a direct-deposit option for my checks," she deadpanned.

"We'll see if you still have your sense of humor after tomorrow night."

Chapter Two

Grier's number. On his phone. For the first time in a goddamned year.

She hadn't shown at Mace's wedding, even after Kell had invited her behind Reid's back. Reid could understand why, probably better than any of the others. Grier didn't mind being vulnerable, telling him about her past, her reasons for becoming a marshal, but she couldn't shake off her sense of right and wrong. She was black and white, with no gray . . . and he definitely lived the majority of his life there.

She knew she'd wounded him by pretending to die. Good reason, of course, but he could've been let in on the plan. Should have been.

Dammit. Grier might not mind the vulnerable shit but Reid sure as hell did.

Now he sat with the phone next to him, Grier's message unplayed.

But a year and six days . . . *why now, Grier?*

He stared down at the screen stupidly, ready to press the voice mail button.

He took a deep breath and hit redial instead. When

a man answered, he clutched the phone so hard he was sure he'd broken it.

"Reid, is that you?"

"Jack?"

"Didn't you listen to my message?"

"Obviously not."

"Shit. Sorry, man . . . I didn't think—grabbed her phone and figured you'd know it was important." Jack was Grier's partner.

"Figured this was faster. Fill me in." And fuck, this wasn't good.

"She's gone. It hasn't hit the papers yet, but it will within the next few hours and then all hell's going to break loose. I need your help."

Reid shoved a hand in his pocket, the other kept the phone to his ear. He was convalescing at Mace's bar—Doc's orders after an unfortunate incident on his last job with Dylan.

Thankfully, the human traffickers had been hurt far worse than either he or Dylan had been. The girls they'd rescued were now recovering with their respective parents.

He and Jack had kept in touch over the year. Rather, Jack kept in touch with him. Reid wasn't sure if Grier put him up to it or if he did it on his own. He'd also given Reid a few tips on some recent cases and leads to others that the law couldn't get involved with. Even Dylan had to grudgingly admit that the guy was good.

"Is this another near-death experience?"

"No, man, I'd know. She and I were charged with a witness. A few months of babysitting. She was getting him settled and now they're both gone. The room's trashed and there's blood on the carpet near her phone. This is some bad shit, Reid. The FBI and the marshals are on it, but . . ."

Yeah, he got it. They could get places those agencies couldn't. "How long?"

"I'm assuming five hours, give or take. I wouldn't have known if I hadn't gotten to the motel where she was staying earlier than expected."

"Where are you now?"

"Heading back to my apartment. You gotta meet me."

"I'll be there tonight," he promised.

Time was critical. He packed—flying commercial with weapons wouldn't work, so he planned to buy some in Texas. Dylan wouldn't let him out if he didn't leave before anyone noticed him. He heaved the bag over his shoulder, ignoring the sharp pain in his ribs and punched in flight times on his phone. He'd beg or bribe his way onto the next flight out.

"Where are you going?"

Teddie. He turned around slowly, found her leaning against his doorjamb with her arms crossed. Obviously, she was his babysitter today. As if he needed one. Most of the time. "Ah, just taking a ride downtown?" he offered.

"Try again."

Geez, the women were worse than the men in this group. He had no choice but to come clean. "It's Grier."

"She called?"

"Not exactly." When he finished telling her, Teddie was handing him cash, telling him she'd give him as much lead time as possible.

"Bring her back, Reid."

"I will."

"You love her, you know."

He opened his mouth to say that you couldn't fall in love that easily, but he'd had half of a living, breathing example in front of him. "Thanks for the help."

Three hours later, he was seated on a direct flight to Houston. He'd neither had to beg or bribe, but flirt a little and even though his heart wasn't in it at all, for Grier, he did what he needed to. And got bumped up to first class to boot.

Now he tried to focus himself, to stay calm. He didn't like plane rides under the best of circumstances. Most of the time he was riding in one, he was on his way to fix something, save someone, and the need to be there immediately, if not faster, made him slightly claustrophobic. Driving was his preferred method but that wouldn't get him to Texas quickly enough.

She's all right. She's tough. She can take care of herself.

And he had no real idea what she was up against. Jack didn't want to talk in case his line was tapped. Which meant Grier was in bigger trouble than just being kidnapped. If that were possible.

His phone continued to buzz incessantly. Dylan, again. He stared at the screen, thinking about picking up this time when the flight attendant told him, "Sir, you'll have to turn that off," and offered him a cookie.

"Gladly." He shut it down, took the cookie and looked around, waiting for Dylan or Kell or any of them to storm the plane. They weren't above that, he knew. He wouldn't be, anyway.

Finally, after twenty tense minutes, they were wheels up and Reid found himself unable to sit still. He ended up pacing through coach and sitting next to the air marshal on board, which was an odd coincidence since there was only one on one out of every twenty flights. The guy was a retired Marine, said the gig was good money.

"And boring as shit," Reid added.

"Yeah, but hell, it's necessary." The man stared at him. "You hate flying."

"It shows, huh?" He stared out the window past the guy and wondered if DB Cooper had just been claustrophobic.

"You're going to see a girlfriend."

"That obvious?"

"Yeah." The Marine handed him a mini-bottle of scotch. "You'll need fortification."

Reid opened it and said, *"Semper Fi,"* before draining it in a single gulp.

Also available from

Stephanie Tyler

LONELY IS THE NIGHT

A Shadow Force Novella

AN ORIGINAL NOVELLA
AVAILABLE ONLY AS A
DOWNLOADABLE PENGUIN SPECIAL

Reid Cormier is a recently retired Delta Force Operator.
With his former teammates, he works black ops jobs all
around the world, utilizing his skills. On his last job, he
was sure he'd been too late to save U.S. Marshall Grier
Vanderhall's life. And when he discovers that she faked her
own death without telling him of the plan first, he is
unable to forgive the betrayal. But that all changes when
she's kidnapped and her partner calls Reid for help. As he
tries to rescue her from a dangerous ring of criminals,
neither knows if this will give them another chance to be
together or get them both killed.

Available wherever e-books are sold or at
penguin.com

facebook.com/LoveAlwaysBooks

Also available from

Stephanie Tyler

Dire Warning
An Eternal Wolf Clan Novella

AN ORIGINAL NOVELLA AVAILABLE ONLY AS A DOWNLOADABLE PENGUIN SPECIAL

Immortal and invincible, Rifter is the head of the last surviving pack of Dire wolves—a band of Alpha brothers charged with protecting the Weres. But now that witches have joined forces with nefarious weretrappers, it's a perfect storm for double trouble. When the murder of a human points to a wolf—along with the threat of the packs being outed to the world—the Dires fear that something even more dangerous is out there hiding in the dark, something waiting for the right time to show itself.

Available wherever e-books are sold or at
penguin.com

facebook.com/ProjectParanormalBooks